I0601280

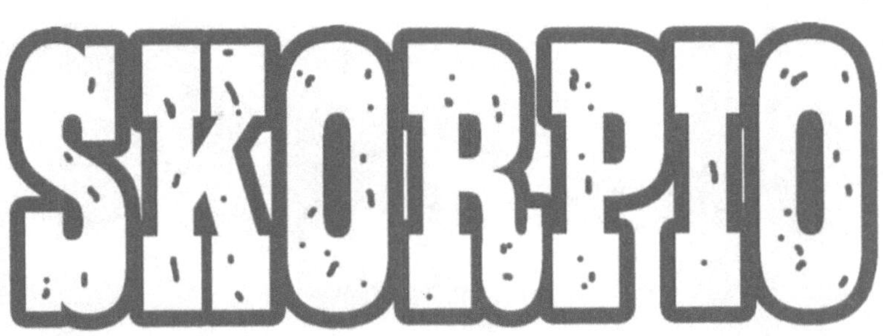

SKORPIO

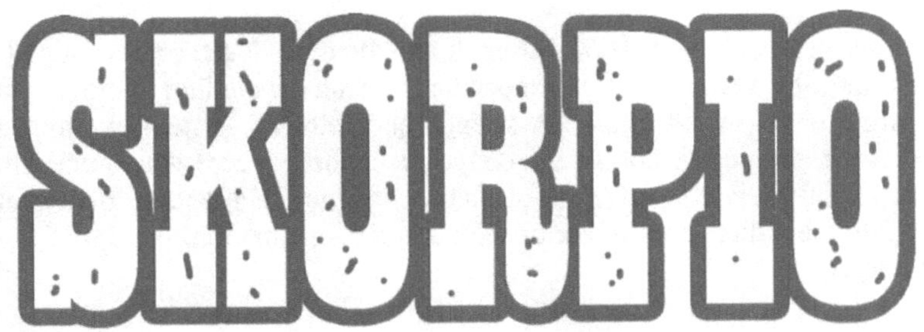

Mike Baron

WordFire Press
Colorado Springs, Colorado

ISBN: 978-1-61475-084-0

Cover painting by Jordi Armengol

Cover design by Bob Garcia

Book Design by RuneWright, LLC
www.RuneWright.com

Published by
WordFire Press, an imprint of
WordFire, Inc.
PO Box 1840
Monument CO 80132

WordFire Press Trade Paperback Edition October 2013
Printed in the USA
www.wordfire.com

CHAPTER ONE

LAST CHANCE

Heat lingered in the desert, even at dusk. The VW bus, wedged between two dusty pick-ups outside the Last Chance Bar & Grill in Gap, AZ, was plastered with Grateful Dead stickers, peace symbols, and flowers, a relic from the dawn of rock and roll. The symbols were barely visible through the patina of dust that descended on any vehicle on the plateau. Even vehicles kept in closed garages were covered with dust.

The Last Chance formed the end cap of an exiguous Main Street stretching for two blocks, consisting of a couple of two story brick office buildings, a feed store, the Last Chance Bank, Vern's Hardware, Vern's Gas, and directly across the street, Vern's Motel.

It was 1985. At Vern's Gas, it was a buck eleven a gallon.

The Last Chance itself was an adobe structure with viga poles protruding from its brow, a plank porch that ran the length, and a landscape window in which the neon Last Chance light flashed over the small Budweiser. The bar had once been pink but now, like everything else exposed to the Sonoran desert, it was sandy beige. Constant wind whipped through the streets sandblasting everything in its path. It was ninety-eight degrees outside, the only living thing an old dog on the bar's porch, which got up and circled five times before settling down on a filthy blanket. A hand-made Navajo bowl held water.

The only sounds were the wind, the whine of the rooftop air-conditioner, and very faintly, Jefferson Airplane's "White Rabbit."

Inside, Curt Mayweather and Ronnie Potts, seniors and roommates at Creighton University in Creighton, IL, sat at the bar. They were stoned to the gills. Each had a sixteen ounce glass of Rattlesnake IPA before them, ten percent alcohol. Curt hunched over the bar, ballpoint pen in hand, sketching in a Bristol board pad he carried with him at all times. Ronnie looked at the stuffed rattlesnake and coyote over the bar, the tin signs celebrating defunct motor vehicles, WW II nose art, and shootin', the sawdust-covered plank floor, the dart board, and the patrons themselves, four cowboys in boots, Stetsons, and bonnaroo belt buckles the size of Texas, and thought, *how cool is this?*

Ronnie was five eleven, second of three children belonging to Marge and Daniel Potts of Evanston. Daniel Potts of Stankle, Murphy and Crowder, Attorneys at Law specializing in corporate litigation. Ronnie was a varsity wrestler at 170, working toward his bachelor's degree in Anthropology. After which he would go straight for the Masters while trying to hitch a ride on every archaeological dig he could find.

Curt bent over his drawing. He majored in psychology but was toying with the idea of changing his major to art. He had always drawn, ever since he was a child. He drew in the margins of his books in grade school. He created little flip books by drawing the same image over and over again—with slight variations—so that when you gathered the pages between thumb and forefinger and let 'em rip, you saw a tiny skeleton dance the hoochie-coochie.

His teachers tried to discourage him at first but by the time he reached Junior High, it had become evident to all, even his parents, that Curt could draw. He was an only child. His father was an accountant for Sheldon Property Management in Evanston, and his mother worked as a librarian. Curt was a round-shouldered hulk with a beer belly and a beard. Unlike the other patrons, the students' faces were as smooth and unblemished as freshly laundered sheets.

The interior winked and gleamed through its gloom—Christmas tree lights surrounding the bar, the neon in the window, and the bubbling Wurlitzer in the corner into which Ronnie had plugged a buck in quarters, a full album's worth. He'd searched among the Hank Williams, Johnny Cash, Johnny Paycheck and Merle Haggard that dominated the little rotating selection menus. Nobody so much as looked up when Grace Slick began to wail.

Herders and cowboys, the patrons were taciturn and tolerant and frankly grateful for a change from the usual fare. The bartender was a middle-aged half-Apache with "Muriel" stitched on her blue bowling shirt in red script. Her long grayish hair was tied in a ponytail and she wore a silver and turquoise brooch around her neck. Her skin was the color of brick yet remarkably smooth. Like the regulars, she viewed the two college kids with bemusement. They were so obviously "not from around here" in their cargo-shorts, high-zoot hiking shoes, and backpacks.

Muriel wandered over to where the boys were grooving and looked at Curt's sketch. Even from upside down it was readily apparent as a butte, beautifully rendered in pencil with shading that looked almost real.

"Whatcha drawin' there, hoss?" she said.

Curt reversed the notepad so she could look at it right-side up. "It's this place I keep seeing in my dreams."

A faint shiver trickled down Muriel's spine. She looked up. Damned condensation from the ancient AC. It seemed to her that she'd seen the butte too, but couldn't recall when or where. Maybe in her dreams.

"You ever see this place?" Curt asked.

"Now how would I see that place?" Muriel said. "You couldn't pay me to go out there. I hope you boys isn't goin' out there."

"That's why we're here!" Ronnie gushed. "I mean, I'm an anthropology major and we hear there are all sorts of glyphs out there." He did not mention the other reason, that they had both read Aldous Huxley's *The Doors of Perception* and wanted to trip in the desert like Timothy Leary and Cary Grant.

"Huh," Muriel said. "Thought you was here for the eclipse. You know not to look directly at the sun, right?"

One of the regulars eased out of his booth against the front wall and ambled to the bar, slightly bow-legged from years of ranch work. He had a face like a Shar-Pei and a white handlebar mustache. He set a glass tumbler on the counter.

"Muriel, my love, if you don't mind."

Muriel emptied the glass, scooped in more ice, and added two inches of Old Buffalo Fine Distilled Spirits. "Here you go, Pete."

Pete gazed over Curt's shoulder at the drawing, which had returned to its original position. "Seems I seen something like that once."

Curt looked up. "Where?"

The old cowboy nodded his head to the east. "Out there. Back when I was young, dumb and fulla come and we used to ride dune buggies out there. Nothin' out there but sand, rattlesnakes and scorpions."

"That's what I'm tellin' 'em, Pete. This here's an anthropologist."

Ronnie turned, grinning, his horn-rimmed glasses reflecting the neon lights. "Ronnie Potts, sir. Student at Creighton University."

Pete took the kid's soft hand in his rough one and shook it. "Anthropology, huh? When I was a boy we studied ranching, business, and water management."

"Understanding ancient cultures is the key to understanding ourselves," Ronnie said.

"Ain't that the truth. Well, you can call me Pete. You goin' out there?"

"We're prepared," Ronnie said. "We've camped before."

"Ahuh. Take plenty of water. I mean plenty. Take .twice as much as you're thinkin' of takin'. Got any guns?"

Ronnie's grin went wide-screen. "No, of course not. We're students."

"Of course not," Pete said. He hefted his glass. "Good luck to ya, son."

CHAPTER TWO

GROOVIN'

They splurged and spent the night at Vern's Motel, $29 for the double. They showered in the morning. They began to sweat as soon as they stepped outside. By eight a.m. it was already in the eighties.

Curt conducted an inspection of his beloved microbus that he had bought from a used car dealer in Midlothian, IL six thousand miles ago for $1,500. It only had eighty-eight thousand miles on the clock, a relative youngster. Curt pulled out the old metal toolbox and removed the air gauge. He worked his way around the car with a hand pump, making sure the tires were inflated to 33 lbs. per square inch. He'd studied the USGA plat maps and determined there were enough old mining trails laid out on the rock-hard sand that they should be able to drive a couple hundred miles without difficulty. Tread was good. He'd brought a sturdy jack, two spares, and shovels.

He opened the side passenger door with a skin-rippling screech. A little WD-40 was in order. He removed the blue can from his tool box, attached the short straw, and spritzed the running tracks and hinges. He worked the door back and forth. Ahhh. Better. Inside he had extra air and oil filters just in case. Two five-gallon picnic thermoses. Curt used his plastic ice bucket from the room to deliver loads of ice from the outside ice machine to each of the thermoses. He used the bathtub faucet to fill four half-gallon canteens swathed in canvas he'd purchased at an army surplus store.

He checked his copious supply of dehydrated meals, cheese and cold cuts in an ice chest that was half melted. He would have liked to replenish the ice, but the old machine had barely filled the two buckets before grinding to a halt. Ronnie emerged from the room into bright morning light, bare-chested and toweling off his mop of auburn hair. Catnip. Catnip to the girls. Curt had always envied Ronnie's easy way with women but Ronnie wasn't stuck-up or greedy and Curt did all right on the leftovers.

He'd been Ronnie's wingman since freshman year.

Ronnie placed his hand over his eyes and squinted east into the sun looking past Vern's Hardware at the distant, hazy mountains. The landscape was unrelieved by plant or water. Nothing stirred, nothing moved except for a pair of turkey buzzards hovering in the middle distance. He smacked his hands together and inhaled.

"Smell that desert air!" He looked up and down Main Street. "Jesus. They never heard of McDonald's?"

"We'll eat on the road. Come on. I want to find some shade before we stop for the night."

The VW's twenty-gallon gas tank had a range of 350 miles. Curt also carried two steel five gallon gas tanks on the roof next to their camping gear. They'd topped off when they hit town last night. They did not plan to roam the plateau, but rather to seek out an interesting site and camp there. It was Ronnie's idea. It was he who first came across the Azuma in an obscure conquistador's diary in Seville, when he and Curt had back-packed across Europe the previous summer.

He'd been studying maps of the area and Anasazi texts the whole semester and thought he had the site narrowed down to a ten square mile area. The Spanish breached the Azuma stronghold in 1542. Ronnie had a thousand dollar Nikon his parents gave him for his birthday and he had been putting in long hours at the dark room in the Student Union. Dreams of *National Geographic* danced in his head.

Aside from fantasies of fame and riches that every young man possessed, he was driven by a burning desire to know. Ronnie had been hooked when his parents took him to Colorado's Mesa Verde National Park when he was twelve years old.

The sight of the ancient cliff dwellings enraptured him. A deep bell rang in his heart. As a boy he had always played the Indian in cowboys and Indians. Between high school and college he'd spent a summer volunteering on the Pine Ridge Reservation in South Dakota. The Indians he met were not the Indians of his imagination. The Pine Ridge Indians seemed enervated, passive, and inured to subsistence living. They drank and did drugs. They were a sharp contrast to the warriors of his imagination and perhaps it was this desire to uncover those warriors of old that drove him.

For Curt, it was all about dropping acid in the desert. He'd always had that mystic bent. His drawings were getting spacier.

They saddled up and headed out, the microbus making its characteristic grinding noise. Five miles out of town on County Highway BB the pavement ended and they rode on the hard flat surface of the desert consisting of silicon, crushed pyrites, sand and gravel. Vegetation was sparse and hardy. It had been a dry year and the desert stretched before them sere and forbidding.

Curt plugged the Kinks into the 8-track and cranked it to drown out the engine noise, which sounded like a cement mixer filled with metal. "You Really Got Me." They rode without speaking, each lost in thought, chewing beef jerky, sunflower seeds and quaffing water. The old microbus had no air conditioning and they rode with the windows open. It was like sitting near a blast furnace. The air was sweet and dry with a hint of mesquite.

Ronnie rolled a joint on a copy of *Rolling Stone* and they lit up. Suddenly they were loquacious.

"This is gonna be so cool," Curt said.

"What about rattlesnakes, man?" Ronnie said. "We got to be wary of those suckers."

"Just watch where you step. We'll sleep in the bus. Shouldn't be a problem."

"And scorpions. You heard what the man said."

"Scorpions are generally afraid of humans and their stings are rarely fatal."

"They give me the creeps," Ronnie said, turning around and digging through his backpack for the snakebite kit he'd purchased at a sporting goods shop in Denver.

Within an hour they'd left all traces of civilization behind save for the ruts and grooves of the road itself. The microbus jounced across broad stretches of washtub surface. Ronnie pulled out his Zeiss binocs and sighted in on the distant mountains. He thought he saw a communications tower but he couldn't be sure. The distance was clouded in heat haze.

The Kinks finished with "Sunny Afternoon." Ronnie popped them out and replaced them with New Riders of the Purple Sage.

It was just past noon, when they saw the old woman.

CHAPTER THREE

CLARITY

Curt couldn't believe his eyes. How did she get there? They were miles from nowhere in a desolate wilderness, yet there she stood by the side of the road as if waiting for a bus. He looked at Ronnie.

"I see her," Ronnie said, quickly closing the ashtray to hide the joint. As if an old woman standing in the desert had any interest. He felt anxious, foolish and absurd all at once. He laughed at himself.

"Maybe she's lost," Curt said.

"How did she get out here?" No car. No bike. No horse. She stood next to the road with her wizened face turned expectantly toward them.

"Maybe we should ignore her," Curt said.

"No, man. We can't just leave her standing there. She might need help."

"We are not heading back into town," Curt said with finality.

"No, man. Let's just ask her if she's all right. She looks like she's waiting for us."

Curt stopped the microbus by the side of the road. The pale cloud of dust they'd been trailing slowly overwhelmed them, pouring in through the windows and covering them with grit. The old woman stood on the right, or south side of the road. She was about five two, wore a shapeless potato sack dress and her head was covered in a beaded shawl. Ronnie didn't see how she could stand it.

Up close it was obvious she was Native American from her coppery skin and bulbous nose. She could have been anywhere from fifty to a hundred.

"Are you all right, ma'am?" Ronnie said through the open window.

She came close and peered in through the window, standing on her toes to glance in the back. She had mismatched eyes; one brown, one silver. Like a Malamute.

"Have you seen my son?" she said.

Ronnie and Curt exchanged a glance.

"No ma'am," Ronnie said. "You're the first person we've seen since leaving Last Chance this morning. How did you get out here? Did you come with your son?"

"I warned him. I warned him about that woman."

"How did you get out here, ma'am? Did somebody drop you off?"

"He is very tall. His father was a shaman too."

The old woman was obviously touched.

"Give her one of the canteens," Curt said. "We've got plenty."

Ronnie leaned back and snagged one of the sweating canteens, covered in canvas. He held it out through the window. "Here take this. Are you sure you're all right?"

The old woman took the canteen and looped it over her shoulder. She shrugged, turned and walked into the blazing heat.

The boys stared.

"Maybe we should go after her," Ronnie said.

"And do what? Forcibly restrain her? I don't think that's a good idea. Listen. If she's still here when we come back we'll take her into town with us."

They watched for a few minutes as she receded into the sandy landscape. Curt put the VW in gear and they headed east toward the mountains.

Two hours later they found themselves running parallel to a gash in the earth when the road forked. The left turn laid a beeline for the horizon. The right veered toward the chasm.

"Take the right," Ronnie said.

"You sure?"

"Take it."

Five minutes later they came to the chasm and a precarious-looking wooden bridge that spanned a ten foot gap to a free-standing butte. And from there, another ten-foot bridge to undulating desert. They got out of the bus.

The chasm was twenty feet deep at that point but they could see where it dropped lower up ahead.

"I don't know, man," Curt said.

Ronnie walked out on the bridge. "Feels solid." He jumped up and down in the middle causing pebbles, gravel and dust to gyrate. "It's good. Let's take it."

The bridge creaked ominously as they traversed it. Ronnie relit the joint and passed it to Curt. The land descended toward a series of buttes and crevices in the distance. They drove down a switchbacked slope and their ears popped. It felt as if they were below sea level. A half hour later they spotted an odd rock formation off to their right. Ronnie got out the binocs. "Looks like a decent spot to lay up."

The microbus jounced and jittered over the rock and sand. The formation, which looked like a mushroom, was further than it first appeared and it took them forty-five minutes to finally pull up beneath the overhang of a sandstone ledge that jutted from the earth like a natural Stonehenge. It was a little after four.

The boys got out to stretch their legs and walk around the odd formation. It was bigger than it looked, with several jagged routes up and into the crown. Ball cap pulled low over his forehead Ronnie boosted himself up onto a boulder to climb inside the crown.

"Careful of rattlers, hoss," Curt reminded him.

Ronnie hesitated. "It's hot and sunny. Hopefully they're all sleeping."

"No man. They lay up at night. They like the heat."

Ronnie wore over-the-ankle hiking boots. They wouldn't do much good if a rattler lunged for the calf or thigh and he paused before each step. There were numerous cubby holes in the rock, dark places where snakes could hole up. He wished he'd boned up more on rattlesnakes.

"Wait a minute," Curt said from the ground. "I'll get the snakebite kit." He returned to the bus and located the plastic, lozenge-shaped capsule. Carrying a backpack and canteen he followed Ronnie into the crown. It only took a few minutes to reach the summit, an uneven confluence of two rounded boulders leaning together and surrounded by jagged shards of granite and sandstone that formed a natural parapet.

They scanned their surroundings. No snakes. Curt reached into the backpack and removed an aluminum foil bindle. He unwrapped it, revealing two beige capsules.

"Ready to launch?"

Ronnie reached out and took one of the caps. "Let's do it."

The boys swallowed the acid. Ronnie took out the Zeiss and leaned against the waist-high stone, slowly examining the horizon. Curt sat in the shade cast by a broad shingle, took a fat doobie from his shirt pocket and lit it with a Zippo emblazoned with the Grateful Dead symbol.

Soon they were mellow. They waited for the acid to kick in. Ronnie took long swigs from his canteen, got up again and resumed his watch. Afternoon sun lit the desert like the Radio City stage, the crown of rocks casting a long shadow to the east. Pale cumulus hung on the horizon glowing gold in the lowering sun. It was October and the desert would grow cold at night but they had plenty of sleeping bags in the bus.

Curt's gaze focused in on a half inch crack in a roundish boulder and he saw a large black spider with gold markings industriously wrapping a beetle in silk. He knew the acid had kicked in. Here was life in all its horror and glory. He reached for his backpack and withdrew his sketch pad and a mechanical pencil.

They grooved in a timeless space. A tendril of chill insinuated itself up Curt's shirt like the breath of a waking ice giant.

"Curt."

"What?"

"Curt."

"What?!"

"Come look at this, man! Look at this fucking butte, man! It looks like that drawing you made!"

It took Curt a couple seconds to remember how to move as he shifted first to one hip, then to his feet. He joined Ronnie at the rail looking east at the distant violet mountains.

"What?"

Ronnie handed him the Zeiss. "Five after twelve, man. Doesn't that look just like that butte you drew?"

Curt took the glasses. His wavering grip found the rock at his waist, the sand, the horizon. The butte escaped him.

"Can't see jack shit, man."

"Here," Ronnie said, taking the binocs and laying them on a flat shelf, a giant chipped tooth. He crouched and carefully adjusted the binocs. "All right. Don't touch 'em. Just carefully get down here and look?"

Curt did as he was told. As usual, he saw nothing at first but he kept looking and the flickering trick mirror coalesced—a minor distortion revealing the tiny, quavering chimney-like rock of his dreams.

"Whoa."

"Yeah. Let me see that sketch."

"I gave it to the bartender."

Ronnie did a double-take. "What?"

"Yeah. She asked for it. I didn't have tip money anyway."

A dark blue crept behind the mountains indicating the night to come.

"That's where we're going, man," Ronnie said.

"Bullshit, Ronnie. Look at these canyons."

Ronnie turned toward him with feverish eyes. "Don't you see? There's a reason you drew that place! It's too similar to be a coincidence. Someone or something is telling you to go there!"

"Oh. Wow," Curt said as revelation dawned. He stood and stretched. His up-thrust arms topped the long shadow of the crown like horns. "The only place we're going is back to the bus. Aren't scorpions nocturnal?"

"We been out here all afternoon and ain't seen diddly. I say we build a fire and camp up here, man."

All they had was a small camp stove. It would take hours to gather enough scrub brush from the desert floor to build a fire that would last minutes. There was nothing resembling a branch much less a log.

"No fire. It would make the stars more difficult to see."

Ronnie nodded. "That's right, man."

Curt seemed to have modified his earlier policy. As the sun settled into the west they climbed down to the bus, retrieved their sleeping pads and bags and returned to the crown. They set the camp stove up in the center of the crown on a flat spot but now the acid raced through their veins and neither was hungry.

As twilight gave way to night, they lay back with their heads on their rolled up bags and gazed at the celestial display. Back in college, they may as well have been in a tent when the stars came out. Light and air pollution had dimmed the heavens to a faint backgrounds glimmer.

Out here, miles from the ubiquitous neon and spotlights, the stars spanned the heavens to infinity. Millions of them. The whole Milky Way, a carpet of diamonds. Far to the east a meteor fell to earth leaving a blazing trail.

"Wow," Ronnie said.

"Yeah," Curt said. "Clarity."

Ronnie looked down. A pale scorpion hustled across his ankle. It tickled.

Far out, he thought.
Eventually they fell asleep.

CHAPTER FOUR

SAND STORM

The sun woke them. The sun and the wind. Because they were surrounded by abutments, it was past ten before the sun struck Curt in the face. He groaned, wiped a hand across his eyes and reached for his sunglasses. The wind was out of the east playing the crown like a flute. The clefts emitted dissonance as the wind ripped through. Sand flew.

Curt splashed water in his face from the canteen, took a healthy swig and shook Ronnie awake.

"Wha—?"

"Get up. Wind's picking up."

Curt stood and looked over the stones to the east. A roiling brown wall concealed the mountains. It filled the sky until it tapered off in a pale yellow.

"Fuck," Curt said. "Sand storm coming."

"What?" Ronnie said getting to his knees and unsteadily to his feet. He looked over the wall and turned away at once blinking and rubbing his face. "Ow."

"Yeah. It's a sand storm! We'd better get to the bus."

They gathered their things, rolling the sleeping bags sloppily, hanging backpacks and canteens around their necks, and scrambled down the pipe to the desert floor on the west side of the crown where they were shielded from the brunt of the wind. The bus was at six, shielded by the outward leaning sandstone shelf.

Ronnie paused to piss. "Fuck, man I'm still tripping."

Curt stared at the rock. Tiny whorls of gray/green lichen rotated in spiral nebulae. They walked around the base, drew open the side door and threw in their stuff. They got in the van. Ronnie was first to pop the red and white Igloo and pull out a slab of cheddar wrapped in cellophane. Curt found a loaf of California sourdough they'd bought two days ago and tore off a chunk. Next they hit the jerky.

Twenty minutes later the boys belched, satisfied. The wind had picked up and even here, behind the crown pinpricks of sand peppered the bus. The push-out vents howled when the wind hit the right resonance. A fine grit entered through the open windows, but even in the shade it was hot and neither was eager to close the windows.

Curt grabbed a handful of Arby's napkins and opened his door. "Roll up a doobie. I gotta take a dump."

He let himself out and looked for a place out of the wind. Underneath the shelf was best. He duck-walked back and looked around for a pair of rocks on which to crouch, eyes glossing over a peculiar pattern in the stone. Then back.

Curt couldn't believe it. There were pictographs under the stone. They were hard to make out due to age and shade but when he got close they were plain as day. A cluster of conquistadors in their distinctive peaked caps riding horses. The lead conquistador held a curved saber overhead. Two feet away crouched behind a peculiar rock formation stood an Indian firing an arrow. The Indian seemed like a giant compared to the tiny Spaniards but perhaps that was due to perspective. Yet the Spaniards were drawn as if moving right to left in the middle distance—not coming toward the Indian.

Perhaps it was symbolic.

Midway between them, a wagon wheel.

Curt found a different place then returned to the bus.

He opened the door. "Hey man! Get your camera and follow me. You've got to see this."

Ronnie looked up from his reefer works spread on a shopper, carefully finished the doobie and set it in the ashtray. He grabbed the Nikon.

"What's up?"

Curt led him under the ledge and showed him the pictographs.

"Wow," Ronnie said focusing. He took pictures at a low exposure to take advantage of the limited light. "Surprised they're not defaced or something."

"Yeah, well you know with the wind around here man, the sand could have covered them up."

"It's gonna cover us up if we don't get back in the bus."

The desert plowed through them. Sand began to accumulate beneath the ledge due to back drift. They got in the bus. Ronnie pulled the doobie from the ashtray and lit up. Soon they were mellow.

"What about that old woman, man?" Ronnie said. "I hope she isn't out in this."

"For all we know she lives nearby. Walked there."

"Lives nearby where? There's nothing on the map."

"Ronnie. You're not going to obsess about that old woman, are you? Look outside. It's fucking opaque."

Visibility was maybe ten feet. The desert was moving west. A choking cloud of dust enveloped the crown leaving a bubble of slightly dense air in its lee. Sand flew into the bus through the open windows and at last the boys cranked them closed leaving only the rear flaps open. Their gear was covered in grit.

"Fuck! What if we get covered with a fucking dune or something?" Ronnie said.

"We got shovels, dude. Remember? For digging up shards and shit?"

Ronnie thought about Terry, his svelte blond girlfriend. She'd wanted him to go to Playa del Carmen this summer. He closed his eyes and pictured turquoise pools beneath swaying palm trees, surf rolling in off the Caribbean. He'd never been to Mexico. They would have been a mere day trip from the pyramids and Tulum, the fabled Mayan outpost on the sea.

The bus began to rock on its springs.

"Man that wind is strooong!" Curt said. "Grab me one of those sodas, wouldja?"

Ronnie turned in his seat and stretched for the cooler. A three inch scorpion the color of discarded skin dropped on his wrist.

"YAHHH!" Ronnie jerked his hand back so hard it struck the windshield. Curt twisted in his seat, a spear of anxiety rising from his shades.

"What?"

"A fucking scorpion just dropped on my hand!"

Curt half-turned and put one knee on the seat. "What? Where?"

Fearfully they surveyed the jumble of rubble that filled the bus' interior. No way would they know if the scorpion were inside. The junk could be hiding a dozen scorpions.

"Fuck," Curt said. "What do we do?"

"We gotta get it outta here, man, or we can't stay in here."

"Aren't they supposed to be frightened of people? Maybe it'll just hide and leave us alone."

Ronnie looked up hopefully. A scorpion crawled from between the folds of a sleeping bag and climbed to the top raising its tail in victory. Sir Edmund Hillary. This one was orange.

"That's not the same scorpion," Ronnie said.

"Fuck."

"Yeah."

Now there was no question. They had to clear the bus of scorpions or they were fucked.

"Get that Off! out of the glove compartment," Curt said.

Ronnie retrieved the orange and blue aerosol can. He read the directions. It said nothing about scorpions. It wasn't a poison—it was a repellant. But he couldn't think of a better idea.

Curt picked up a pair of two foot barbecue prongs. "Okay. I'll lift the shit with these and shake it out. You blast it with the Off!"

Ronnie aimed the aerosol at the red scorp, still posing on its hill, and let fly. The scorpion scrambled off the mound, tried to make the seams but Ronnie was right there dousing it. It struggled feebly against the side door. Ronnie opened the door and used his foot to shove the arachnid out. He followed it out. It would be easier to avoid them out here than in there.

Curt followed. They faced the interior. Curt used the barbecue tongs to drag his sleeping bag from the bus. It was light—made of nylon and filled with down. He whisked it away.

"Fuck it. We'll just leave 'em."

He extracted Ronnie's and did likewise. The interior was still filled with fast food wrappers, magazines, maps, Ziplocs, backpacks, shoes and other bric-a-brac but at least they could clear a space to stand.

Something heavy hit the windshield with a crack. Both boys' heads swiveled in unison.

"What the fuck was that?" Ronnie said.

Curt got down on his haunches and peered beneath the bus. Sand had built up around the perimeter and he couldn't make anything out.

Another report, this one unmistakable.

"That's a fucking rock!" Curt declared.

"Come on, man. No way the wind is hurling rocks."

Curt looked at Ronnie with an expression close to panic. "There's somebody out there," he said so softly his voice was drowned by the wind.

Ronnie caught the vibe. They leaped back into the bus and shut the door. Curt went for his White Stag bowie. Ronnie picked up the tire iron, which floated around the back with everything else.

Curt had wanted to bring guns but Ronnie talked him out of it. They froze, waiting for the next rock. The wind turned the crown into a madman's pipe organ. The bus howled and whistled. Ronnie thought about shutting the back vents but was afraid to move. For long minutes nothing happened.

Could they have been mistaken? Could it have been something else?

"Maybe they fell off the ledge," Curt said.

A shadow fell across the windshield. A mailed fist punched through the glass and uncoiled. Each finger was a scorpion's tail. The hand extended and seized Curt by the throat.

CHAPTER FIVE

THE COLLECTION

aughan Beadles beamed at his students on the last day of the semester. The finals were over, the grades issued, the i's dotted and the t's crossed. They were a bright, resourceful bunch destined to do great things. Some in anthropology, which he taught, and some in completely unrelated fields. At six foot one with wavy dark hair, Beadles did not resemble a stereotypical university professor. More like a runner, or a boxer. He wore a wine and green Hawaiian shirt over creased Dockers and the tan of an outdoorsman.

"Why did the Mayans disappear? Basic sanitation, or the lack thereof. That's my guess."

Rob Whitfield, one of his best students, raised his hand. Beadles recognized the bookish young man in wire-rimmed glasses. "Rob?"

"What about the possibility they were conquered and absorbed into a more warlike culture, like the Toltecs?"

"If you can prove that, you'll be halfway to your PhD. And on that note, I wish you all success with your finals and I'll see you next semester."

The 126 students in Emory Lecture Hall gave him a standing ovation. Beadles was an extrovert and easy to like. He invited favorite students to go biking with him on weekends on the many bike trails in and around Creighton University, in the heart of sylvan Creighton, IL. CU was a private liberal arts school with outstanding anthropology and engineering schools.

A half dozen students gathered at the foot of the stage to speak with Beadles including two co-eds who might arouse suspicion in a less than trusting wife. Like Betty. Betty was a bombshell and she knew it. The whole faculty knew it. A gorgeous wife could be an asset or a detriment in academia depending on the character of one's colleagues. Thus far Betty had been an asset.

Beadles chatted with one of the co-eds, a brunette stunner from Wyoming. She left no doubt about her availability. Beadles waved his wedding ring in her face until she got the hint.

Ten minutes later only Whitfield remained.

"What's up, Rob?" Beadles said.

"Hey Professor, can I take a look at the collection?"

Beadles swung his backpack over his shoulder and headed up the aisle. "What collection?"

Whitfield scampered after. "Come on, Professor! Everybody knows you've taken possession of the Lost Tribe collection! There was an article in *National Geo* about it."

"'The Great Lost Azuma Collection.' It was never lost. Mr. Hayes knew about the collection since he was six years old. Kept it secret his whole life, a family tradition, I gather. The only reason he turned it over to Creighton was because his granddaughter came here on a basketball scholarship. She's a senior now."

"Yeah. Roberta Hayes. She's phenomenal. I've seen her play."

"Bright girl. I gave her an 'A' last year."

"Wow. You know what that means, Prof? It means you're the reason that rancher chose Creighton!"

They had left the Emory Building and walked across the quad, crisscrossed with pathways and students, shaded by centuries old oak and elm. They headed diagonally across the quad toward Merrill Hall where the collection was kept under lock and key.

The University had scheduled a press conference for next Friday, one week from today, to announce the acquisition. Beadles would formally take charge. Six years ago Beadles had written *In the Footprints of Ghosts*, an inquiry into the existence of a heretofore unknown tribe of the Anasazi, a loose configuration encompassing numerous Indians who roamed the Southwest prior to the Navajo and Hopi. It had been a critical and popular success and had unleashed an undertow of fear and loathing among his colleagues that flowed to this day.

Beadles recalled Sayre's Law; "Academic politics is the most vicious and bitter because the stakes are so low."

Particularly apt re: Head of Anthropology Herr Professor Joel Liggett with whom Beadles was expected to celebrate tomorrow night.

Merrill Hall was a four story red brick Victorian monster with turrets at the corners. It had previously been an armory. It now housed the Museum and various collections. It had been retrofitted with cable, sprinklers and New Age light bulbs but the main doors were still iron and looked capable of withstanding the Crusades.

It was a warm day in early June, but the foot-thick walls kept the high-ceilinged interior cool. They entered the vast foyer and inhaled the smell of centuries. Dust, graphite, a hint of sage. The tile floor was checkerboard. Framed black and white photographs of pioneers, Indians, famous persons lined the corridor cutting through the heart of the building. They passed the Lecture Hall and Library, went through a set of double doors and down a concrete stairwell to the basement.

The basement floor was gray painted concrete. Fluorescent bulbs in aluminum hoods lit the way past several locked doors to a metal door marked B-12. Video cams watched the hall discreetly from the corners. Beadles removed a set of keys from his pocket and was about to insert one when the door swung inward.

A stout Native American, long gray hair tied in a ponytail, wearing a blue workshirt and Dickey's gray work pants stepped aside. His coppery face was as lined as old gloves.

"Professor," he croaked.

"Hello, Anatole," Beadles said entering the long, low-ceilinged chamber followed by Whitfield. A series of rectangular tables covered with sheets of brown paper held the new collection. Pottery, woven goods, shaped stones and flint arrowheads seemed to stretch to the end of the room. It smelled like a dig, like fresh-turned earth with a hint of sage.

"Anatole, Rob Whitfield. Rob, Anatole Cerveros. Anatole's been a custodian here for, what, fifteen years?"

"Sixteen," the old Indian replied. "But who's counting?"

"We're just going to take a look. If you want to leave I'll lock up."

Cerveros shut the door. "Gotta stay, Professor. Them's the rules."

Beadles was surprised. He was not yet in charge of the collection but he assumed he was in the loop. "What rules?"

"Professor Liggett's."

"I see." He hoped Whitfield hadn't seen him grimace. He shouldn't let the little toad get to him. Joel Liggett. Even his name was chinless.

"Don't touch anything," Beadles said.

The room was well lit with fluorescents. Whitfield stared down at the first table.

"Holy shit. Look at the fluting on this arrowhead, Professor."

Beadles joined him and looked at the beautifully shaped shard sitting on a sheet of white paper. "It's certainly unique. I wonder how they worked that squiggle."

"Why do you call them the Azuma?"

"It's as close as I can get to a translation of the petroglyphs discovered in 1938 in Corkindale, Arizona. Of course this is assuming a cultural basis in ancient Pueblo. That one site was the foundation for most of my research. The rest is from a sixteenth century Spanish diary."

Beadles turned toward the janitor. "What do you think of all this stuff, Anatole?"

The old Indian shrugged and crossed his arms. "They're all ancestors far as I'm concerned."

"You're Navajo, aren't you?"

"That's right."

"You ever hear of the Azuma?"

Shrug. "My father and grandfather told me and my brothers and sisters all sorts of stories when I was growing up. Most of them were bullshit."

Whitfield's scream split the air like a cleaver. A pot fell to the concrete floor and shattered with a sharp report. Cerveros and Beadles whirled in shock to see the undergrad dancing away from the table frantically shaking his arm. A pale scorpion dropped and skittered along the baseboards.

Beadles raced around the table to his student whose back was against the wall staring in horror at a tiny red dot on his wrist.

"I told you not to touch anything!" Beadles said grabbing the wrist.

"I didn't! It leaped out of the fucking pot! It stung me! Am I going to die?"

"Don't be absurd. Scorpion stings are rarely fatal for adults. Come on. Let's get you to the ER."

As Beadles led the stunned and shocked Whitfield through the door he saw that Cerveros' face had blanched almost white.

CHAPTER SIX

CLOSE CALL

eadles sat Whitfield down on the shaded stoop and used his cell phone to call campus police. It was against policy to admit anyone to the collection not personally approved by the department head but that never occurred to him. Within five minutes a new Chevy Impala with Creighton University Police on the door pulled up on the sidewalk in front of the hall. The officer got out and walked around the car. He was an older man with a belly and a walrus mustache wearing the beige university police uniform and a ball cap.

"What's the problem, Professor?" he said looking at the seated Whitfield.

"Hello, Phil. We've got to get Rob to the ER. He was just stung by a scorpion."

The cop's bushy eyebrows hunched. "A scorpion?"

"Long story. It came in a pot."

Together they eased Rob into the backseat. He seemed dazed and his arm had begun to swell. The cop switched on the lights and took the shortest route back to Storrow Drive which wound through the campus. Once on the road he hit the siren. University Hospital was seven minutes away.

They pulled up in front of the ER behind an ambulance. An orderly in a green smock saw them helping Rob from the back seat and wheeled a chair toward them through the automatic doors.

"Scorpion sting," Beadles explained as they wheeled him inside. The orderly motioned for a lady doctor to come over. She wore a white lab jacket and cat's-eye glasses, her blond hair pulled back in a severe bun.

"He was stung by a scorpion that crawled out of a pot," Beadles said.

"Oh my," the nurse said. "Let's get him back there and see what we can do. Sir, are you a relative?"

"I'm his professor," Beadles said. "His name is Rob Whitfield. I think he's from Paducah."

"You'll have to stay here," the doctor said. Her label said Musgrove. "Would you notify his next-of-kin if you think it's appropriate?"

"He's not going to die, is he?"

The nurse checked Whitfield's pulse. The patient's eyes followed her fearfully.

"I doubt it, but the quicker we act the better chance he'll have."

Beadles watched them wheel Whitfield through the automatic doors into the interior. What did he do now? He had work to do but it didn't seem appropriate to simply abandon Whitfield while he went about his business. He checked his Razr. Betty had called. He called her back.

"Vaughan, what are we going to do about a baby-sitter? Cathy can't make it and the Burkes are out of town."

The department party was the following night and their son Lars was two years old.

"Relax. There's a pool of students registered at the union looking for baby-sitter work. I'll find one of my students."

"Please let me know as soon as possible."

"Don't worry about it Betty baby. My students love me. I have a couple in mind."

"When will you be home? I'm making lasagna."

Beadles debated whether to tell her about Whitfield. Better not. Betty was a worrier, an obsessive/compulsive perfectionist. It had made her a star at the mortgage title company where she worked but she could be difficult when fixated. Like a terrier with a bone.

"I'll be home by five, snookums."

"Love you."

"Love you."

Beadles checked his stock portfolio and his Facebook page. He had twenty-two comments, mostly on scholarly matters. He sat in a plastic chair and made notes on a lecture he planned to give on the Azuma. A young Hispanic mother dozed fretfully in another chair while her five-year-old played with plastic toys from a box.

Forty minutes later Musgrove came out the sliding doors. "He's sitting up. He's asking for you."

Beadles stood. "How's he doing?"

"Fine. We got some anti-venom serum into him, basically the same stuff we use for allergic reactions and he seems to be responding. His pulse is back to normal and so is his body temperature."

"Thank God," Beadles said with such conviction the doctor glanced. He followed her back through the medicinal-smelling halls to a room. Inside Whitfield was sitting up in bed watching Judge Judy.

"Professor! Man, I'm sorry about this mess."

"Rob, don't be silly. I'm just glad you're okay. You want to notify anyone? Your parents?"

"God no. They said if I'm still stable in an hour they're going to release me. You don't have to hang around."

Beadles looked at the arm. The sting was covered with a white bandage and the swelling had gone down. He felt massive relief. That will teach him to violate the rules.

Yeah right, he thought. *As if I ever learned to toe the line.*

"Give me a call in a few days. We'll go riding."

"You bet, Professor. And thanks again for letting me see the exhibit and getting me in here so fast."

Beadles waved. "All in a day's work."

He took the bus back to campus, walked up the hill and unlocked his Trek 10-speed which was chained to a rack outside the Emory Building. Riding through the shaded streets, Beadles reflected on how lucky he'd been. He'd always had good luck.

Plus, he made his own luck, often recklessly. He'd first spotted Betty in a supermarket aisle. He'd followed her through the parking lot with a grocery cart which he "accidentally" let slide into her car.

That was six years ago in Elgin. They dated. They clicked. She was the most exciting thing in his life. Beadles had never had trouble attracting women. It was getting rid of them that was the hard part. He didn't see himself getting married before age forty, but after a year of dating, Betty said, "Either we get married or I'm out of here."

Beadles did that quick calculation so many make. Can I do better? Like staring at a Ferrari with the keys in your hand. Yeah it goes like hot stink and it's beautiful, but think of the upkeep! Mechanics alone are 250 an hour. Premium gas. Thousand dollar tires. Limited utility.

He was an up and coming academic star with pop success. She was an ambitious, gorgeous, intelligent and charming loan officer with a future. What could go wrong? It wasn't until a week later he realized she smoked.

She'd tried to keep it hidden. For awhile. He could taste it on her lips but never said a word. God knew he had his own vices.

Their anniversary was coming up. They planned to drop Lars with Betty's parents in Rockford and spend a week at Sandal's in Jamaica.

Six years on and he still couldn't get enough of Betty's world-class body and bedroom flair. It blinded him to a certain selfishness. He pulled into the driveway of the Craftsman-style bungalow he'd purchased three years ago when he'd joined the faculty and there she was, hoisting Lars from his car seat in her Ford Edge, tailgate open revealing two sacks of groceries.

He swung his right leg over while still in motion, came to a halt next to Betty and kissed her while she held the babe. He tasted cigarettes. She'd velcroed an ashtray to the console in the Edge.

"Guess what?" Betty said. "Got a baby-sitter. I went to that university site listing undergrads and found someone who was your student last year."

"Great? Who is it?"

"Stephanie Byrd."

Beadles shook his head. "Doesn't ring a bell."

"She has excellent credentials. Liggett endorsed her."

"Oh, well, if the great Liggett himself endorsed her…"

"Grab the groceries, wouldya?"

CHAPTER SEVEN

SOUVENIR

etty baked lasagna, Lars went down for the count. They watched *Ghost* on cable with Patrick Swayze and Demi Moore, and made passionate love on the king-sized bed in the master bedroom. Betty went out on the porch and smoked a cigarette. Lars slept in a crib in the dressing room that dog-legged off the bedroom. Betty returned and crawled into bed.

She slept.

She ground her teeth. A low wave irritation accompanied by atonal humming. It did no good to wake her. Beadles had begged her to visit a dentist, a psychiatrist, someone to stop the grinding. Betty flew into a fury the second time he did this. It was better to just keep his mouth shut and put up with it even if it did cause him many a sleepless night. A big part of marriage was overlooking your spouse's irritating habits.

Lars woke around one a.m. and squawked. Betty heaved herself out of bed and pulled on a flannel robe. "Your turn next time, buster."

Beadles got out of bed too. "I'm going to do a perimeter check."

"That's good. There might be Injuns."

Beadles slipped into his sheepskin moccasins, went into the kitchen and opened the refrigerator. He removed an open carton of orange juice, drank directly from the spout and put it back. He opened the basement door, turned on the lights and went downstairs where he had a makeshift office: a desk, computer, and table covered with books, papers and artifacts. He sat at the desk and opened the center drawer, reaching far back behind the pens, paper clips, flash drives and post-it notes to a small cloth bag in the rear. He pulled it out, opened it, and shook a quarter-sized gold object into his hand.

He held the softly gleaming gold medallion between thumb and forefinger. Squiggly lines radiated from a turquoise center. He had discovered the medallion the first day the Azuma Collection had arrived, before anyone else had seen it. Before Liggett and his apes raced over, even before Anatole had unlocked the door.

Uncataloged. It had fallen out of a pot filled with beads and shards. One tiny little item. He deserved it for his devotion to his students and the prestige he brought the University. It was otherwise destined to be cataloged and shut away—or perhaps put on display in the university museum—forever to gather dust. No one would miss this one little item out of so vast a collection.

Don't kid yourself. It's stealing.

He planned to mount it on a gold chain and give it to Betty on their anniversary. Betty loved her bling. She had twenty grand in jewelry stashed in an ivory-inlaid dowry box. He tossed the medallion up and down in the palm of his hand, feeling its weight. Now that he'd had an opportunity to open up the whole collection he'd found there wasn't much gold. The Azuma were not big on ornamental jewelry.

It was the squirrely fluting on the arrowheads that convinced him the Azuma were a heretofore undiscovered tribe. He saw the pattern repeated on some of the pottery and woven baskets. No other tribe to his knowledge had ever used it. A squiggly line embossed in gold and worked into stone. How had they done it?

He turned the disc over. The back was flat and rough. He planned to epoxy a small gold loop on the back through which to run the chain.

The old floor creaked as Betty comforting Lars came to the head of the stairs.

"What are you doing?"

"Just checking on a few things. Go back to bed. I'll be right up."

She padded away. Beadles slipped the gold bead back into its pouch and replaced it in the back of his drawer.

Tomorrow was the department party and he had to get some rest.

CHAPTER EIGHT

BABY-SITTER

eadles rose at six and did three miles on the green streets of Creighton. At thirty-eight, he was determined not to slide into middle-aged professorship like the well-fed burghers who surrounded him. He entered through the kitchen door puffing.

Betty was giving Lars his breakfast. "My turn. Can you watch Lars while I go to the gym?"

"Sure. Just let me take a quick shower."

Beadles showered and dressed in slacks, sandals, and a guayabera he'd purchased in Guatemala. It was a typical early May morning, temperatures in the sixties and expected to hit the mid-seventies. When he returned Lars was strolling the living room hanging onto the furniture and gurgling.

Beadles retrieved his backpack from the entryway, sat on the sofa and removed a stack of term-end papers. Minutes later Betty breezed through in a Bruce Lee jumpsuit and blew him a kiss.

"Back by noon. You want anything from the deli?"

"Bring me a club sandwich."

"Love you."

"Love you," Beadles said. He placed the stack of papers on the coffee table while Lars amused himself with a primary-color Lightning McQueen that burped aphorisms. "Life is like a highway. You've got to stay on the road."

Lars gurgled in delight.

"Lars, you are one swell kid," Beadles said.

He picked up the first paper, "Did Mongolians Discover America?," and started to read. Every year at least five papers about Asians crossing over into the Americas via the Alaskan land bridge, each student reinventing the wheel. Not that this was a knock—it was becoming increasingly difficult for students to come up with fresh anthropological angles. Beadles didn't know whether it was the times or the students. There would be at least a dozen papers every year on the Vikings discovering America. Several maintained ancient aliens sowed the seeds of civilization. Erik Von Daniken was very popular. Invariably Beadles gave these papers low grades. He had little patience for ancient aliens.

One student had turned in a paper claiming seventh century Druids had not only discovered America, they had deposited a despised wizard as far inland as Wisconsin. The student had spent his summer searching for the grave. Beadles suggested he switch his major to creative writing.

Beadles got through six papers before Lars confronted him and said with the utmost seriousness, "Daddy, I have to go poop now."

Beadles set the papers aside and scooped Lars up. "All right little man. Let's get 'er done."

They spent a little time in the back yard and when they came in Lars was down for a nap. Beadles returned to the living room and phoned Rob Whitfield. It rang five times before he got the recording.

"Rob, it's Vaughan Beadles. Give me a call when you get this."

He phoned the hospital. Whitfield had been discharged last evening shortly after Beadles had left. He would not shed a tiny spasm of anxiety until he heard from Whitfield himself.

Beadles went back to grading papers. Betty returned at three, fresh-faced, pumped, and toting a big paper bag from Norm's Deli. "Ran into Liz Maroukis at the gym. She wants me to try out for *Taming of the Shrew*."

Both Betty and Liz were members of the Hometown Players' Theater Guild. Betty had played a small part in last year's production of *The Crucible*, and had been active in high school and college drama.

"Do you have time to do that?" Beadles said from the couch.

"I don't know."

"Do you want to do that?"

Betty gave him a wide-eyed look and a Bronx cheer. "Do I want to do it? Of course I want to do it! Shakespeare! The big time! But I don't have time. I barely have time to do my job and take care of you two. Where's little man?"

"Down for the count."

"Mommie!" squealed in. Betty dropped the paper bag on the table and went down the hall. Beadles took his lunch out on the front porch and ate it there, sitting in an Adirondack chair he'd purchased from Lowes. School had just let out. Beadles watched the kids heading home on foot, skateboard and bicycle, some chauffeured from Montessori school in their parents' SUVs. The air was sweet with honeysuckle

Yet that one nagging little doubt kept Beadles from fully savoring the afternoon.

His phone chimed "Baba O'Riley." He scooped it up and looked at the panel.

Thank God.

"Professor, it's Rob. What's up?"

"How are you feeling, Rob?"

"A little sluggish but I think that's the anti-inflammatory they gave me. Otherwise I feel fine. The swelling's virtually disappeared and now it just itches like hell."

"That's great, Rob. That's great. Listen. If you haven't already told anyone about this…"

"No problem, Professor. It was wrong of me to wheedle my way in there."

"Bike ride next week?"

"You bet. I'll call you."

Beadles hung up with a vast sense of relief like a long-dried lake bed suddenly filling with rain. That left Anatole, the campus cop, the orderly, Dr. Musgrove, and whoever else had treated Rob at the hospital. They would be unaware of the protocol.

Hopefully that was the end of it.

"Professor Beadles?"

A young woman stood on the sidewalk wearing a backpack, shapeless in an oversized Banshees T-shirt and baggy slacks with a round head, a Beatles cut, and round sunglasses. She looked vaguely familiar. She held the handlebars of a mountain bike with a dished frame and knobby tires.

"I'm Stephanie Byrd. I took your course 'Populating the Americas' last year."

"Of course." He was surprised he remembered her at all. She hadn't asked a single question all semester and he could barely remember their two personal consultations, which he held with every student.

"I spoke to your wife earlier. I'm your baby-sitter."

"Of course! Come in. Come in."

Beadles stood and glanced at his watch. It was almost five. They were due at the University Club at six. It was a good thing the girl had come by. He led her into the house. Stephanie hoisted the bike effortlessly to her shoulder and carried it up the steps.

"May I leave this here?"

"Of course. Betty! The baby-sitter's here!"

"Just a minute!" came back from the hall.

Beadles gestured to the living room. "Make yourself at home. There's the TV. Help yourself to whatever you fancy in the fridge. Would you like something to drink?"

Byrd set her backpack on the coffee table with a thump. It was designed to look like an Ewok with furry head, ears and little limbs clutching forward. Something a 7th grader might cherish.

"May I use the bathroom?"

"Down the hall, first door on the right."

While Beadles was in the bedroom changing his clothes he heard Betty sorting things away.

"Now you have both our cell phone numbers. Don't hesitate to call if anything happens."

"Nothing's going to happen, Betty. I've been baby-sitting half my life."

Beadles emerged wearing a crisp white short-sleeved sport shirt with arrow collars and creased cream-colored Calvin Klein trousers. Betty was a knockout in a little black cocktail dress that stopped at mid-thigh, her long auburn hair done up in a wave, simple gray pearl earrings. With her high cheekbones, turned-up nose, and wide, generous mouth she was cover girl worthy, every man's dream of a sexy tomboy.

Byrd talked nonsense to Lars on the sofa. Lars laughed, giggled and squealed.

As they pulled out in the Ford, Beadles said, "Who are the Banshees?"

"Oh, some awful heavy metal band. At least it's not rap."

Betty rolled down her window and lit a cigarette, blowing the smoke out.

CHAPTER NINE

DEPARTMENT PARTY

The CU Anthropology Department had benefitted munificently in the past year. In addition to Jepson Hayes choosing them as the custodians of the Azuma Collection, an alumnus named Daniel Potts had bequeathed them two million dollars. The End of Semester party was a tradition among most departments at CU and each celebrated in its own way.

The Athletic Department held theirs in a beer hall with brats and deep-fried cheese. The English Dept. celebrated at an Italian restaurant. Anthropology always held theirs in the tony University Club, hub of the University Golf Course. Joel Liggett was a longtime member and avid golfer.

The Beadles turned their car over to the chauffeur under the Frank Lloyd Wright-designed porte cochère and entered the club through double oak doors. The tinkle of ice and of laughter drifted out of the Lake Tipton room, down the hall on the left. Inside, three dozen people had gathered in clusters, some at the square tables or in the booths overlooking the lake, some at the curving bar. White liveried waiters circulating among them were distributing canapés.

There was a minute rustling as the Beadles entered, like sunflowers turning to the sun. They looked so glamorous, more like celebrities than faculty. Beadles sensed admiration, fear, envy and loathing. The rotten fruit of academic infighting. Donations from the Alumni Foundation were down across the board due to the economy and disagreement with school policies. The Creighton Catamounts' football team had pieced together three losing seasons. The B-ball team was mediocre. New speech guidelines enraged some alumni who held to the quaint proposition that universities should be laboratories of free speech and open inquiry.

Anthropology was the exception due to the Azuma Collection and the Potts Endowment. Beadles and Betty glad-handed their way through the crowd accepting backslaps, hugs and accolades.

An already boozy Wilmar Childs, specialist in Early Mesopotamian Society, weaved through the crowd with a silly grin. Wilmar looked like a parking meter, skinny as a rail with a big bald dome.

"Beadles, old boy! Congratulations on landing the Azuma Collection! I don't suppose there's any chance getting a peek this week?"

Beadles shook Childs' clammy hand. "You know the rules, Wilmar. No one is supposed to go in there except the curators until we know what we've got. However I intend to spend the next month going through the collection. I'd like to open it up as quickly as possible."

"Do you think," Childs said weaving slightly, "that your status as an American Indian had anything to do with Mr. Hayes' decision?"

A warning bell went off in Beadles' skull. Childs was one of Liggett's cronies. Beadles had marked that he was part Native American on his application.

"I doubt it, Wilmar. Mr. Hayes made it clear he was honoring Creighton because his granddaughter, Meredith Hayes, played varsity basketball here."

"Well good for you. I've always thought the department was too damned white!"

Beadles knew Childs wasn't kidding. Childs carried White Guilt around like a shroud. He'd urged the department to add a Professor of Hip-Hop.

Betty to the rescue. "Hello, Wilmar!" She kissed him on the cheek and took his arm. Childs was undone. He would have swooned if Betty hadn't held him up.

"Vaughan, I hate to break this up but there's someone I want you to meet."

Beadles excused himself and let Betty lead him to the bar.

"Cavalry to the rescue," he murmured.

"Oh, Wilmar's harmless." She led Beadles to a tall old man with a silvery widow's peak in a somber banker's three piece.

"Vaughan, this is Daniel Potts, class of '64."

Beadles and Potts shook hands. "That was a very generous endowment, Mr. Potts."

"Call me Dan. They tell me you're in charge of this new Anasazi collection."

"The Azuma Collection, yes."

"And you think it may be evidence of a previously unknown tribe?"

Beadles nodded, wondering how Potts had known. His theory was of little interest outside rarefied academic circles.

"My son Ronnie thought the same thing. He lost his life trying to prove it."

"I'm so sorry," Beadles said. "What happened?"

The old man was clear-eyed and sober. "He would have been fifty had he survived. Ronnie and his best friend Curt went out into the Arizona desert in 1985 searching for proof the Azuma existed. They were never heard from again. We searched for days by land and air. To this day, we haven't a clue as to what happened. I have offered a fifty thousand dollar reward to anyone who can tell me what happened to those two boys."

"Does this have anything to do with the endowment?" Beadles said.

"In a way. But of course this is my alma mater and I've always been proud to be a Catamount. I was track and wrestling. I've been blessed to have a successful career, a son and daughter who survive and eight healthy grandchildren. I'm afraid one of them is going to turn me into a great-grandfather shortly."

"Congratulations."

The old man shrugged. "I'd be happier if she were married but at my age I'll take what I can get. I read your paper in the summer '11 Journal of *Anthropology*. I always believed Ronnie was right. I would welcome proof of the Azuma."

Beadles had been planning a fall expedition if he could get the funding. "Funny you should mention that, Dan."

Twenty minutes later a spoon tapping crystal drew everybody's attention. Liggett stood at the entrance to the dining room chiming away. He was a round little man, bald on top with a fringe of hair, a bulbous nose and close-set eyes.

"Folks if we can start moving into the dining room?"

Liggett stood at the entrance, greeting everyone as they passed through. He shook Beadles' hand warmly.

"Here's our star professor! Can't wait to see what you come up with, Vaughan. Betty, beautiful as always."

"Thank you, Joel," Betty replied.

They filed in and took a seat at a round table in the back with a couple of department newcomers, Adjunct Professor Clayton Gray and his wife Doris. Gray was a pale and nervous young man with round glasses. Doris was a thick young woman in an oversized shirt.

Gray turned to Beadles with a worried expression. "Did you hear? They're thinking of reducing our hours to comply with the new health care law. We will no longer be eligible for university health insurance."

"I've heard," Beadles said. "It's bad news for everyone. They've put a freeze on hiring."

"We hear they're going to start laying off faculty," Gray said.

Doris put her hand on his arm. "Clayton, can we talk about something else?"

A waiter appeared and plopped down salads. A young teaching assistant and his boyfriend joined them, both with long hair and bangs. All expressed delight at the Azuma acquisition and confidence that Beadles would produce a world-class collection.

Shortly after dessert, Liggett struck his crystal wine glass with his silver spoon. It was time for the department speech.

CHAPTER TEN

SPEECH

nthropology!" Liggett boomed in a surprisingly deep voice. "The science of humans and their works!"

Betty elbowed Beadles in the ribs.

"I have always considered it the noblest of professions save for perhaps medicine. I am thrilled and honored to welcome you to our annual dinner. As I gaze out among you, I see so many of you who have become more than colleagues: you are my friends and together we share not only a passion for learning, but a burning passion for justice and a better tomorrow, for it is only through understanding the past that we can endure the present and confront the future."

Teaching assistant Ben whispered in his friend's ear and they giggled. Beadles knew just how they felt.

"It has been an astonishing year by any measurement," Liggett continued. "From the discovery of a Mayan pyramid in Georgia to new evidence that South Sea islanders may have settled South America, the revelations have been unrelenting. As you all know, Mr. Jepson Hayes of Cross Creek, Arizona has chosen Creighton to be the recipient of the Azuma Collection, a treasure trove of what many believe to be a heretofore unknown tribe. This was due in no small part to the ongoing research of our distinguished Professor of Anthropology, Vaughan Beadles! Stand up, Vaughan."

Smiling good-naturedly, Beadles stood to enthusiastic applause. None clapped harder than Liggett, although Betty was close. Vaughan did a formal little bow in three directions and sat.

"As many of you know, Vaughan's 2011 paper, "Lost Tribe of the Southwest," appeared in the February issue of *Modern Anthropology* and inspired a Discovery Channel Special."

They'd filmed it in the desert. It had been 110 degrees.

"It is this type of research that brings credit to our college and fills the seats with students. Anthropology has been doubly blessed this year. As some of you already know, Mr. Daniel Potts, Class of '57, has generously endowed our department to the tune of two million dollars! Stand up, Dan."

Liggett already had him scoped. Beadles followed Liggett's gaze and saw the tall man shaking his head no and waving off the suggestion but his tablemates thought otherwise. Reluctantly he stood, essayed a chilly smile and sat.

There was more boilerplate and a couple of deans spoke. It was nine by the time the Beadles finally pulled themselves free and drove home. Lights glowed softly from the little house on Maple St. They parked the Ford in the drive and entered through the front door so as not to wake Lars. They could see Stephanie Byrd watching *Game of Thrones* on the flat screen TV through the big front window.

She got up to greet them as they opened the door.

"Hello. How was your evening?"

"Very nice, Stephanie. Thank you. How's Lars?"

"He's a little sweetheart. We played with some of his toys for awhile, I gave him the warm milk and he fell right asleep."

Betty checked the kitchen. Everything ship-shape. Beadles pulled out his wallet and paid Stephanie forty bucks. "Thank you very much."

"Thank you, Professor. And if you need me again, please call."

Betty went to check on Lars. Beadles waited until Stephanie had taken her bike down to the street and left before turning off the outside lights and locking the door. He went into the bedroom and took off his sports jacket. The disconnect between Liggett's effusive praise and their personal chemistry bothered him. The department head didn't like him. There had been nothing overt. A few disparaging comments about their own "GQ celebrity," an instant of undisguised lust directed at Betty.

Mrs. Liggett was bigger than her husband and had a sour expression. Beadles had no doubt their home life was less than ideal.

Betty swept into the room. "Lars is down for the count! Give me a minute to slip into something more interesting…"

Bam. Just like that he had a stiffy. Beadles peeled off his shirt and trou. Betty came out of the bathroom wearing a filmy black baby doll. As they made love he couldn't help thinking does it get any better?

"Did you see Doris Liggett?" Betty said, lying in his arms after. "She looked like she was training for a pie-eating contest."

"Now, Betty. Be nice."

"The Haverhills are going to have us over for dinner."

"Who's that again?"

Betty stretched languidly. "Ollie Haverhill runs Madwire Media. I ran into him at the bar. His wife Lois heads the Illinois Women of Influence. They've asked me to join them."

"That's great, Bet!"

"So all of a sudden you're an Indian?"

Beadles felt a ripple of shame. "I thought you knew that."

"Let me guess. Cherokee."

"Yes, that's right. I knew I told you."

"No you didn't tell me. I guessed Cherokee because every white American who claims Indian blood says Cherokee. Don't ask me why. Maybe it's that long march. Maybe they impregnated every farmer's daughter along the way."

"My mother told me I had Indian blood," Beadles said in a slightly defensive tone. "It's part of our family history. I think my great, great grandmother on my mother's side was a full-blooded Cherokee."

"Show me the papers."

"I don't got to show you no stinkin' papers!" Beadles said.

Heavy pounding on the door.

Beadles and Betty looked at each other in astonishment. Who could it be at that hour of the night?

The pounding resumed. A muffled shout.

Betty looked at Beadles with bafflement. "Did he just say it was the police?"

Beadles pulled his trousers on and threw on a Catamount T-shirt. He padded through the darkened house. The living room danced gaily with red and blue strobes through the front window. Beadles looked out the front door. Two police cars had pulled up, one in front and one in the drive. Three police officers stood on the porch waiting to be let in.

CHAPTER ELEVEN

NIGHTMARE ON MAPLE STREET

The cops were big. They were city cops, unknown to Beadles. Beadles opened the front door. The lead cop handed Beadles a folded warrant.

"Mr. Beadles, I'm Officer Whitaker of the Creighton Police Department. We have a warrant to search your home for artifacts believed to be taken from a collection owned by the university."

Beadle's face looked like counter-rotating gears. "Are you serious?"

"We're very serious, Mr. Beadles. If you'll please step aside."

Beadles looked at their uncompromising faces and stepped back. They all looked like linebackers. Betty appeared in the hallway wearing a terrycloth robe.

"What is it?"

Lars started to cry.

"These gentlemen have a warrant. They think I've stolen artifacts from the university."

"That's ridiculous!" Betty snapped, whirling and heading toward their son. One cop moved as if to stop her but Whitaker put a hand on his arm. A lady cop appeared. Her tag said Gonzalez.

"Officer," Whitaker said, "follow Mrs. Beadles and keep her company."

Like she was going to take the baby and run. Beadles watched in horror as the fat-hipped lady cop walked down the corridor, her black service shoes echoing on the hardwood floor. Soon Betty reappeared holding a fussy Lars accompanied by Officer Gonzalez.

"Do I have the right to know who's accused me of theft?" Beadles said with a self-righteous stain.

"The document was generated by a credible but confidential source," Whitaker said. "We're only following the judge's orders."

A cop went to the basement stairs and turned on the light. Drawing a flashlight, he descended followed by a fourth cop who had come in the door. Beadles felt the bottom drop out of his stomach. It wasn't possible. How could they know? The moisture fled from his mouth as he listened to the cops opening drawers and moving boxes.

"This is ridiculous," Betty hissed. Lars kept up a low level sob. "Do you mind if I put my child back to bed?"

Whitaker nodded at Gonzalez. "Please accompany Mrs. Beadles."

They disappeared down the hall leaving only Beadles and Whitaker.

"This is somebody's idea of a malicious prank," Beadles said.

"Sir," the cop said, "do you have any firearms in the house?"

Beadles goggled. "What? What is this, a fishing exhibition? No, I don't have any firearms in the house!"

There was a grunt from below. Minutes later the two cops emerged, the one in front toting a cardboard box. He set the box on the floor between Beadles and Whitaker and shined his flashlight in it. The interior contained an Anasazi pot, six inches tall by seven wide, decorated with the characteristic squiggle of the Azuma. Beadles had never seen it before. It easily could have come from the collection. He hadn't even started to catalog and had only looked at a small portion.

"I've never seen that before!" he protested.

Whitaker drew his cuffs. "Sir, you're under arrest for theft. Please turn around."

In a stupor Beadles turned his back. He felt the cold steel of the cuffs clamp around his wrists. Like some stupid nightmare.

"Sir, I am advising you of your Miranda Rights. Anything you say can and will be used against you. You are entitled to have a lawyer present during questioning. If you cannot afford a lawyer, the court will provide one. Do you understand these rights?"

"Yes. Yes, goddamn it! Betty! Call Mel Berenson! Tell him what's happening!"

Betty ran down the hall sans Lars, terrycloth robe flapping. She looked at her handcuffed husband. "Oh no. Oh no. There's got to be some mistake."

"Betty! Did you hear what I said? Call Mel! Get him out of bed! Have him meet me down at the fucking jail! Where are you taking me?"

"Steubenville Justice Center on 10th Street. I doubt a judge will be available to grant your bail at this hour. The earliest that could happen would be nine Monday morning."

Betty watched in shock and disbelief as the cops took Beadles, one at each elbow, led him down the stairs and put him in the back of one of the cruisers.

"Jesus fucking Christ!" Betty said.

"Ma'am," Officer Gonzalez said coming up behind her. "There's no call for that kind of language."

CHAPTER TWELVE

JAILHOUSE TALK

The cell was made of yellow-painted cinderblocks and contained two steel bunks on opposite walls, hanging from chains. It smelled of piss and disinfectant. There was a stainless steel toilet with a sink over it on the wall between the cots. Beadles, deprived of his belt, sat on one cot with his head in his hands. A black kid with an explosion of weasel tails on his head sat opposite. He wore a gray wife beater exposing blue tats, a cut torso and baggy cargo pants.

"Hey man, whatchoo in for? They holdin' me on a federal beef. I hacked into Homeland Security's Atlanta Fusion Center. Man, I had those babies looking at naked women on rooftops! They think I'm some kinda terrorist threat all I want to do is look at naked women! I could shut them all down I wanted."

Dude had to be piped on meth. He radiated a raw animal odor as he gesticulated like a signer for the deaf.

"Hey, my name's Ninja. Whatchoo in for?"

Beadles looked up. "They think I stole a pot from the university."

Ninja snapped his head on his long neck like a towel. "Whaaaaat? You stole pot from the u-ni-VERS-ity?"

"Not pot as in reefer—a clay pot."

"That's fucked up man."

"I didn't! It's some kind of set-up! I've been framed. Now I'm trying to figure out who and why."

Certainly the distinguished head of Anthropology would never stoop to such a thing. Why? Out of pique? Because Beadles had once made fun of him? That would make Liggett a psycho, and psychos didn't get to head major anthropology departments.

"Hey man, what's your name?" Ninja said with a hint of impatience.

Beadles looked at him. Two men in a cage. It always came down to this. Can I take him? Beadles thought that he could. Beadles had boxed in college and still sparred regularly at the University Health Club. He had a black belt in karate. He was four inches taller and had Ninja by at least forty pounds. Ninja looked like a Mad Max extra but his brain was probably fried on meth.

"Vaughan," Beadles said.

"So what were you gonna do with that pot, Vaughan, fence it or what? It must be some kind of rare sumbitch like something you'd see on Pawn Stars or something 'cause fucking pots are hard to fence, y'know? I mean, it's bulky, it's breakable, it's a piece of shit! I was gonna steal something it would be something valuable like a diamond or some gold or something, you know what I'm sayin'?"

Beadles was developing a healthy loathing for his cellmate. A baton banged against the barred door. Outside stood a jailer the shape and size of a refrigerator. "You two lovebirds shut the fuck up," he said, "or ahmina come back and mace ya. That means you, Preston."

He glared to punctuate his message, satisfied when the occupants had turned away.

As soon as the guard moved on Ninja spoke in whisper. "Hey man you gotta mouthpiece? I know a Jew lawyer slicker 'n' a preacher. Name's Feldstein—you want I could put a word in for you. He's my lawyer."

"I have a lawyer," Beadles replied lying down and staring at the ceiling. Maybe motor mouth would get the hint.

No such luck. "Yeah? Who's your lawyer? I know a lot of lawyers in this town."

I'll bet you do.

"Does it matter?" Beadles said softly willing Ninja to shut up.

"Fuck it matters! You probably got some high-priced corporate asshole or tax lawyer don't know shit about the criminal justice system."

Snap! Ninja was exactly right. But Mel also knew most of the lawyers in the city and if he didn't feel capable of handling the situation he would pass Beadles on to the right man.

Ninja suddenly got to his feet and in one smooth motion dropped his trousers and swiveled his ass onto the stainless steel toilet. Seconds later, he exploded, releasing a cloud of poison from which there was no escape. Beadles buried his mouth in his sleeve and turned to the wall.

"Sorry, man. I had a peristaltic rush. When you gotta go you gotta go, you know what I'm talkin' about?"

Beadles willed the man gone.

"Hey," a guttural whisper. "Hey I'm talkin' atchoo."

Beadles sat up and faced his cellmate who had returned to his cot. Beadles held his sleeve in front of his face. "I don't wish to appear unfriendly but this is extremely difficult for me. Could you just give me some space here to figure it out?"

Ninja put his hands up, a placating manner. "Okay. Okay. Don't go all gangsta on me, y'hear?"

Beadles lay back down with his arms crossed and stared at the ceiling. He could hear Ninja muttering to himself but as long as he wasn't interactive that was enough. He remained awake all night until pale morning light crept in through the cube-like window high up on the outside wall. They'd taken his watch so he had no idea of the time.

About an hour after sunrise, when Ninja had finally run out of fuel and was contorted on his cot facing the wall, two guards came by and delivered two box breakfasts consisting of cardboard coffee cups, packets of creamer and sugar, a cold, uncooked English muffin, a small tin of Philadelphia cream cheese, an apple, an individual tub of applesauce, and a napkin. No utensils.

It was Sunday.

Beadles mutilated his cream cheese tin to spread it on the cold English muffin. He ate the applesauce directly from the tub. He poured all the packets of creamer and sugar into the coffee which still tasted like cardboard. He rinsed out the cup and used it to drink water from the faucet above the toilet.

Ninja awoke with a jolt, looked at Beadles as if seeing him for the first time, saw Beadles' empty breakfast box, looked down and saw his own beneath his bunk. He picked it up and looked inside.

"Why you not eat my breakfast?" he said, honestly bewildered.

"It's your breakfast," Beadles replied.

"Shit. I woke up first, I would have eaten yours."

Beadles crossed his arms, sat back and stared at the wall.

"Okay," Ninja said. "Okay." He ate his breakfast.

There was a blessed five minutes of silence filled with the echoes and shouts from other inmates.

"My man Feldstein gonna get me outta here," Ninja said. "You got a mouthpiece?"

"We had this conversation last night, don't you remember?"

"I don't remember nothing, man. Whatchoo in here for anyway?"

Beadles felt as if he were trapped in a bizarro version of *Groundhog Day.* "Theft. A pot."

Ninja' face lit with recognition. He pointed. "That's right! You stole the fuckin' pot from the university! You a gangsta!"

Twenty-four hours later the door opened. "Let's go, Mr. Beadles," said the refrigerator.

CHAPTER THIRTEEN

INITIAL APPEARANCE

el Berenson waited in the jail foyer to accompany his client across the street to the courtroom. Berenson was a tall, dignified man with glasses and a Roman nose. He'd handled the closing on Beadles' house and other matters that had come up over the years. He watched as a jailer returned Beadles' belt, watch, and wallet.

Beadles remained uncuffed, accompanied by a policeman as they took the elevator to the second floor and from there an enclosed pedestrian bridge over 10th Street to the courthouse, a Georgian revival with fluted columns. The streets were alive with vehicular and pedestrian traffic, people going about their Monday morning business.

"Vaughan," Berenson said. "I read the warrant. I assume you had nothing to do with this."

"Absolutely not. It's a frame-up."

"Well, let's just let that slide until we get you out of here. Considering your lack of record and standing in the community I don't think we'll have to wait too long."

"How's Betty?" Beadles said.

"She's coping. She called her parents who are driving down from Elgin to be with her."

Great. Betty's parents had never really warmed to Beadles, although they put up a good front. They were hide-bound conservatives who were not shy about expressing their opinions and turned every family get-together into a harsh debate.

They joined a half dozen supplicants, their lawyers and police in the corridor outside the courtroom and sat on marble benches beneath a painting of Lincoln.

"You need anything? Coffee? There's a vending machine downstairs."

"No thanks, Mel. Let's just get this over with."

Shortly the bailiff called them into the court. Judge Shirley F. Black was a wizened crone with pince-nez peering down at them like a hawk at a mouse. The bailiff called their case.

"Creighton University versus Vaughan Beadles."

"This is grand larceny, Mr. Beadles. How do you plead?"

"My client pleads not guilty, your honor," Mel said.

"I'd prefer to hear that from the client if you don't mind."

"Not guilty, your honor."

Black pored over papers four inches from her nose. "Very well, Mr. Beadles. I'm not going to set a trial date because judging from your history I expect you and the university to come to some kind of agreement before then. Bail is hereby set at five thousand dollars."

"Five thousand dollars, your honor?" Berenson said. "Isn't that a little steep for a first-time offense?"

"Well according to my documents Mr. Beadles was arrested for shoplifting in Rockford in 2005."

"That was a misunderstanding, your honor," Beadles said. Berenson looked at him reproachfully.

"We're satisfied with the bail, your honor," Berenson said.

Black nodded her head. The door to the hall popped open with a degree of urgency. Whitaker appeared before the judge clutching a warrant.

"Your honor, if I may?"

The judge nodded. "Go ahead, officer."

"Last night one of Professor Beadle's students, Rob Whitfield, died from a poisonous insect sting that occurred when Beadles violated university policy and a non-disclosure agreement he had signed and admitted Whitfield illegally to view a closed exhibit. That makes Professor Beadles an accessory to manslaughter. Professor, I'm placing you under arrest for involuntary manslaughter."

Whitaker whipped out his handcuffs.

CHAPTER FOURTEEN

PHIL RUBY

This time Beadles had a cell to himself. Betty came to see him in the afternoon. They ushered him into a common room with a Formica counter running down the center and individual cubicles separating the inmates from visitors with a thick, Plexiglas shield. There was a slot at the bottom like they have in box offices but everything was done under the watchful eyes of two armed guards and cameras in every ceiling corner. There were three other guys on his side spread out among the six slots.

Betty wore jeans and a loose-fitting plaid blouse and looked worn without makeup, her hair gathered in a ponytail. They pressed their palms together on the Plexiglas.

"How's Lars?" Beadles said.

"He's upset. He knows there's something wrong, but Mom and Pop arrived and are trying to jolly him up."

"How you holding up, baby?" Beadles said.

"I can't believe this is happening. Don't worry. Mel is getting Phil Ruby, a big-time criminal attorney to take over."

Beadles did a mental audit of his bank account and assets.

"We can afford him," Betty said. "Mom and Pop are willing to help out if it goes to trial."

"It won't go to trial. This is absurd. Listen. I've had a lot of time to think about this. You've got to find that girl Stephanie."

"The baby-sitter?"

"Yes! She had plenty of opportunity."

"But why, Vaughan? Why would she do something like that?"

"I don't know. Maybe Liggett put her up to it. He's hated my guts ever since he overheard me doing my impression of him at a faculty meeting."

Betty bit her bottom lip. "That thin-skinned son of a bitch."

"I don't know it's him. It's all I've got. Maybe the girl had her own motives. Maybe I flunked her, I don't know!"

Betty nodded. "I understand. What was her name again?"

"Stephanie Byrd. First thing you do, tell the new attorney about her, okay?"

"You got it, big guy."

She looked like she was going to say something else but she didn't. "I love you," she mouthed as she stood and went to the door, waiting for one of the guards to buzz her out. Three other guys on Beadles' side of the partition watched her go.

Beadles was released into the day room with the other non-violent offenders. Three blacks, two Mexicans and three white guys. The three blacks huddled together laughing loudly with big hand gestures. The three white guys sat in plastic chairs bolted to the Formica floor in front of the flat screen television fastened high up on one wall watching the Quality Value Network. Two breathless blond cougars hawked ersatz emeralds in Empire settings.

Beadles had no intention of joining the Aryan Brotherhood. The two Mexicans sat in the back row talking quietly in Spanish. Beadles sat in the back row at the opposite end. The Mexicans glanced over once and looked away. Nobody else paid any attention. Cameras hung from the ceiling corners.

Was it possible? Was Liggett a psycho who would plant stolen goods in his house? It was the move of a desperate man and not something that could withstand scrutiny. If Liggett were responsible, this would mean the end of his career. Beadles expected full exoneration and permitted himself a daydream of assuming the chairmanship of the department.

Why not?

It was only just. He was the star academic. He was the one who'd landed the Azuma Collection. He'd even been in talks with the Discovery Channel about doing his own show, out in the field. People loved that sort of thing. They were willing to watch men fish off Alaska, surely they would watch anthropologists and archaeologists uncover lost civilizations.

Mel would know a good show biz attorney. At six, everyone returned to his cell and received a boxed dinner: two Arby's roast beef and cheddar sandwiches and a bag of chips. Beadles drank water directly from the faucet.

He fell into a shallow sleep near dawn and dreamed he stood in a desert as flat and as hot as a restaurant griddle. The sun blazed so brightly that he couldn't see. Something was coming for him but he couldn't see it because the glare was everywhere. The glare surrounded him as if he were standing inside the sun. He tried to run away but he could barely move—like a cripple dragging one leg. That thing was closing in. Anxiety, sweat, thirst, running in place.

A baton running across his barred window woke him. His clothes were drenched with sweat.

After breakfast a guard took him to the visitor room where Phil Ruby waited. Ruby was a short man with a full head of wavy hair over a boxy face and square glasses. He had a surprisingly high voice.

"How are you doing, Professor Beadles? I'm Phil Ruby."

"Thank you for seeing me."

"I'm sorry I couldn't get here any sooner. I was downstate. Your wife told me about the baby-sitter. Ms. Byrd seems to have disappeared. Her roommate said she left late Saturday night right after coming home from your house. I have contacted the state police and informed them that she is a material witness. Unfortunately, they pointed out that since she is our witness, it is up to us to produce her. With your permission I'd like to hire a private investigator."

The words echoed from a great distance. Beadles felt trapped. How had this happened? "Are you shitting me?" he said.

"No sir."

"What about Liggett? Did he split too?"

"No, but Professor Liggett has not returned my phone calls. I believe he has retained an attorney of his own."

"Why does he need an attorney?"

"To protect himself from false accusations, he said."

Beadles felt a vein throbbing on his forehead, sending jabs of pain into his eye. "You don't think I did it, do you?"

"It doesn't matter what I think, Professor. But I must warn you—if this goes to trial that old shoplifting charge is bound to come up. They will go over your past with an electron microscope. If you were ever stopped for a traffic or drug beef they will find out. I hate surprises. So I want you to tell me the straight story. What are they going to find?"

The throbbing had assumed Olympian proportions. Beadles felt as if his head would explode. "Can't that wait until I'm out of here?"

"You're scheduled for arraignment this afternoon. I'll see what I can do."

CHAPTER FIFTEEN

DEAR VAUGHAN

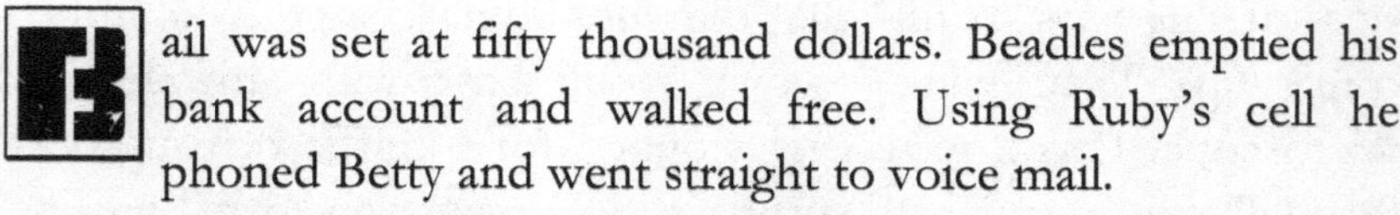

Bail was set at fifty thousand dollars. Beadles emptied his bank account and walked free. Using Ruby's cell he phoned Betty and went straight to voice mail.

"Miss you, babe. I'll be home shortly."

A talon of concern sunk into his neck. Betty should have been there to pick him up. Her folks were watching Lars, weren't they? Ruby offered Beadles a ride home.

"So what's the story, Professor? What else is lurking out there aside from the shoplifting charge?"

Beadles ran a hand through his hair, which felt both greasy and gritty. "I got busted for grass in college. I did community service and it was supposedly expunged."

"Holding or selling?"

Beadles stared out the window. "Selling. A goddamned ounce to some fuckin' weasel who turned out to be a police informant."

"How'd you get out of it?"

"I had good grades. It was a first offense. My dad had some clout."

They traveled south on Raymond Road. Shops dwindled to schools and then neighborhoods. Ruby turned west onto Maple St.

"Your folks still alive?"

"Dad passed away four years ago. He was seventy-eight. Mom lives in a retirement community in Naples. I was a late baby."

"Siblings?"

"None that I know of, Phil! No. They were pretty damned surprised when I came along."

"Okay, here's the deal. This manslaughter charge is bullshit. It's going away. They're left with grand larceny, which is debatable, and violating university policy. A case could be made that the university itself is liable for not insuring the collection did not contain noxious pests.

"I doubt you'll serve any jail time."

"Great. I'll lose my fucking job."

"Probably."

"Did you talk to the maintenance supervisor? Anatole Cerveros?"

"I was told Cerveros walked off his job on Friday and hasn't been heard from since."

A brain freeze descended on Beadles' skull.

He looked out the window. A little boy menaced his GI Joe dolls with a plastic scimitar. Beadles shook it off. Anatole was an Indian. There was no point trying to understand them.

So much for anthropology.

Beadles was glad his father wasn't around to see this. But some malicious bitch at The Hamlets was bound to find out and spread the news. He faced a grim choice—let his mother Ethyl find out from malicious bitches or tell her himself. The early signs of Alzheimer's had appeared and the doctors warned him what to expect. He'd been planning a July trip but now he had to see.

Beadles vowed to phone his mother.

They pulled up in front of the house. No police tape. No Ford or the folks' Buick either. Beadles got a queasy feeling in the pit of his stomach.

"Have you been in touch with Betty?"

"No, I have not. Haven't you spoken to her?"

"Not today."

Ruby shut the engine off. "Would you like me to come into the house with you?"

"I'm fine."

"Well okay. I'll let you know as soon as the PI comes up with anything about the Byrd girl."

"Oh god, the PI. What's his name?"

"Rolf Panny." Ruby dipped his fingers into his inside jacket pocket and produced a card.

Beadles took it and got out of the car. "Thanks for the lift, counselor."

"I'll be in touch," Ruby said.

Beadles sensed neighbors' eyes as he walked up his steps. Certainly the Carsons across the street, whose twelve-year-old son Beadles had caught trying to take his bike one night when he'd accidentally left the garage door open. Beadles let the kid go with a warning but he was the type of pasty-faced little loser who would poison the whole neighborhood if he could.

Beadles resisted the impulse to turn and look. He glanced up and down the block. Couple small children playing with a puppy four houses down. A couple cars. He removed his keys, unlocked the door and went inside.

The house was empty. And there it was. A white envelope on the dark dining room table. Betty wouldn't just leave a note. No. It had to come in a fine linen envelope. He opened it up.

Dear Vaughan:

I've accepted Mom and Pop's offer to stay with them in Elgin until you get this thing under control. You know I love you and I have always supported you but I feel that Lars and I would only be a distraction to you during this difficult time.

I will call you tonight after we have settled in.

Talk soon.

Love,
Betty

So much unsaid. Betty was about to become a vice president at Jackson Loan and Guaranty, an extremely conservative organization. Was it possible she was laying the groundwork for a divorce?

Of course it was possible. Betty had always looked out for Number One. As long as the good times lasted she would cling to the last drop but once the bank account was emptied she was outta there. She wasn't about to support some unemployable academic thief.

It was crazy! Whom the gods would destroy they first make mad. Beadles was furious all right. Furious at his faithless bitch of a wife. Furious at Liggett and the university. Finally, he was furious with himself. He'd flown too close to the sun. He never should have tweaked Liggett or courted that reality show. The alumni considered it vulgar.

He wanted a shower and a drink. He went to the basement door and turned on the lights. He went downstairs. The room had been turned upside-down and his hard-drive was missing. He sat in the old kitchen chair in front of his desk, opened the center drawer and reached all the way to the back. His hand closed around the velvet bag and felt a hard disc inside.

A tremendous relief flooded through him, a cleansing rain. At least this larceny had escaped notice. He pulled it out and shook the medallion into his palm. Well fuck you, Creighton! And fuck you, too, Professah Liggett, you sea slug! This was the least the university owed him.

Byrd, Byrd, Byrd. He dug around in his files until he found copies of last year's essays, which counted for thirty percent of the student's grade. Over 300 essays caused the file to bulge like an accordion. He flipped through them one by one until he found Byrd's essay. "Did Ancient Aliens Populate the Americas?"

He'd given her an 'F.'

Upstairs he heard the kitchen phone ringing.

CHAPTER SIXTEEN

CHARACTER

They'd kept the land line because it went with the house. Betty predicted the Chicoms were going to explode a huge electromagnetic pulse over the continent and fry all the satellites and wireless systems. That's why she kept vinyl LPs as well.

Vaughan took the stairs two at a time and scooped up the antique Bakelite receiver.

"Betty?"

"Hello, Vaughan," Betty said, voice oozing concern. "How are you?"

"I stink but I'm outta jail. When you coming back?"

"I think I made that clear in my letter, Vaughan. Not until you have this under control."

"Ruby says I'll probably just have to pay a fine."

"Vaughan, I don't see any way the university can keep you on after this."

He eyed a block of butcher's knives. "Come on, Betty. You're my wife."

"Vaughan, there are trust issues."

"Come on! You know I haven't looked at another woman since that one incident! How many times do I have to apologize?"

He felt her cover her phone and hunch in a corner of her parent's house as she lowered her voice. "I'm not going to argue with you. This isn't about your affair." With just the smallest emphasis. "It's about character. I thought you'd changed."

"You don't believe I stole that pot, do you?"

The pause was Brobdingnagian.

"Please just settle this as quickly as possible," she said and hung up.

Beadles clutched the receiver with white knuckles and made a low growling sound in the back of his throat. He replaced the receiver and poured himself four fingers of Macallan and added some crushed ice from the fridge. Carrying his drink he went down the hall into the master bedroom.

Bitch couldn't even make the bed. He went into the bathroom, stripped, and stood under a hot shower for ten minutes. He drank two fingers, toweled himself off and put on clean jeans and a Sturgis T-shirt. Thought about ordering out but didn't want some kid gawking at him as he forked over the pizza.

Beadles returned to the kitchen and poked around in the fridge. He found some frozen lasagna and popped it in the microwave. In a wooden chair with his feet up on the kitchen table he finished the Scotch.

That hard drive was going to kill him. Why would a guy with a wife like Betty even download all that porn?

Most of his research was on the hard drive. And the laptop, which they had taken as well. It was also up in the Cloud due to his file saving program. He could access it from other computers.

He got up to get more Scotch and nearly fell on his face, barely catching himself on the table.

"Whoa there, pardner," he muttered, knowing he'd poured a shitload of Scotch into an empty stomach. Well, he wasn't going anywhere. He was in no condition to pull his Bullitt Mustang out of the garage and add to his woes. He'd probably have to sell it to pay his legal fees.

Carefully, Beadles edged along the counter, grabbed the Scotch and returned to his seat while the lasagna pirouetted in the microwave. Time to think about a new career.

"You want fries with that?" he said. Just trying it out. If the university fired him for cause they were still required to pay three months' salary.

If he could prove someone planted that pot, he could sue them. But if it was only Stephanie Byrd there would be nothing to collect. If, on the other hand, it had been Professor Liggett, he could sue the university.

For millions.

Enough to fund an expedition to find the Azuma stronghold, the sweetest vindication of them all.

"This is what I do," he said to the room.

The microwave dinged. He let it sit.

He needed to prove his thesis. It was as simple as that. He'd been carrying it with him since undergrad days, since he first stumbled upon an obscure sixteenth century Spanish text. The diary had allegedly been discovered by a Benedictine monk in a mountain cave in Arizona in the nineteenth century. He turned it over to the Vatican which in turn sent it to the library in Seville.

The diary began with Don Felipe's birth and upbringing in a small town in Catalonia to his volunteering to travel to the New Land.

Beadles learned of Don Felipe Balmora's diary at the New York Public Library which had one of two known print copies, the other in a museum in Seville. In 1894, a volunteer polymath named Edgar Saucier translated Balmora's diary and issued twelve leather-bound copies. Eleven disappeared without a trace. The New York Public Library had the twelfth.

CHAPTER SEVENTEEN

DON FELIPE BALMORA

May 5, 1540. *Under glorious blue skies and through the grace of God Almighty who shines His Fortune upon us today we set sail from Compostela in New Spain in four stout caravels in search of the Seven Cities of Cibola under the guidance of Governor Coronado.*

May 19. Blessed with Divine Guidance and good winds we have made landfall. All our horses and men survived, thanks be to Almighty God. Governor Coronado has made friends with the local Indians who are called Zuni.

May 20. Governor Coronado has agreed to Captain Lopez da Gama's request for a small expedition to cut into the mountains northeast of us to search for the Seven Cities of Cibola. Captain da Gama has chosen me to be his lieutenant. We leave in the morning. I pray to God Almighty that I may perform my duties to His satisfaction, and to the satisfaction of Captain Da Gama and our King.

May 27. By the Grace of God Almighty, we have left behind the friendly Zuni and turned away from the river. The Indians run in fear from us. We must present a very strange breed to them—they have never seen horses before and some of them believe man and beast to be one. We have traversed twenty-five miles of the most desolate terrain, filled with poisonous vipers that will announce their imminent attack by rattling a series of calcified rings surrounding their tails. These are called rattlesnakes. One such viper bit Paulo Vatine's horse which went mad, broke its leg and had to be put down. Captain da Gama sent Vatine back on foot. We pray for our brother's safe return.

There are also venomous arachnids similar to those found throughout the Holy Land. There is nothing in this desiccated land, it seems, that does not bite, sting, or poison you to death.

I would write more often but long days in the saddle and the work of finding water and setting camp is exhausting. A rare storm blew over this afternoon, bringing much needed water into gulches and arroyos, thanks to God Almighty.

May 28. We have entered an eerie landscape. Fierce winds tear down hills in one place and deposit them in another. The Indians call these "walking hills." We see mountains in the distance and many shimmering mirages but there is no water to be found. Captain da Gama scans the skies with his glass upon the hour searching for buzzards or a speck of green. He is a skilled cartographer and makes extensive notes in a leather portfolio, fixing landmarks by the light of the sun or with his sextant. It his desire to present Our Most Holy Father in Rome as well as King Philip with a map of this previously unknown land.

At night we hear strange noises from the arroyos that cover the earth like a fisherman's net, but never a drop to be found. The men talk fearfully of devils and demons. Father Dominguez is sorely-tried and himself given to melancholy. He seems to have lost enthusiasm for blessings, prayer and consultation. I fear the Father may not last long without food and water and will be the first among us to go.

My thoughts are never far from God Almighty and His Infinite Mercy.

May 29. Father Dominguez fell off his horse. When we got to him he was dead. May God have mercy on his soul. We buried him beneath rocks and made a cross from driftwood left from long ago flood. I now carry the Father's Bible in my saddlebags. We are reduced to eating snakes.

May 30. God in His Infinite Mercy has blessed us with a drenching downpour. We were able to fill all the canteens and satisfy the horses. Indeed, they had to be restrained lest they burst their bellies. Captain da Gama has ordered us to rest for the day. In the morning we will head for an odd rock formation he spotted in his glass.

May 31. We covered 18 miles today and are no nearer to the butte upon which Captain da Gama has set his sights. At night we hear the call of coyotes and other beasts we are at pains to identify. It is up to me now to lead the men in evening vespers, those who are interested. I did not think that at the tender age of seventeen I would be called upon to minister to these hardened warriors, all so much older than me, but if it is God's Will so be it. May His Mercy continue to shine on us.

June 1. Oh Horrible! Oh Demon from the darkest pit of hell! It is our brother in arms Paul Vatine whom we found spread-eagled in the sun, mutilated in the most horrible way! His blood was fresh! What manner of fiend has tracked us through this fearful land keeping Paulo alive until such time as they could torment him in the most vile manner, to taunt us, to warn us, to wish us dead! Captain da Gama has ordered 3 men to stand guard throughout the night. May God have Mercy on our Souls.

June 2. We came upon a village of the savages hewn into the walls of a canyon, like certain towns in Portugal. Driven by a Righteous Fury of Vengeance we attacked with musket and halberd, showing no mercy. We killed twenty-seven that day including eight children and nine women. Captain da Gama showed the survivors no mercy, as they had shown none to Brother Paul. Surely God in His Merciful Wisdom guided us in this endeavour for hidden among the pots in one of the cliff dwellings was twelve pounds of gold in the form of heathen images.

June 5. The Fiend who has been stalking us has showed himself. At noon he stood atop a ridge a mile distant surrounded by lessers of his tribe. He stood for an hour as if deliberately giving each of us a chance to look through the Captain's glass, and so we did. This Fiend is a very tall Indian with long waving hair, broad of shoulder and stout of thigh. He and six or seven warriors are armed with bows and arrows, but stood beyond the reach of our muskets. Oh that we had brought a cannon! Yet no cannon could have made this journey. Captain da Gama was prepared to order a cavalry charge were it not for the rough ground. The Fiend taunted us in the most vulgar and obscene manner. He and his tribesmen dance in merriment.

June 6. The Fiend has agreed to a meeting. Through means of sign language, which I understand as well as some Zuni, Captain da Gama will advance on foot with only three soldiers and his cavalry sword. Captain da Gama has asked that I accompany him for my language skills and to judge for myself whether the Fiend and his tribe represent Satan. The Fiend will bring three of his tribesmen.

The remaining pages had been removed by the Vatican.

CHAPTER EIGHTEEN

WRONGFUL DEATH

eadles' research had only fueled suspicion that the diary was "incomplete." He'd queried the Vatican numerous times and always been told that the Vatican Library had no knowledge of any remaining pages.

Beadles felt this was a lie and believed the Vatican had only surrendered the diary because the Benedictines had informed Spain that it existed, and it rightfully belonged to them. The Balmora Dynasty had generously bequeathed the diary to the Universidad de Seville. Beadles had reached out to them but never received a reply.

A thump from the front porch. Beadles stared dumbly for a second before getting to his feet and going to the door. He turned on the lights and looked out. No one. He opened the door. A dead cat lay at his feet. His eyes swept the street first one way then the other. His heart accelerated. It was that Carson kid he was certain. Cowardly little shit.

Beadles got a plastic supermarket bag from the trash, picked up the cat in the bag and put it in the garbage in the garage. He made sure the garage was locked, pausing for a minute to admire his British racing green Mustang Bullitt. A powerful urge descended on him. Just get in the car and go! Leave it all behind. But he'd learned from bitter experience that he couldn't do that. They'd track him down and extract their pound of flesh. The university had its reputation to consider. Hayes could always withdraw his gift.

Beadles retrieved his Scotch and returned to the bedroom. He went into the dressing room and looked for Betty's bling box. Gone. Not a good sign. He wouldn't be pawning any jewelry for get-away money. He'd need every dime he had to pay the lawyers. He mentally touted his assets—the bank account, the retirement account, the vacation property in Wisconsin.

Hell. Attorney fees would piss through that in a New York minute. He would discuss suing the University with Berenson in the morning. His hand went in his pocket and removed the medallion. Too late to return it. It would only add to the fire.

He opened the top drawer of Betty's bureau, rummaging among the panties and bras for any jewelry she might have forgot. He inadvertently peeled up the flowered contact paper that lined the bottom. A yellow piece of foolscap peeked out. He pulled it out. It was in Betty's handwriting.

"Someday I will meet my soul mate and give up smoking."

Galactus' fist closed on him squeezing out all breath. His knees buckled. He caught himself on the edge of the dresser.

Get over it.

He clenched the gold coin tightly. They could take his livelihood, his dignity and his marriage but they would never take this! He peeled off his clothes, got in bed, held the coin and went to sleep. Shallow, restless dreams. He was at a faculty party. People kept telling him that the President was looking for him. Filled with anxiety, Beadles sought to escape the party but he couldn't find his car. He couldn't remember where he parked it and he found himself walking up and down the streets near the University Club looking.

The sun came up. It was so bright he couldn't see. How was he expected to do anything if he couldn't see?

Beadles woke up with the light shining in the bedroom window. He felt like crap. His throat was dry and he had a pounding headache behind the eyes. He looked blearily at the empty tumbler on the bedstand.

Idiot.

He had drunk himself to sleep. Rubbing his temples he sat up. He went into the bathroom and splashed cold water in his face. It was ten-thirty. After a cursory breakfast of cheerios in milk he phoned the PI Panny and left a message. He phoned Ruby but the lawyer was in court all morning. He phoned Berenson.

"What if I can prove Liggett had that pot planted? Can I sue the university?"

"That is certainly an option," the lawyer replied. "But it seems dubious. Professor Liggett is a highly-respected academic. You'd have to come up with some pretty solid proof."

"I'm working on it, Mel."

"Well let me know if you find something. In the meantime, you're in good hands."

Beadles didn't know what to do so he went for a run. For the first mile every footfall sent a needle through his temples but after that it got easier. You could always kill a hangover if you were willing to put in the work.

He took a shower and when he came out his cell phone, which he'd left charging on the bathroom counter, rang. It was Ruby.

"The University has obtained a restraining order preventing you from entering the campus until this matter is resolved."

Beadles sat heavily on the bed suddenly exhausted. "Can they do that?"

"Yes, they can. You might want to think about sending someone over to claim your personal effects."

"Jesus Christ."

"The good news, they're eager to settle and put this matter behind them. We have a meeting this afternoon at two at the law offices of Strunk and White. Can you be there?"

There was a knock at the door.

"I'll be there, Phil. Excuse me. There's someone at the door."

It was UPS delivering one of those high-velocity letters. Stan and Mary Whitfield of Waukegan were suing him for the wrongful death of their son.

CHAPTER NINETEEN

FLEW THE COOP

Strunk and White's offices were in an old two-story Victorian off Courthouse Square on Mason St. Beadles parked his Mustang down the block, waiting until he saw his lawyer arrive before getting out of his car. He met Ruby on the stoop and they went inside. The middle-aged secretary ushered them into a conference room looking out on a rose garden and asked if they wanted something to drink.

Beadles asked for a Coke. Ruby sat pat.

"I've spoken with Asst. DA Nancy Warner and the state has agreed to reduce the charges regarding Mr. Whitfield to criminal negligence. The state has no desire to crucify you for something that was obviously out of your control," Ruby said softly. "You'll be sentenced to six months community service."

"If I plead guilty."

"That's right. As for the Whitfield suit, I'm not qualified to speak to that. Ask Mel. He'll know."

The door opened admitting a slight senior citizen with close-cropped white hair and rectangular glasses.

Old Elihu White himself, class of '51. His body was frail but his mind was as sharp as ever as laid a manila folder on the mahogany table and shook Ruby's and Beadles' hands.

They all sat.

"Gentlemen," White said in a phlegmy voice. "The University will drop all charges if Professor Beadles will turn in his letter of resignation."

Beadles started to speak but Ruby laid his hand on the professor's wrist. "Mr. White, we have reason to believe that my client was framed. Will you give us a week to prove it?"

White held the manila folder. "Gentlemen, the University is very eager to put this behind them. As you know, this is a critical time with the upcoming Alumni Foundation meeting. You have until the end of the week. I'll need your decision Friday."

Outside they walked to Ruby's Lexus.

"Have you heard from Panny?" Beadles said.

"No. He'll phone me when he finds something. He's a good man. If anyone can find this girl he can."

Beadles had turned his cell off during the conference. He got in his car and turned it back on. The PI had returned his call.

"I'll try again later," the man said with a faint Germanic accent.

There was also a call from a reporter for the *Creighton Sun Courier* which he did not return.

Beadles drove by a sub shop near campus. Some idiot started pointing at him and whispering as he stood in line. At home he sat on his front porch and ate his sandwich. Let them stare. He couldn't control anybody's behavior but his own. It was his house. It was his porch. He had a perfect right to be there.

He was innocent of grand larceny, innocent of manslaughter.

He felt the warmth of the medallion through the pocket of his blue jeans. As if it had been sitting in the sun.

The university owed him that.

There was still the matter of his ethnicity claim. It had seemed like a no-brainer at the time. Native Americans were automatically fast-tracked so the university could wave the all important banner of diversity. And his mother did used to joke that he must be part Indian.

The phone rang. Berenson. His civil attorney as opposed to his criminal attorney.

"Vaughan, what about this janitor who was there? We'll need to get a statement from him."

Beadles explained that Cerveros had vamoosed.

"Phil has a private investigator he uses."

"Already on it, Mel."

"All right. Let me know if there's anything I can do."

A couple kids cruised by on their boards with a glance-over. The living room drapes across the street at the Carsons' moved a little.

Beadles phoned Betty and got her voice mail.

"Call me."

It wasn't a conversation he should have on the front porch anyway. He went inside. His cell beeped and this time it was Panny.

"Professor Beadles, Stephanie Byrd boarded United Flight #2658, O'Hare to Belize City by way of Mexico City, at 9:15 Sunday morning."

Beadles collapsed onto the living roof sofa, jerking it back into the wall. The air flew out of him.

"What?"

"I have confirmed her arrival in Belize. The US has no extradition agreement and she's wanted for no crime. It would be very costly to go after her if only for a statement."

"Jesus."

"I'm sorry to be the bearer of bad news. I know some people in Central America who might be able to help."

Beadles was already counting his losses. He'd have to sell the Mustang.

"I don't know what to do, Mr. Panny. Wait! Wait. There's someone here in the United States, I pray to God, who's still here. I want you to find him."

"Who, Professor?"

"Anatole Cerveros. He's a Navajo Indian used to work at the university. He was there the day the scorpion bit Rob."

"Can we meet? I'm available this afternoon."

CHAPTER TWENTY

PANNY

They met at LaLuz, a Mexican cafe on the north side among the trailer parks and discount tire stores. Panny was a neat little man with a gray Van Dyke. They sat at the patio in the rear and sipped Dos Equis.

"Phil Ruby hired me but I am really working for you. If, as you surmise, the Byrd girl smuggled the pot into your house at Liggett's behest, and she is willing to testify, it would certainly behoove you to pursue her. It is my impression that she suddenly came into some money. But let me ask you this. Why would Professor Liggett, no matter his distaste, go to so much trouble and expense?"

"I don't know," Beadles said.

Academic politics is the most vicious and bitter form of politics, because the stakes are so low.

"Maybe he's insane," Beadles said.

"Maybe there are things Liggett wishes to keep hidden."

Beadles looked at the PI. Was he trying to drum up work? "What am I paying you?"

"Two fifty a day plus expenses."

Beadles took a slug of his beer. "I can't just go on a fishing expedition for everyone involved in this case! God knows what my legal fees are."

"I understand. I may just take a look for my own satisfaction. I believe you were framed, Professor. I came to this country because I believed in truth, justice, and the American way."

"Superman."

"Yes, I watched it as a child in Germany. Do you want me to pursue Miss Byrd? She adds credence to your case by fleeing. The court may very well see things differently."

"No, no, let her go. See if you can find Cerveros."

"Tell me about him."

There wasn't much to tell. Beadles had exchanged pleasantries with the custodian on numerous occasions but Cerveros was not a talkative man. "He said he had a son back on the rez."

"Reservation?"

"I don't know. He said he was Navajo."

Panny made notes in a spiral pad. "The University should have that information."

The PI laid a twenty on the table and rose. "I'll be in touch. Please feel free to contact me if something new comes up."

Beadles shook his hand again. "Thanks for doing this. Looking into Liggett, I mean."

Panny twirled a finger. "Piece of cake." He left through the bar.

Some day laborers fresh off work were laughing at another table. A couple mariachis emerged and set up on a small stage made of moving pallets covered with plywood. Trumpet and guitar. They weaved a spell of such sadness and beauty that the day laborers fell silent and Beadles found himself weeping uncontrollably.

He used a napkin to wipe his tears, fearful that someone had seen him. If they had they gave no sign. This was a place where men came to forget.

He finished his beer and left. His cell rang on the way to his car. The reporter again. He took the call.

"Professor, this is Don Mullaney of the *Creighton Sun Courier*. Would you answer a few questions regarding Rob Whitfield's death and the accusations that you…"

"I have nothing to say, Mr. Mullaney." He broke the call.

There was a death threat on the home answering machine. "You fucked up Whitfield you motherfucker and now we're gonna fuck you up!" The voice sounded young. Beadles phoned the police and reported it. They told him the threat was probably a prank but that if they persisted, Beadles should bring them the tape and they would try to ascertain from where the calls originated.

"Could be weeks, Mr. Beadles."

He unplugged the phone. Betty had his cell. But she didn't call. And he'd be damned if he called her and got the Big Chill. He dreaded turning on the news. And yet he must.

Beadles sat in the living room and used the remote to turn on the free-standing flat screen television angling out from one corner. He and Betty had had a knock-down drag-out fight over it. She had decreed that under absolutely no conditions would there be a television in the living room.

Beadles won that fight but not without casualties. The cold treatment persisted for a week.

The local CBS affiliate began their five o'clock news. Seven overnight shootings in Chicago led. Beadles remembered J-school. "If it bleeds, it leads." When the segment ended he heaved a sigh of relief. He'd fallen out of the evening news, for the time being.

There was a thump against the front door. Another dead cat? In broad daylight?

Beadles got up and went out on the porch. The afternoon edition of the *Sun Courier* lay at his feet.

CHAPTER TWENTY-ONE

THE SUN COURIER

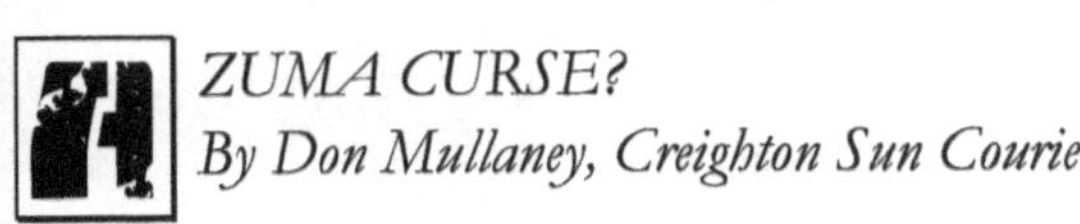

ZUMA CURSE?
By Don Mullaney, Creighton Sun Courier

The CU Anthropology Dept. broke out the champagne bottles this summer when it was announced that Arizona Rancher Jepson Hayes, of Cross Creek, Arizona, had chosen them as the recipient of an uncataloged collection of Native American artifacts. Mr. Hayes' family had known of the collection for two hundred years and had deliberately kept it secret to protect it.

Mr. Hayes said that he had chosen CU not only because his granddaughter had played on the varsity basketball team, but because he had seen a National Geographic article about CU Professor of Anthropology Vaughan Beadles, who has been conducting research on the Azuma.

Now Beadles stands accused of stealing priceless artifacts from the collection and of being party to the death of undergraduate Robert Whitfield of Waukegan. Whitfield was bitten by a scorpion last Saturday. The scorpion was alleged to have arrived as part of the Azuma Collection. The collection is kept under lock and key in Merrill Hall. Professor Beadles broke university rules in admitting Whitfield to see the collection before it had been examined by a panel of experts.

Mr. Hayes told the *Sun Courier* that there have been other deaths associated with the Azuma over the years, which have contributed to his desire to donate the collection. In 1889 Mr. Hayes' ancestor Prudence Wipperfurth, whose sister Joan married Nathaniel Hayes, picked up one of the pots and was bitten by a rattlesnake. She died two days later.

"We considered the collection bad news," Hayes told the *Sun Courier*. "Some of the Indian folks we knew said it had belonged to a bad tribe and they prayed the tribe would never return."

It was Professor Beadles who gave the Azuma their name, based on petroglyphs he found in the Sonoran Desert. Professor Beadles declined to be interviewed for this article.

CHAPTER TWENTY-TWO

BEADLES RESIGNS

He turned in his letter of resignation Friday morning. It wasn't just the alleged theft. It was the diversity claim and the porn on the hard drive. When he got home a process server handed him divorce papers.

You think you know someone. You marry them. And you find you didn't know them at all.

He spent the weekend putting things in storage and listing items on Craig's List, including the Mustang. Two of his students, Bob and Frank helped. On Monday the court released his hard drive and laptop. He spent the evening transferring data to flash drives and drinking. There was still a chance Dan Potts would help him.

If he could prove the Azuma were a distinct tribe, and more importantly find the center of their ancient civilization, it would be the greatest story since the moon landing.

He would break the Curse.

He had to know more. Much more. By this time his legal bills were fast approaching six digits. He'd been forced to hire a lawyer to defend himself from the Whitfield's wrongful death suit. It wouldn't matter if he won. By the time it was over he would be so deep in the hole it would take a miracle to dig out.

The Azuma were that miracle.

On Wednesday, Panny phoned to tell him that the PI had tracked Cerveros to a PO Box in Durango. "Mr. Cerveros is not Navajo. It says Ute on his application form."

Beadles was shocked. Why would Cerveros lie to him? But was it a lie? Hadn't he in fact assumed the man was Navajo? The janitor obviously didn't think it worthwhile to correct Beadles' impression.

Maybe it was because the Indian had no respect for Beadles. Maybe it was because he regarded all white interest as patronizing. Wasn't it racist and condescending to even entertain such explanations?

"I also learned something about Liggett. I won't have time to pursue this further. I'm devoting all my resources to a missing dog starting tomorrow. I'd like to give you what I have in person."

They agreed to meet at La Luz.

A dozen choppers lined the curb out front. Los Negativos, a Mexican biker gang, had taken over the back patio so Beadles and Panny sat in a booth in the dim bar as Los Lobos wailed on the juke.

Panny's bill came to $1,256.75 including expenses. Beadles wrote him a check. He now had a balance of $200 in his checking account.

"I found out something about Professor Liggett," Panny said craning his neck. No one paid them any attention.

Beadles' face spoke for him. Panny reached into his jacket pocket and slid a folded sheet of white paper across the tabletop. Beadles opened it up. It was a black and white photo of what at first glance appeared to be a Nazi SS party, with a half dozen improbably young looking Nazis goose-stepping around a beer hall. The uniforms were comically exaggerated like something in a Mel Brooks movie.

"What is this?"

"Liggett attended the University of Wisconsin and was a member of the Tau Ceti Fraternity. This is a photograph of their end of semester party, May, 1990." The PI's finger fell on a plump young Nazi throwing a sieg heil. "This is young Herr Professor."

A phosphorescent light ignited in Beadles' chest. "Holy shit. Where did you get this?"

"I have friends in Madison. I don't know how he obtained the photograph. He scanned it and sent it to me. I also sent a copy to your email. You may keep that."

There were no identifying marks on the photo but the figure was unmistakably Liggett. But what could he do with it, really? Anything he did now would be perceived as sour grapes. His brand had been tarnished. Even were he to convince the university that the photo was genuine the most he could hope for was a forced resignation but Liggett had become so important to the university they would probably brush it over as a childish prank. Which it was.

When Beadles thought back on his own college career, he cringed at the shit he'd pulled. That pot bust was just the tip of the iceberg. He was in no position to throw stones. He refolded the paper and slid it into his pocket.

"Thanks, Rolf. Good luck on your new hunt."

CHAPTER TWENTY-THREE

COURTESY CALL

Potts agreed to see Beadles Thursday afternoon at his home in Evanston. Beadles had a buyer for the Mustang but had to hold off until the following week because he needed transportation. He was already downsizing in his mind. The court had granted Betty primary custody of Lars. His phone calls were not returned.

Three p.m. on a bright June, Beadles drove the Mustang between the stone pillars marking the Potts residence, a Taliesin design made of fieldstone and shingles shielded from the street by a stone wall and a line of poplars. He parked his car in the brick turn-around. Potts came out of a glass door to the right of the main entrance and waited for Beadles to follow him into a home office. Potts shut the door behind them. A window was open admitting a cool breeze. Potts sat in a leather chair and motioned Beadles to a sofa.

"Would you like something to drink?"

"Got any Coke?"

Potts got up, opened a refrigerator in one corner and pulled out two cans of Coke. He handed one to Beadles and sat. They popped their cans. It was the loudest thing in the room.

"Thanks for seeing me, Mr. Potts."

"What can I do for you, Beadles?"

"I didn't steal that artifact. I was framed."

Potts just looked at him.

"Who would do such a thing and why?"

"I don't want to speculate. I have an idea but I'm going to keep it to myself until I have proof."

"Good luck."

Potts' manner had obviously cooled. He was being courteous, nothing more.

"Mr. Potts, your son was right. The Azuma were real. I know they're out there. I am going to prove it."

"While proving you were framed?"

Beadles colored and he sat back. "This is outrageous. The university forced me out on the most specious of grounds."

"Then why aren't you fighting back? I've spoken to several members of the faculty who told me some things about you. Things that don't go with the whole academic image."

Beadles couldn't defend himself without looking guilty as hell. He saw his chances slipping away.

"Ronnie learned about the Azuma from the same obscure Spanish text I did. Did he ever say anything about a map?"

Potts' eyes narrowed and he looked up. "He did mention a map."

Beadles' heart quickened. The diary spoke of a map but the expedition's fate was unknown. "Did he have any leads?"

"He said he spoke to an old guy—a WW I vet he encountered in some little town outside of Breckinridge, CO. The old guy was a member of the County Historical Society. Said they had a whole warehouse of stuff they'd bought off Indian scouts, prospectors and the like who spent their lives searching for gold in the Marble Canyon area—all over northern Arizona. The old guy—look who's talking—said they had a bunch of Spanish artifacts including manifests and maps but hadn't got around to sorting it all out. Ronnie was going to do that the following summer as part of his senior thesis."

"Did he have a name, or the name of the town?"

Potts heaved himself out of the chair and Beadles saw age pressing down on the old man. He went behind his cherrywood desk, opened a bottom drawer and pulled out a binder filled with letters. He returned to his chair and opened the binder.

From where he sat Beadles saw that they were letters from his son. For a moment the old man got misty eyed and had to put a hand to his face. He shrugged it off and began going through the letters. Beadles waited in silence.

After a few minutes Potts held one much folded letter up. "Dear Dad: Great news! I ran into a WW I vet in Permission which is just west of Nederlander outside Boulder! Nederlander is where Chicago, Fleetwood Mac, and a whole bunch of great rock bands recorded.

"The old dude is a member of the Permission Historical Society. He's heard of a lost tribe and told me that the HS has a warehouse filled with old maps and manifests they'd been purchasing from desert rats since the nineteenth century! He invited me to come back next summer to help him sort through it."

Potts set the letter back in the folder and closed it.

"There you are. Permission."

"Mr. Potts, would you still be willing to underwrite my expedition?"

Potts stare icily. "I care about the University. It's reputation matters to me. Are you planning a protracted battle over your resignation? Are you planning to sue?"

"Never crossed my mind," Beadles lied.

"I'll tell you what I'll do. I will give you a one-time stipend of five thousand dollars if you'll use it to solve this mystery. Naturally if you come across evidence of what happened to Ronnie and Curt, that's another story."

"Thank you, sir."

Potts got up and retrieved his checkbook from the desk.

CHAPTER TWENTY-FOUR

LEAVING LAS VEGAS

Summer knew Vince was going to hit her when she saw the little vein popping over his narrow hillbilly eyes.

"You fucking whore," he said and smacked her hard with the back of his hand. She stumbled but she didn't go down.

"I wasn't coming on to him! He was just another drunk!"

"Is that why you let him stuff his hand up your pussy?"

"He was giving me a twenty, Vince!"

Vince grabbed her hard by her slim but muscular bicep and twisted her around, shoving her into the hot little bedroom of the hot little apartment they rented in North Vegas not far from the Speedway. You couldn't fight Vince. He was a force of nature. He shoved her down on the unmade bed, ripped off her shirt, shorts, and panties and stuffed himself into her like she was some kind of appliance. Summer gritted her teeth and turned away. Vince put his hand on her face to wipe her out, to depersonalize her, so he didn't have to look at her.

After five minutes of grunting he couldn't come so he pulled out, flipped her over like a pancake and reached for the Vaseline in the bedside table drawer. He fucked her up the ass until he came, stiffening like a garden hose, then collapsed with his full 230 lbs. on her. Biting her lip to keep from crying, Summer crawled out from under him, onto the floor where she panted on hands and knees. Vince's hand shot out and grabbed her by her long straight black hair.

"Bring me a fucking rum and coke. I'll give you a boost."

Summer got to her feet and went into the bathroom. She turned on the shower.

"RUM AND COKE, YOU FUCKING WHORE!" Vince bellowed.

Wrapping herself in an old Lakers jacket, Summer went into the kitchenette. She looked out the window at the parking lot filled with used and broken-down vehicles. The dealer cars were all hot—300s, Chargers and Camaros. Their homes were shit, their children lived away with their mothers without adequate medical care, but the dealers had nice whips.

Summer opened the cabinet and took down the bottle of Ron Rico. She opened the refrigerator and took out the once-opened liter bottle of Coca-Cola. She reached into Vince's leather jacket and took out a small plastic baggie filled with six black capsules. Rohypnal.

She didn't want a bump from Vince. Ever again. She had had it. Ma Funderburk's little girl was a slow learner but she did learn. It was time to cut her losses and run.

Vince sold roofies to tourists down on Fremont Street. Coke, speed, whatever you need. Back when they first met, he'd treated her like a queen, but little by little, as she got to know him, Vince revealed himself to be just another psychopathic asshole. He'd picked her up at Dante's when she was feeling particularly weak and vulnerable.

"A broad looks like you shouldn't have to beg," was his line. Picked her up, treated her to a decent meal, hosed her down and made her his woman. She'd done his coke and even tricked for him a few times. The money was good and she didn't have to trick if she didn't want to. Unless Vince made her.

Vince had a deal with Alex, the greasy pig who owned Dante's. Vince sold Alex the blow he used to control his girls. The deal was, Summer would dance for Alex but would only get her blow from Vince. And she didn't date customers. Unless Vince said so.

Summer mixed two roofies into the rum and coke and hoped it would be enough. She didn't want to kill the guy. She took it into the bedroom where Vince lay on his back, his left arm inked like a boa constrictor. He sat up, took the drink and downed half in one gulp. He opened the bedside table and took out an amber vial and a small mirror. The mirror's surface was smeared. He dumped a mound of white powder on the mirror and began to chop it up with a knife. He divvied it up into two lines and handed Summer a cut soda straw.

"I can't Vince. We're outta rum and tequila. I need to make a run."

Vince leaned over the lines and did them both. "More for me."

"Can I take your car?"

All anger had left him. It was party time. He reached down to his jeans on the floor and pulled out the fob. "Don't crack it up."

He finished off his rum and coke. Would the roofies overcome the coke? He'd been up for thirty-six hours running from pawn shop to storage unit, convinced he could make a fortune because he was such a great trader. He watched *Pawn Stars* and *Storage Wars* frequently and loudly. He'd visited the Pawn Stars store and made a scene when they declined to meet his price on a Civil War era pistol he'd taken in trade from some addict.

"Oh man, I gotta lie down," he said.

"I'll be right back," Summer said clutching the keys tightly. She was all packed. She had four hundred dollars she'd managed to keep hidden plus another eight hundred she'd taken from Vince's wallet. This was it. Adios you flaming asshole. She would run so far and so fast he'd never find her again.

He might not even report the car as stolen. He was already on cop radar for a bust last year in the Luxor parking lot. The lot attendant spotted him doing a deal and reported him to the LVPD who swooped down and caught him with 200 hits of Oxycontin still in their pharmacy bottles. Vince side-stepped by turning in his source, an assistant pharmacist with a habit.

It was eleven p.m., Summer had come off her shift at nine. Shortly before quitting time, Vince entered Dante's and saw the guy stuffing the twenty down her crotch while she played kissie-poo with the john. It was all an act. But Vince was crazy jealous.

She could only fuck the guys he chose and they were all unattractive because of his immense ego.

Well fuck that shit.

She was outta there.

She let herself quietly out of the apartment. From what she knew about roofies, he would be out for at least twelve hours. Maybe forever. Summer was not a vindictive woman but Vince had brought it on himself.

She went down the stairs, out into the parking lot and beeped open the Camaro. It was a yellow and black LT 1 with over four hundred horsepower and a six speed transmission. Summer had learned to drive a stick back on the rez.

The engine snarled to life, she snicked into gear, chirped the tires and headed toward the Hoover Dam.

CHAPTER TWENTY-FIVE

SALINA

eadles put the house on the market and sold the Bullitt. He bought a Jeep Cherokee with 85,000 miles on it. His combined legal fees came to $38,000. He owed 25. Betty agreed not to press for child support in exchange for primary custody. Beadles didn't contest her. It wasn't that he didn't love Lars. He had learned to love him.

When Lars was born Beadles' initial reaction was a certain relief that it was a boy and anxiety on the coming struggle to raise a child. Presented with the newborn in the delivery room, Beadles held the bundle in his arm and felt nothing. Certainly not love. He wondered how he got in this mess. He'd never wanted to be a parent.

Betty had always said she had no interest in children until she became pregnant. Like strapping a turbo to her self-absorption.

It took him a year to warm up to the idea.

Now he felt only relief. The last thing he needed was parental responsibility. He wondered if he had sociopathic tendencies.

The Whitfields' wrongful death suit was a constant drain on his resources.

No one would hire him and he'd become notorious. The university claimed he'd falsified his job application and credentials. The Cherokee Nation disavowed any knowledge of his membership.

He made a few calls. His old grad school prof had died last year from a stroke. Beadles hadn't even sent the family a letter of condolence. He called a few other academic pals but each had multiple excuses. Times were tough. They were thinking of cutting the anthro department. They were laying people off. Too many qualified candidates who hadn't been accused of larceny and manslaughter.

Last year Lucasfilm flew him out for an interview. They wanted his take on a sci-fi fantasy. *Avatar* meets *Alien*. The lawyers soaked up his fee like the Gobi Desert.

Finally there was only one thing left to do.

Find Anatole.

Beadles planned his trip as carefully as a space launch. He filled the old Jeep with camping gear, research materials, batteries. He would drive through Permission on the way. The night before he left he had that dream again, with the glare. Only this time the everywhere-glare disappeared, as if a curtain had been drawn, leaving the after-image of a rock butte burning red on his retina. As a child he had suffered night terrors in which he found himself trapped in some ancient cliff dwelling—walls the look and texture of reptiles that oozed the oil of age, death, dust, destruction. The idea that something so old existed was in itself terrifying. It continued to haunt him until well into his teens.

It was partly as an attempt to come to grips with his terror that he became an anthropologist. The way so many messed up people go into psychotherapy.

He left Creighton on a Sunday morning, hit the I-70 and got all the way to Salina before checking into a Best Western. He'd thought about camping at KOA to save money but that was already thinking like a loser.

All he had to do was prove the Azuma were real, find the center of their universe and he could write his own ticket. The book deals, the movie deals. Now that he'd had a taste of pop success, he wanted more. There was nothing like it. Certainly not the staid and constricted academic world.

Beadles thought of himself as a serious scholar with a pop flair and a sense of humor. He'd begun making notes in a journal on the book he planned to write. He canceled all his credit cards but one on which he put his internet service.

Anasazi referred to ancient Indians who lived in the "four corners" region, where Utah, Colorado, Arizona and New Mexico meet. The Anasazi were eventually displaced by the Pueblo, Hopi, Navajo and Zuni. Scarce resources, especially water, led to war and some tribes relocated to remote areas to avoid all conflict. In the nineties, a dig outside Dolores, Colorado produced twenty-four skeletons which bore the unmistakable mark of cannibalism.

The Anasazi were not the only Native American tribes thought to practice cannibalism. Far to the north and one thousand years ago, the Aztalan Indians settled in Southern Wisconsin, built pyramids and ate their neighbors. In all fairness there was evidence of cannibalism among the Jamestown settlers too.

Beadles used his laptop to stay in touch with people and organizations he thought could help him in his search. Unfortunately, Permission, CO was now an official Ghost Town. No one ran the Historical Society. The county had the town listed on Craig's List as a potential tourist attraction and casino. No takers so far.

Beadles was cagey about his internet persona and took pains to disguise himself, often working through aliases. Anthropology was a little like international treasure hunting. It was difficult to keep a big hunt under wraps and, if you weren't careful, you'd find a dozen parties nipping at your heels either trying to beat you to it or suing you. Although well known in anthro circles, Beadles had already begun downsizing his social media presence hoping to travel under the radar.

The Azuma had virtually no internet presence—a few news items about the collection.

Beadles flipped through the TV channels. Even here in East Bumfuck there were three dozen channels. He'd fallen out of the news. He watched *Judge Judy*. Why were so many of the guests morbidly obese?

Beadles walked across the swooshing highway to a Cracker Barrel and had dinner. It was a relief to be out of academia, among normal people who worried about the rent and what was on TV that night. His meatloaf and mashed potatoes were delivered by a fresh-faced girl with a smile and a Midwestern twang. Sated, he darted back across the highway and collapsed in his room, lulled by the sound of passing traffic.

He dreamed of the desert.

CHAPTER TWENTY-SIX

HAVA

ummer drove straight through to Hava, stopping only for potty breaks and to renew her supply of Monster energy drinks, Weasel Peters, Cheetos and bananas. She pulled into the barren lot in front of the doublewide Holmes Elegance house trailer in which she'd grown up with four siblings. The stoop was made of cinderblocks covered with plywood. An old propane tank peeked from one end. Six other trailers clustered around the sand common which held a half dozen discarded tires and a rusting jungle gym. The ground was hard-packed earth. There were no signs warning parents that the jungle gym was potentially hazardous and they were not responsible for injuries.

Rusting pick-ups sat in front of some of the trailers. A dun-colored '68 Camaro with the side windows smashed out rested on cinderblocks in front of her own ancestral home. It had been her father's pride and joy. Summer had given no warning because the trailer had no phone.

It was seven-thirty and still light as she got out in the baking heat, lugged her overnighter up the creaking stoop and tried the door. Locked. She knocked on the thin aluminum door. Footsteps caused the old trailer to list and squeal. The door opened revealing the blotto face of her younger brother Ethan, who'd been in jail the last time she checked for stealing copper wire. He was tall and skinny with a Beatle mop and a furze of black hairs clinging to his upper lip.

"Look what the cat dragged in," he said returning to the sprung sofa in front of the flat screen TV. He plopped down and picked up his gaming yoke. A half empty bottle of malt liquor sat on the thrift store coffee table next to a bong. The TV emitted muted gunfire, roars and screams. The room smelled of beer and reefer. It was cooler inside the trailer, filled with the whine of a window-mounted AC.

Ethan's thumbs worked the yoke. Onscreen, a First Person Shooter mowed down Al Qaeda types with a machine gun. Ethan reached for the bong, lit it with a Bic and inhaled, exhaling a plume of gray smoke.

"Want a hit?" he said without taking his eyes off the screen.

"No thanks. Where's Ma and Pa?"

"Ma's in the bedroom. She ain't been feeling right. Pa's dead. Didn't you hear? Drifted across the centerline last week and hit a semi head-on. Didn't anyone tell you? I thought Mary was gonna phone."

Mild shock, relief, and a deep burning shame all ignited within Summer's heart. Her father had been an abusive drunk and her mother never said boo about it. You were supposed to feel something when your father died but all Summer felt was a faint sense of relief. He was a rotten failure for whom his children never measured up.

"Did they already have the funeral?"

"What funeral? We let the county take him."

"Jesus that's cold," Summer said.

"What the fuck do you care? Mary didn't get hold of you, huh?"

"I change phones a lot."

For the first time since she'd entered the trailer Ethan looked at her. "Jesus, sis! What happened to you? You look like you've been in a fight."

"Vince beat me up. I left him."

"Who's Vince?"

Summer plopped down on the sofa next to her brother. "Some loser I was dating."

'Yeah, well I hope you cut his balls off."

Summer smiled grimly. "Not quite. But he's going to be pissed when he wakes up. I took his car."

"Wondered where you got that bitchin' Camaro. Maybe you'll let me take it for a spin? I got some shit to pick up in town."

"You got a license?"

Ethan made a motion and resumed shooting. Screams and explosions.

She'd told Vince about growing up in Hava. He might track her down. She'd have to move on but she figured she had a grace period—at least twenty-four hours—for Vince to wake up and get his shit together.

She knew a truck stop down the Interstate where she could sell the Camaro. It would be dangerous but she did not intend to go there unprepared. That was one of the reasons she'd returned to Hava.

"Pa still had his guns?"

"I ain't sold 'em yet if that's what you mean."

"Good. 'Cause I'm taking one."

Ethan set the yoke down and looked at her. "The fuck you are. I need that money!"

"For what? Drugs? I'm just as entitled to his shit as you are. All I want's one pistol. You can keep the rest."

"I'm gonna crash here tonight. I'll take the sofa."

Ethan shrugged. "Whatever."

Summer got up, went down the hall and softly opened the door to her parents' bedroom. Her mother lay on her side like a manatee snoring. Summer shut the door and went outside. She opened the Camaro's trunk. That new car smell smacked her. Inside the trunk was a cardboard liquor box. She picked it up. It was heavy. Paper heavy, not metal heavy. She set it down and peeled back the flaps releasing the smell of a mummy's tomb. Inside were stacks of telegraph messages bound together with faded ribbon. She picked them up and looked at the top message.

Will arrive Flagstaff noon the 24th stop hope you have contracted for mules and equipment stop I remain your obedient servant Wilbur H. Addison stop

It was dated May 8, 1897. The rest were similar. Vince must have picked them up on one of his free-lance picks. There was also a leather portfolio containing black and white photographs of Indians. Maybe they were worth something. She set them aside and kept digging. An old miner's hat, bills of sale from a dry goods shop and at the very bottom, a leather portfolio so ancient only a brown patina remained. It was held shut by an ancient black ribbon. She unwound the ribbon and carefully opened the portfolio on top of the box.

Inside was a desiccated sheet of deerskin that had been folded innumerable times. She began to unfold it and saw that it was a map. A hand-drawn map made with a quill pen. The cartographer was gifted not only in his elegant penmanship but in his drawings of landmarks. In the fading evening light the paper was the color of goat's milk. The writing was in Spanish.

The ancient map felt like felt. A wind blew up and threatened to tear it out of her hands. Summer carefully folded the map, returned it to the portfolio and took it into the house.

CHAPTER TWENTY-SEVEN

JACKPOT

eadles pulled into Aurora, Colorado at five p.m. Tuesday evening and checked into a Motel 8 next to Fergie's Bar and Grill, a sports bar with a dozen TV screens surrounding the vast open room divided by an island counter next to the horseshoe bar. Beadles took a table in the rear. The waitress gave him a funny look when he ordered an Absolut martini. She was young, stacked, brunette, and reminded him that he hadn't been laid in a week.

She also looked like she was barely twenty-one. Beadles took his drink to the bar. Three stools down hunkered a clutch of thirty-something women cracking each other up. Beadles had often observed how women tended to gather in homogenous groups. These women were all attractive, well made-up, with expensive but not flashy clothes. Realtors, shop owners, sales persons.

He watched them in the mirror behind the bar, making eye contact with a pert redhead with slightly crazy eyes. He knew about women with crazy eyes. Easy to get, hard to shed. That was all right. Once she found out what a loser he was she would rabbit for the tall timber.

He ordered a hamburger at the bar and another martini. Basketball bounced from the walls, sound turned off to accommodate four feeds. Beadles looked around. It was a young, upwardly mobile crowd, guys and gals unwinding after work, laughing and gossiping. Some solitary souls buried their snouts in their Razrs and Droids, texting, tweeting, and Facebooking. Beadles had held onto his internet account. It was the only way he could stay in touch.

He took out his Razr and checked his messages. The realtor indicated they might have a buyer. Creighton was a hot market because of the university. Cialis spam. He used to compulsively check his investments but there was no point to it now that he was broke. He'd had to sell everything to pay the lawyers and he still owed them money.

By his third martini two of the women were gone and the redhead was on the adjacent barstool. Hester sold Venetian blinds for I Heart Windows and was a passionate Broncos fan. Beadles, who took zero interest in sports, agreed with her that telling Manning to take a knee with thirty-one seconds in the fourth quarter had been a bonehead move.

"I mean, what was Fox thinking?" Hester demanded. "Peyton Manning! He could have got them into field goal range on the next play."

Beadles shook his head in dismay. "You can't fix stupid."

"So what do you do, Vaughan?"

"I'm a professor of anthropology at Creighton College." A venal sin.

"Anthropology…"

"The study of humanity. I specialize in Anasazi Indians—the people who originally settled this country—Colorado, Utah, New Mexico, Arizona."

"My folks took me to Mesa Verde National Park when I was little. Place gave me the creeps. I still get nightmares."

Beadles looked at her with bemusement. "What's scary about Mesa Verde?"

"Those ruins? Carved out of the rock? I had a terrible fear that if I stepped inside I would never get out. The walls would close in on me and I'd die of thirst or suffocate. They were just so old. I don't know why but it frightened me. I remember crying and my parents taking me back to the car."

By ten they were back in his room where he showed her the gold medallion. By ten-thirty they had done the dirty deed and she lay snoring in his bed. Her purse sat open on the dresser next to the big screen TV. He stared at it. He stared at her. He was down to his last hundred bucks minus the five thou in the trunk and the Visa was maxed out.

Quietly he rose, went to her purse, and fished through it for her wallet. Hester was flush. She had over six hundred dollars in her wallet. She wouldn't miss a hundred. He stealthily transferred the twenties to his own wallet, went to the bathroom and returned to bed.

CHAPTER TWENTY-EIGHT

VINCE WAKES UP

ince woke with the mother of all headaches. He lay there long minutes watching the ceiling pulse like gecko neck. WTF? His throat felt like a shop drain. His tongue was a fuzzy caterpillar. He started to sit up. Whoa.

Waves of nausea roiled. He lay back down. What had he done? At least he was home in his own bed. Good sign. The last thing he remembered was seeing that dipshit Rotarian trying to cop a feel off Summer. And the bitch was leading him on with a lascivious grin, tongue running the keys like Liberace.

They'd argued. The argue escalated at home. He'd hit her.

Fuck.

FUCK!

The bitch drugged him! He knew the signs, he'd been there before.

Not Summer. Not sweet, passive little Summer. Where did she find the guts to slip him roofies? What else had she done?

A pearl of dread grew in his gut.

Vince roared off the bed like a Sea World porpoise. Nausea drove him straight to the porcelain god where he knelt and made his stutter-chuck offering, washing the bile out of his mouth with Scope and draining three glasses of water.

He stumbled back into the bedroom, scooped up his jeans and sat heavily on the bed. He pulled out his wallet and opened it.

"FUCK!" he said.

She'd cleaned him out. He'd had eight hundred dollars in there. At least she'd left the credit cards and cell phone.

His keys were gone.

Oh no oh no. Grunting, Vince pulled on his jeans, did a quick canvass to make certain he hadn't dropped them in a drawer or in the kitchen. Grabbing the spare house key, he surged out of the apartment nearly colliding with Marisa Guttierez who worked as a maid at Caesar's, sidestepped and ran down the cinderblock stairwell two steps at a time to the ground floor where he exploded through the parking lot exit, eyes going to where he'd parked his sweet Camaro diagonally across two spaces at the back.

Gone.

The bitch took the car.

"GNARG!" Vince said, shaking his shaven head. A couple skate punks looked over then away. Vince was cut like a con with tats covering his arms and torso. Snakes encircled his biceps, barbed wire his wrists. There was a star on each shoulder and BRAWLER emblazoned across his chest in biker Gothic. It was his nickname when he was a cage fighter. He went four for seven before hanging up his gloves.

Vince stormed back into the house meaner than a rabid vole. He slammed the apartment door shut behind him. The construction was so cheap it wasn't even a satisfying slam. Just a soft click when the hollowed-out door hit the frame.

Surrounded by cheapness and failure, Vince reviewed his options. He owed Luca Bonamici $18,000. Chump change to the high rollers but it was worth Vince's life. Luca looked like a popover but he employed heavy muscle and had pulled the trigger on guys who owed less.

Vince had three days to come up with the cash. He'd hoped to use the proceeds from the Camaro's trunk to pay if off. He'd hooked up with some batshit millionaire, lived in Palm Springs filled with Western memorabilia, items stolen from the Smithsonian including Ulzana's skull. Ulzana had been a Chiricahua warrior who led a raid in 1886 killing twelve farmers. You could call them atrocities but that wouldn't be sensitive to the pain and suffering of Lo, the Noble Red Man.

As far as Vince was concerned, Lo, the Noble Red Man was a lazy, shiftless, easily intoxicated and prone to drug abuse slacker like Summer.

She sure could shake her booty.

Maybe he'd throw her a fuck when he caught up with her. One she wouldn't like. And he was going to catch up with her if it's the last thing he did. She had no idea the value of the contents of the Camaro's trunk. That Palm Springs geezer was salivating like a hungry dog, waving a hundred gees.

All over an ancient map of some obscure shithole in the desert that Vince took in trade from a cat burglar that owed him four grand. Vince could be pretty fucking scary. Dude wasn't really a cat burglar, just a meth addict who would lift his own mother's dentures. But he'd had some pretty sweet scores, Vince had to admit. One of them was the contents of a storage locker in Aurora, CO, which contained the artifacts, including the map.

There was also a model 72 Winchester which the cat burglar sold to a collector in Aspen before he blew all the money on whores, booze, and meth, which Vince was happy to supply. Then the guy went in the tank.

Vince couldn't report the Camaro as stolen. They both carried too much baggage. Nor was Summer stupid enough to keep it for long. First things first. Vince had to find a new set of wheels. He phoned a dealer he knew and left a message.

He needed a gun too.

CHAPTER TWENTY-NINE

ONE LOUSY LITTLE AUTOMATIC

Arthur Funderburk had kept his guns in a cabinet in a corner of his bedroom. Arthur Funderburk only used them on his birthday, the 4th of July and New Year's Eve when he fired them in the air, drunk as a sailor. Summer's friend Eunice had a cousin who was killed by a falling bullet on New Year's Eve.

Summer went into the bedroom where her mother Maria lay snoring like a beached whale. The gun cabinet stood in the corner.

Summer took one look and said, "Ethan I thought you said you didn't sell the guns!"

The upper part which used to hold a Remington 12 gauge and a Springfield 30.06 was empty.

"Just a sec!" Ethan squeaked through his inhale. A moment later he appeared in the bedroom and went up to the cabinet.

"Well, shit. Ma or June musta took 'em or something. Try the bottom drawer. What you want guns for anyway?"

"I would just feel safer."

Summer crouched and drew the bottom drawer. She had to fight with it because it was a cheap cabinet and somewhat warped. The drawer suddenly popped free with a rattling sound. Inside lay a gun cleaning kit, a couple of loose brushes, a leather holster, a dozen bullets in different calibers, and a Beretta .25 in its original box.

"What happened to the Glock and the Mag?" Summer said rhetorically.

"Fuck if I know. What's wrong with that Beretta?"

Summer plucked the tiny black handgun from its box and put it in the pocket of her cargo pants. She grabbed a box of Wolf .25 ammo.

"Don't shoot yourself," Ethan said, returning to his game.

Maria snorked, opened her eyes, and sat up in bed. "Hello, baby," she said. "What are you doing here?"

Summer sat on the bed and hugged Maria who smelled like cigarettes and stale bread. "My boyfriend beat me up so I left him."

"Oh, dear," Maria said, holding Summer's chin in her hand and looking at the shiner. "Oh, dear. Are you all right?"

"I'm fine, Ma. He might come here looking for me."

"Did you tell the police?"

Summer just looked at her.

"Never mind. I'd fix you something to eat but there's nothing in the house."

"That's all right, Ma. I got money. You want to give me a list I'll drive down to the Bosselman's and pick shit up."

"That'd be swell, Summer. Just swell. Maybe you could get me a bottle of Four Roses."

"Sure, Ma. What happened to Pa's truck?"

"It's out back. Needs a battery and a couple of tires. You ask Joe Jeffords, he'll get it running for you. Just give him twenty."

Joe was an itinerant mechanic who lived two trailers down. Summer was going to need transportation. Pa's old Ford 150 hadn't been licensed in years. But first she had to sell the Camaro.

It was six-thirty when she knocked on the door of Joe's faded turquoise and white trailer. She heard a grunting noise and the trailer creaked as someone came to the door. Joe looked like a russet potato, long black hair gathered in a ponytail. He squinted at her hard for a minute before his face cracked in a broad grin.

"Summer! What are you doin' back in town? How the hell are ya?"

"Hi, Joe. I wonder if you could fix up Pa's truck so it runs. I got money."

Joe opened the screen door. "Come on in."

He went to the ice box and took out a six pack of Coors, held it up.

"No thanks."

Joe popped one loose then popped it open. He chugged half the can and sank into an old over-stuffed chair with cotton ticking peaking out at the seams. His trailer smelled of stale body odor and cigarettes. He reached for a pack of Pall Malls next to an overflowing amber ashtray and lit it with a match.

"Needs a battery and two tires. I was just waitin' for Maria to come up with the money."

Summer removed her wallet form her front pocket and peeled off two hundred dollar bills. She reached over and set them on the cheap coffee table next to the ashtray. "Here's two bills. That should cover it. You think you can have it up and running by tomorrow morning?"

Joe puffed and grabbed the money. She could see the calculations behind his eyes. Joe knew where to get discount auto parts. Possibly the same place she planned to sell the Camaro.

"Sure, sure, I got to go into town anyway. You want to ride along?"

"No thanks, Joe. I got stuff to do. I'll check with you in the morning."

Summer went through the Camaro carefully, checking to see if Vince had concealed anything in the door panels or beneath the seat. She found an ounce of primo in the center console, took it in the house and tossed it to Ethan.

"Holy shit! Thanks, Sis!"

She loaded the Beretta's tiny magazine, jammed it in and jacked one into the chamber. She stuck it in her front pants pocket. She got in the Camaro and drove fourteen miles to the Bosselman's at the intersection of State Highway 89 and Cross Creek Road. The Bosselman's stood in the Southeast quadrant surrounded by big rigs, pick-ups, and two non-chain motels. The kind of places they didn't vacuum under the beds. As dusk settled in, the Bosselman's lit up like a refinery. The smell of gas lingered in the air. Summer drove around to the back, a broad parking lot that melded into the desert. There were dozens of cars parked in clusters and at the very rear, adjacent to the sand, a couple low riders, some souped-up Civics and WRXs and a dozen gangbangers slouching around in drooping pants and hoodies to the subterranean beat from the open hatch of an Eclipse.

Summer drove right up to them. The boys saw the car first and liked what they saw. Then Summer got out and they liked it even better.

"Hey there, pretty mama, whatchoo need?"

"You can roll with me anytime."

"Oye guapa!"

One thick as a brick Aztec rolled up to her with his hands in his pockets. He had a silver stud through his nose and a sideways Diesel hat. "Whassup, pretty lady?"

"I don't know, pachuco. You tell me."

"Tha's some bad ride."

Summer grinned and leaped onto the hood. "You like this ride? 'Cause I'm looking to deal."

CHAPTER THIRTY

PERMISSION

Permission was a ghost town. Population: 126, mostly retirees. The wood bones of dead cabins announced the town seconds before Beadles reached the epicenter, the only part that remained alive. Quint's Cafe and Convenience. It was right across the street from the long boarded Permission town hall, a nineteenth century Quaker-like structure with a bell tower and stained glass. It had also doubled as the Lutheran Church.

Once, Permission had been a bustling town of 20,000, the gateway to the Permission Gold Mine, which had yielded over a ton of the precious yellow metal until the vein petered out in the sixties.

The town hung on as a tourist haven, a cheap alternative to Breckinridge although the slopes weren't as good and the ski lift broke down a lot. Permission was the scene of Randall F. Fitzroy's shoot-out, resulting in his death. Fitzroy was buried in the town cemetery on a plateau overlooking the basin. Fitzroy had been a notorious gun slinger and bank robber, although he did serve a brief stint as sheriff of No Go, Wyoming in the eighteen nineties.

His final shoot-out took place July 1, 1901. Fitzroy got his man, a bounty hunter by the name of Earl Goodwood, but Goodwood got Fitzroy. They were buried side by side.

Beadles had learned all this from the internet. He parked diagonally across from Quint's next to a Yukon Denali. It was evening and Quint's was by far the brightest thing in Permission. Beadles got out and headed across the street toward the one-story red brick emporium. Light shined from the cafe, a couple of cowboys joking with the waitress behind the bar. They were the only patrons.

They glanced at Beadles as he took a seat three stools down at the end of the bar.

"Getting' feisty, arentcha Al?" the waitress said. She turned and came toward him with a big red smile, a plump woman of about fifty, wearing a peach-colored dress, white apron, gray hair done up in a bun. Gold stitching on her left breast said "Madge."

"Hello, cowboy," she said. "What can I get for you?"

Beadles read the menu on the back wall over the counter. "I'll take the Quintburger, side of coleslaw and Coke please."

"You bet."

One of the cowboys swiveled toward him on the red naugahyde stool. His face was broad and friendly beneath the wide-brimmed Stetson. His belt buckle was saucer sized. "What brings you to Permission?"

"I wanted to visit the State Historical Society."

The cowboy smiled sympathetically. "Hell, that's been closed for years. Ever since old McGill died. He was the only thing kept it goin', ain't that right, Bob?"

The cowboy next to him who looked to be in his sixties cradled a cup of coffee between his elbows. "Ahuh, that's right," he said without turning his head.

"That's a shame," Beadles said. Madge placed a cold glass of coke before him.

"Do you know what they did with its contents?"

"What's your interest," Al said.

"I'm an anthropologist. I'm doing research on an American Indian tribe known as the Azuma."

Al's face wrinkled like the Mississippi Delta. "Azuma? Ain't never heard of 'em. You heard of 'em Bob?"

Bob didn't move. "Nope. Never have."

Beadles stood up and stuck out his hand. "Vaughan Beadles."

Al shook. "Al Barnes. And this here fossil is Bob Woodley."

Madge put the burger down next to Al and moved Beadles' coke.

"Only reason we stick around's 'cause we're hermits. Ain't that right, Bob?"

"Mm-hm. That's right."

"Ol' Pete McGill died back in '08. Christ, he musta been ninety if he were a day. Colorful character. Actually served as a deputy sheriff back in the day. That would be in the fifties and sixties, I reckon."

Beadles could not prevent himself from downing half the burger. "Any idea what happened to the contents?" he said while chewing.

"County cut a deal with some wholesale junk man to come and haul it off."

Beadles set the burger down, anger flaring. "How could they do that? From what I understand the collection contained priceless artifacts! They would have been worth a fortune in a straight ahead auction!"

Al was nodding before Beadles finished. "It seemed mighty fishy to some of us too, friend. That was County Executive Meredith Martin. She got indicted for bribery and I believe she did some time in prison."

Beadles removed a small spiral pad and a pen. "Meredith Martin?"

"Yessir. Her husband was Cole Martin. They owned that big spread up Cold Canyon Road, but he sold it when she got sent up. God knows where he went. Bob, you know where Martin went?"

"Nope."

"You can always check with the County Assessor, but they won't be open 'til tomorrow. Where you stayin'?"

"Best Western Breckinridge."

"Well good luck to you, Vaughan. Hope you find what you're looking for."

CHAPTER THIRTY-ONE

WHEELS

ince's father walked out when Vince was nine, leaving his mother to raise Vince, his brother Luke and sister Frances on her own. South End, Boston, 1990. Vince grew up on the streets with the Southies, a white trash street gang that fought turf wars with the blacks, robbed convenience stores, sniffed glue and shot dope. A lot of those guys were dead or in jail—Vince did four years at Billerica for aggravated assault.

He tried enlisting but his record kept him out. He drifted west working a variety of hustles including fake roofer and fake asphalt repair, usually on seniors. He'd worked construction a couple summers, just enough to sound like he knew what he was talking about. He'd landed in Vegas six years prior and took to it like a journalist to an open bar.

Vince hustled. He worked as a bouncer at a dive on Fremont, dealt a little meth on the side. Dealt a little more. Picked up a couple girls whom he ran at mid-level hotels like the Golden Nugget. He stole and he fenced. He was smart enough not to steal in Vegas—unless some mark was just begging for it. He would drive to Arizona and Colorado, case the big summer homes abandoned in winter, cut the power, break in and loot the place.

Almost got caught a couple times, once by a big dog.

Vince learned a lot in Billerica, including how to shut off home alarm systems and how to deal with aggressive dogs. You gave them hamburger mixed with roofies or ketamine if you could get it. He burgled a couple veterinary clinics and sold the stuff to the Playboy Bloods who used it to induct runaway girls into their stable.

Eventually Vince got his own stable—four hos who kept him in a style that was barely tolerable. They were junkies, but he lost them when an undercover Narc saw him waling the shit out of Brigit one night in an alley behind the Hard Rock and he ended up doing thirty in County.

When he got out, his hos had gone elsewhere.

He tried the fight game, training at Pitbull's Gym and managing himself. His first three fights in Fight League West ended in first round knockouts. *Well, all right* he thought. *Here we go. Success at last.* He moved up to International MMA Promotions and got submitted in the second round by some cowboy from Idaho. He overextended his Achilles tendon and was told he'd be out for at least twelve months. The fights paid shit anyway. He couldn't cut it in the UFC so there went that.

His luck changed when he wandered into Dante's. Blistering September day, the sun so hot you could cook flapjacks on the sidewalk. The interior was cool, dark, and fragrant. Mid-afternoon, the usual collection of pathetic losers, Arabs and blue collar stiffs watching a Rubenesque blond five years past her sale date spread it from table to table. Vince was just going to grab a quick beer and leave.

Summer took the stage like a thunderstorm. She crackled with wicked good looks and that smile. She was way above his grade but he had to try. She wasn't using when he picked her up. The trick was to make them come to you. The next day he was back, sitting at a table near her stage reading a comic book. *Mars Attacks*

Popeye. Never looked up. He came back the next day and did it again.

She never so much as glanced at him. Like she was too good for him. So he cooked up another scheme.

Now the bitch was just another ho, only she had his car and goods. And she'd slipped him a roofie. No one did that to Vince and lived. The ungrateful bitch. He got hard just thinking what he was going to do with her when he caught up.

Emilio phoned back at noon. Emilio owned Emilio's Auto Emporium.

"Vince, mon, how you been, man? You still shackin' up with that hot broad Summer?

"I need a set of wheels, Emilio."

Emilio heard the impatience in Vince's voice and didn't ask about Summer again. "Whatchoo need, mon? Come on down. I just scored a sweet little Porsche Boxster. This baby'll do 180."

"I need something that can hold shit and go anywhere."

"Mon, I got Jeeps, Hummers, Range Rovers, I got 'em in every size and color. Come on down."

"I gotta take the fuckin' bus. I'll be down around two."

Vince showered, put on a clean set of clothes, grabbed a leather backpack and walked—WALKED!—twelve blocks to the Wells Fargo Bank where he kept a safety deposit box. Some fag with a rivet through his ear walked him back. When he was alone, Vince drew out the deep box, sat and opened it. He took out fifteen thou leaving five for emergencies. He took the kilo of pharmaceutical grade coke he'd taken from a dentist passed out in his room at The Hacienda, Vince's ho, Shameeka, having slipped the dentist a roofie. It was a pain-free removal.

Vince caught the Bernstein Boulevard bus, rode it twelve miles through town, transferred to Airport Road and got off at the bus stop a block from Emilio's. The sight of Vince approaching via prison stroll, wide-brimmed Stetson set low over the sunglasses, the gaucho mustache, the jeans and boots caused Emilio's new salesperson Sally to chirp like a frightened bird and rush into the showroom to inform her boss that bad news was on the way.

Emilio was hustling a young Iranian drooling on the Enzo. $265,000. The Persian had come straight from Caesar's Poker Tournament where he'd walked away with a cool half mil.

"Emilio," Sally twerped in kewpie doll voice.

"What is it, Sally?" Emilio said, looking up and past her shoulder to where Vince had just entered the showroom. "It's all right. I know him. Would you help Mr. Viderous with this item? He may want to take it for a test drive."

Sally turned her charms on the Persian who grinned like a flower opening to the sun. Emilio intercepted Vince by a knee-high Lamborghini.

"Vince, mon, you're scaring the customers."

Vince stopped, shook himself, pasted a waxen smile across his puss. "Sorry. Let's go talk." Vince led the way toward Emilio's glassed-in office. He'd been promising to set Emilio up with Summer for months. Emilio had a nose for the candy too. Emilio followed him inside and shut the door.

"Have a seat, mon. What can I do for you?" Emilio went to a cube refrigerator on the wall, pulled out a couple of RC's and tossed one to Vince.

"I need wheels, ese. Four wheel drive. Something big." He popped the can and glugged.

Emilio sat behind his desk and put his feet up. He popped his can and drank. "Everything irie?"

"Summer walked out on me. She took my Camaro."

Emilio put his feet back down and leaned forward, eyes wide. "No shit? That was one sweet ride. Why'd she do that, mon?"

"She got pissed 'cause I slapped her around a little. I caught her making googly eyes at some linoleum salesman at Dante's."

"You got to slap 'em around now and then just so they don't start getting ideas," Emilio said. "She took that Camaro, huh. Emilio's eyes narrowed with concern. "You report it?"

"Do I look stupid to you? Of course I didn't report it! I don't rat out my friends. But now I need something to go chase her down. I know where she lives—over in Navajo Nation. Nothing but sand and scorpions."

Emilio turned to his computer and pecked. "What's your price range?"

Vince grinned bodaciously. "I thought maybe we could do a little horse-trading. You might want to shut the blinds."

Intrigued, Emilio rose, went to the blinds looking out on the showroom, lowered them and closed them. He resumed his seat behind his desk with an expectant smile. "Whaddaya got?"

Vince pulled the freezer-wrapped brick of blow from his backpack and flipped it onto the desk where it thumped solid.

"Pharmaceutic grade blow. Got it from a dentist."

Emilio unwrapped the brick, opened the center drawer of his desk and took out a stiletto which flicked open at the touch of a button. He pulled out a smeared hand mirror and ladled a mound of white powder onto it. He wrangled the line with a business card, pulled out a cut soda straw and inhaled, one line for each nostril. His eyes popped. He stretched backward arms overhead.

"Oh, YEAH!" he said. "That's the real deal! You want some?"

Vince was tempted but he had too much to do. "No thanks, essay. What I need are some wheels. That's got to be worth ten gees, easy. You got something we can just work a trade?"

"Momentito." Emilio reached into another drawer and brought out a small electronic pharmaceutical scale. He set the brick on the disc and turned it on. It read one kilo.

Emilio stood. "Let's take a look." He led Vince out of the office, through the showroom where Sally and the Persian huddled by the Ferrari, out into the yard. Emilio veered right. He lumped all the SUVs together, just as he bunched all his other cars. They passed a dozen Porsches until they came to the SUVs including Porsches, Beemers, CrosSports, Jeeps, Escapes and Rovers. Vince beelined for the steel gray Hummer.

"That's a real sweetheart," Emilio said talking fast. "Just came in—only 45 thou on the clock and cleaner than a hound's tooth. Fully loaded air, Sirius XM, OnStar, Harmon Kardon speakers, lights, heated seats, bluetooth, 425 HP V8, leather." He opened the door. "Asking twenty-five. It's an '09. Want to take her for a spin?"

"I'll give you that brick," Vince said softly.

Emilio's eyes bugged. He looked around and swallowed. He was ready for his next bump. Cocaine made you feel like a new man. But fifteen minutes later the new man wanted a line. It hadn't been easy lately scoring hi-grade in town. The DEA had been running sting operations up and down the strip and a lot of the cartels had switched over to meth which they could produce themselves in country.

"Let's go back to the office and talk about it," Emilio said.

Emilio ended up paying Vince four thou in addition to the Hummer.

CHAPTER THIRTY-TWO

GLENWOOD

eadles wasted two days tracking the Permission Historical Society Collection to Aurora only to learn that the storage company had gone into foreclosure and sold off the contents of all their lockers several years ago. On to Durango.

He ran into an unexpected spring snowstorm in the Rockies on I-70 and learned that the old Jeep's four-wheel-drive worked as he passed dozens of spin-offs by the side of the road including a couple of semis. Even with four wheel drive he had to slow way down and only got as far as Glenwood Springs where he took a room at the Glenwood Inn, including a free pass to the world's largest outdoor community hot spring—a swimming pool the length of a football field between the mountain and the interstate.

Grabbing his swim trunks, Beadles left his hotel and walked a block to the spring's entrance. He handed his card to a clerk and entered the big men's room where he changed into his trunks. There were at least two hundred people in the vast pool but it was so large it didn't seem crowded. Heated by thermal springs, one end was 106 degrees Fahrenheit, tapering down to 102 at the other end. There were coin operated back-spritzers lining the sides. Beadles sank into the hot water and felt anxiety leave through the pores.

Sure. This was going to be a snap. All he had to do was prove the Azuma's existence, ideally find the center of their civilization, and all doors would open to him, his past transgressions forgotten. He looked up. The moon winked at him through clouds and was gone.

A bitter worm crawled back into his heart. He'd always thought of Anatole as a friend given their class differences. And let's not kid ourselves—America was divided by class as much as anything. Maybe even more than race. Beadles was acutely aware of his "white privilege." It had been a required course when he attended Northwestern. He was also aware that he had been extraordinarily lucky to have been born into an upper middle-class family, that his parents stayed together and loved him, that he was unusually good looking and athletically gifted and had an inbuilt confidence.

It wasn't fair to the deformed or stupid, but that was life. Not all the laws in the universe could make everyone happy. Beadles had been happy. Or at least he thought he was and wasn't that the same thing? Despite his misgivings about Betty and the constant academic jockeying for position, he'd felt secure, loved and respected.

How had Anatole felt? Beadles never asked. Anatole was a janitor. Oh, sure, they could call him a custodian or maintenance supervisor, but the fact was he was a janitor and he was an Indian. Whether he'd lived in a box down by the tracks or a mansion Beadles didn't know. Never asked. He did know that Anatole had a son. When Lars was born they got to talking and Anatole pulled out his phone and showed Beadles a picture of the then-sixteen-year-old Rory grinning on a pony, barebacked. The picture might have been taken a hundred years ago. There was nothing in it to indicate modernity—just the boy smiling on a the pony wearing only blue jeans, his grin a slash of white in the nut-brown face.

White guilt reared its handsome head. Had Anatole squealed because he resented Beadles' success? Had Beadles been condescending? He racked his brain. He didn't think he had, but maybe the false bonhomie of treating the janitor as an equal was a form of condescension.

Anatole's betrayal hurt Beadles more than Betty's. What was up with that? Every now and then Beadles thought maybe he should see a therapist. He'd never talked to one in his life except for a few perfunctory questions when applying for scholarships or jobs. He'd always thought of himself as at peace and comfortable in his own skin. He wasn't one of those emotionally troubled souls who lived in the past or the future. He'd been happy, hadn't he?

Sure, he'd been ambivalent about the birth of Lars, as would any first-time father. It took a while, but he came to love the boy. And yet here he was in a hot tub in Glenwood Springs, a thousand miles from his wife and son, and he didn't miss them.

Maybe there was something wrong with him.

He returned to his room a half hour later. It was a small family motel, no service bar. Exhausted from driving, Beadles went straight to bed and dreamed he was trapped in a vast desert landscape beneath a sun so harsh he could only see by shading his eyes with his fingers and staring at the ground.

Until a shadow crossed the land.

CHAPTER THIRTY-THREE

GRAMPA NED

Summer met Grampa Ned Lead when she was five years old. Her father brought her to the medicine man to be blessed. Grandpa Ned was ancient even then and smelled of Latakia and mints. He had a pet wolf named Wolfie and lived in a hogan.

Over the years, Summer would often seek Grampa Ned out for advice. She couldn't ask Joe or Maria whose own lives were turbulent, and often the source of her distress. She needed Grampa's wisdom now.

Last night the banger to whom she'd sold the Camaro drove her home and helped unload the groceries she'd bought in Bosselman's. Ethan was still up playing video games, a haze of marijuana hovering smog-like around his head. He barely looked as she carried the paper bags into the house.

"Ja get any beer?" he said.

"Sixpack Dos Equis."

Ethan set down the yoke and walked over to the kitchen. He peeled off a can and popped it.

"Hey, is Grampa Ned still around?" Summer said.

Ethan shrugged and returned to his seat. "Fuck if I know."

Summer crashed in her old bedroom. Ethan slept on the sofa. In the morning Summer made coffee and took Maria a cup. Maria sat up and was feeling better. She had been tired as long as Summer could remember. Allergies in the summer, fighting off a flu in the winter.

"Hey Ma, Grampa Ned still around?"

"Far as I know, honey. I saw him at the county fair last year. That man doesn't age. Did you get my Four Roses?"

"In the kitchen."

"God bless you, you're a good girl."

Promising she would say goodbye before she took off, Summer left the trailer and walked to Joe Jeffords' place. Good as his word, Joe had four recapped tires in the back of his Chevy. He and Summer rode back to the Funderburk manse, around back where Arthur's 150 sat. Joe went to work. At ten o'clock it was already in the eighties. Summer went in the house, made a pitcher of lemonade and brought Joe a glass. She took a glass to Maria.

Maria drank thirstily and set it on the bedside table next to a half dozen amber plastic pill bottles. Maria suffered from high blood pressure and fibromyalgia. "Thank you, dear. Where did you say you were going?"

"I don't know, Ma. I got something for you." Summer took out her wallet and counted out three hundred bucks in twenties which she laid in Maria's lap. Maria picked it up hungrily.

"What's this for?"

"Food, booze, bills, whatever."

Maria's eyes narrowed. "You ain't trickin' again?"

"No, Ma. I quit that shit. I'm not going to let a man control me ever again. Listen. It's possible Vince will show up. If he does, call the Sheriff. Don't fuck around. He's a mean son of a bitch."

Maria looked alarmed. "Why would he come here?"

"Because I walked out on him and took his car."

Maria flinched. "Oh honey, why did you do that?"

"I had to get away fast, Ma. He beat me like a rented mule. No man does that to me."

"Why didn't you call the police?"

"Oh, Ma."

"Well I don't have a phone."

"What about Ethan?"

Maria nodded hesitantly. "I think so. But I don't have the number."

Summer rolled her eyes.

From out back they heard the grind of a starter motor. Seconds later, the old Ford roared to life and Summer clapped her hands in delight.

"Ma, I'm borrowing Pa's truck."

"Ain't got no insurance. Those plates are no good."

"That's all right. Gotta go. I'll talk to you soon."

"Ain't got no telephone."

"Ethan does. I'll be back." Summer leaned over and kissed her mother.

In the living room she sat next to Ethan, who was deep in battle. "Listen little bro, if my boyfriend shows up here call the police."

Ethan worked the yoke. "What?"

Summer grabbed the yoke. Ethan turned toward her with outrage. "Give it back!"

"Listen! If Vince shows up here looking for me call the police! Do you understand? Do you know how to dial 911?"

Ethan pouted. "Ain't no 911 out here."

"Well call the sheriff. Do you copy?"

"Yeah, yeah. Gimme the controls back."

Fifteen minutes later, she was on the road with her meager belongings including the contents of the Camaro's trunk, the Beretta a hard chunk in her front pants pocket.

Grampa Ned lived at the end of a winding box canyon. Summer slowed way down and eased the old truck over mailbox-sized boulders, up a dry wadi beneath a couple turkey vultures circling in the azure sky. As she rounded a hairpin curve, two turkey vultures took off flapping from a mound of carrion. It was a harsh country. It was best not to look too closely. Might have been a lamb from a nearby ranch or somebody's dog.

One hour and twenty minutes after leaving Hava, Summer topped a gentle rise and saw Grampa's hogan snugged up against the canyon wall, a couple cottonwood sprouting from a hidden spring. Grampa sat in front of the odd structure in a lawn chair in shades and a Cardinals hat puffing on a pipe, a Buddha-like figure. An old mongrel lay at his feet on a carpet segment. The hogan was actually a geodesic dome put up by some college kids who'd volunteered for Habitat for Humanity decades ago. Two glass triangles, hinged on one side and open, acted as skylights. The thing was surfaced in roofing shingles and about as attractive as a garage but it got the job done.

Summer drove to within thirty feet of the house, parked and got out. She wore sunglasses and had coaxed her long black hair through the back of a Not Lame ball cap she'd found in the truck.

"Hey, Grampa."

The old man exhaled a cloud of smoke like the College of Cardinals. The dog thumped its tail. Summer knelt and stroked its head.

"Hey, Boner."

"Hey, Summer Funderburk," Grampa growled. "Ain't seen you in years. How you doing? Come set with your old Grampa. Got root beer inside. Why don'tcha bring me one too."

She went into the hogan. It was laid out like a studio apartment with only the bathroom walled off. The great room had several Navajo rugs on the concrete floor, an old wood-burning stove against one wall, and mismatched thrift store furniture. It smelled of Latakia and bacon grease. Tufts of dog hair lay on the rugs.

She retrieved two Dad's from the ice box, went out front, handed one to Grampa and sat in the lawn chair next to him. Snugged up against the east wall they were still shielded by the morning sun.

"You're looking good," Grampa said. "Whatchoo been up to?"

"Working as a showgirl in Vegas."

"Ahuh. How that working out?"

"Not too well."

They sat in silence for several minutes sipping root beer.

"Grampa, I got a problem."

"I know."

She looked at the old man, gaze unreadable behind the wrap-around Foster Grants. "How did you know?"

"Been dreamin' about you."

CHAPTER THIRTY-FOUR

THE BONES

"What did you dream?" Summer asked.

"You're running from some white man."

"That's true! How much do you know?"

"Child, I don't know shit. You're out in the sun. Something's chasing you. That's all I know. Why don'tcha tell me about your troubles and then we'll cast the bones."

Summer told him everything since moving to Vegas. "I'm afraid he'll kill me."

She waited for Grampa to respond. He tapped the bowl of the pipe down on the edge of a rock, reached into his brocade vest, pulled out a tobacco pouch and refilled the pipe. He lit it with a kitchen match from another pocket. He puffed and blew a series of perfect smoke rings that hung in the still desert air like UFOs.

"Well let's take a look at the bones," he said, placing his hands on his knees and heaving himself to his feet. He was five six and weighed 185. He returned a moment later with a dice canister from Harrah's. He sat with a grunt and handed Summer the canister.

"Shake 'em."

Summer shook the canister, hearing the rattle of tiny bones inside and handed it to Grampa. He added a shake and prodded Boner with his toe.

"Move it, Boner." The old dog got stiffly to its feet and resettled itself at Summer's feet. Grampa unscrewed the lid and tossed the bones on the carpet segment. Eleven tiny bones gathered from eagle, coyote and rattlesnake. They fell in an odd pattern which could easily pass for art were someone to photograph them, or glue them as they lay to a backboard.

Grampa leaned forward with his hands on knees and grunted. He sucked air through his teeth. He turned to Summer and took off his glasses. His gray eyes were twinkly blue tucked beneath an occipital ledge.

"You're headed for some kinda Gotterdammerung."

Summer blinked. "What's that?"

"This here's bigger than just you and this white man. This here involves Shipapu."

"Shipapu? What's that?"

"Shipapu the gateway between this world and the next. Shipapu the font of life. You're on the great north road now, headed toward Shipapu."

Summer's forehead contracted. "What does it mean?"

"I don't know, but lookit here." Grampa pointed to a formation of four tiny bones off to the side. "This here says you're gonna meet the ghost who walks in the sun."

Despite the heat, Summer felt a copperhead ripple down her spine. "Who is the ghost who walks in the sun?"

The old man gazed into the distance. "When the Spanish came they encountered a tribe whose name we do not know. Sun worshipers, a warlike people. Their leader was a giant. The Spaniards used a woman to capture him. They gouged out his eyes and tied him to a wagon wheel and left him to die in the sun. His mother cursed the Spaniards with snakes and scorpions which rose up out of the earth and killed them all. But when they went to retrieve their leader's corpse it was not there. It is said that Skorpio only appears beneath a blazing sun and still seeks vengeance against the white man."

He shrugged. "It's just a tale."

"What did you say his name was?"

"I said it once. I want you to know. But it's bad luck to name the dead. You know that."

"I was hoping you could give me some advice."

"Well now it ain't all bad. See here?" He pointed to a coyote's tarsal lying inside a section of rattlesnake ribs. "You can defeat the ghost who walks in the sun if you're in the Shipapu."

"How do I find this Shipapu?"

Grampa shrugged. "It will find you. You can run but you cannot hide."

Summer suddenly remembered the map. She got up. "I want to show you something."

She retrieved the map from the truck and spread it out on the baking sand in front of Grampa's boots. He placed his hands on his knees and bent forward fighting his belly. He grunted and stared at the map. His finger traced lines in the air.

"Where you get this?"

"It was in the trunk of Vince's car. Probably something he stole."

"This is a map of that nameless land." He pointed to the odd looking rock formation in the center. "Here is where you want to go."

"Where is that, Grampa? I looked at my *Rand McNally* and I can't find anyplace like this map in it."

"You get the *Arizona Atlas and Gazetteer*. That's a better book. You'll be able to find it then. See these landmarks?" He pointed at a mitten-shaped butte. "This here's Monument Valley."

"But why has no one found anything? They must have flown over it a thousand times. Mapped it from space, I don't know."

"They weren't looking. From space it just looks like the surrounding desert. This is where you have to go. Take plenty of water."

"Well, shit. Why don't we drink hemlock?"

Grampa Ned patted her knee. "Don't fret, little sister. See this here?" He pointed to the bones. "Says here you will find a champion."

Summer laughed. "I've been waiting all my life. I always manage to pick the loser. God I have made terrible choices with men."

"The Lord helps those who help themselves. You packin'?"

Summer reached into her pocket and withdrew the Beretta. She handed it to Grampa who turned it over in his hands and handed it back.

"Mm-hm. That's a real peashooter. I can loan you my .45 if you like."

"Will it fit in my pants pocket?"

"Might cause a lump."

"No thanks, Grampa. Is a bullet gonna stop this ghost?"

Grampa shrugged. "Don't think so. It's for the boyfriend. That little peashooter ain't gonna get it done."

Maybe Ned Lead was right. Maybe she needed a gun with stopping power. She'd heard Vince go off with his druggie pals on what was the best hand weapon. Strictly for personal defense you understand. Stupid conversations about calibers and muzzle velocities.

An old boyfriend had taken her shooting. "Always aim for the greatest body mass and keep firing until you're out."

If eight .25 caliber bullets couldn't stop him, fuck it. Besides. Grampa said she would find a champion.

"I'd just dislocate my shoulder. I don't know where to go."

"You can stay here," Grampa said.

She thought about it. Maria knew where she was. Vince was bound to track down Maria who couldn't keep her mouth shut to save her own daughter if Vince bought her a bottle.

"I appreciate that, Grampa. But I got to keep moving. You're not my champion."

The old man shook his head sadly. "No, I ain't. But wait a minute. I want to give you something." He heaved himself up out of the chair and went in the house. She heard him moving things around and grunting. He came out holding a leather thong from which hung a hammered silver disc with turquoise in the center. He put it around her neck.

"Wear this. Might bring you some luck."

Summer turned the disc up in her hand. A series of squiggly lines radiated from a turquoise in the center. "What is it?"

"Been in the family many years. My great-great Grampa Orrin said it was the mark of the lost tribe and no harm would come to him who wore it. That's true because my brother Carl wore it all throughout World War II and no harm come to him. And he was in the Pacific."

Summer stood and kissed the old man on the forehead. "Thanks, Grampa."

"De nada," he said.

CHAPTER THIRTY-FIVE

UTE MUST BE SERVED

Beadles arrived in Durango, Friday, June 16th, shortly before noon. He took a room at the Morrison Motel a half mile north of the city on 550. It was ninety-two when he took up residence with his laptop and a bottled water in Brookside Park, across Main Street from the Post Office. Durango was a small city of 17,000 nestled among the San Juan Mountains. The scenery blew Beadles away. The way the mountains towered over the town instead of vice versa, like Chicago, where the city towered over the lake.

Beadles' plan was to watch PO visitors and wait for Anatole to show. He planned to follow Anatole at a discreet distance until he followed him home. He was prepared to do whatever was necessary to get the janitor to recant his testimony. More importantly, he wanted to know why.

Why did Anatole stick his neck out on such a controversial matter? Why did he quit and take early retirement?

First day: zippo. The PO closed at five-thirty. Beadles grabbed a sandwich from the San Juan Cafe, holed up in his hotel room and watched *Return of a Man Called Horse* on cable. He was at his station by eight Saturday morning in time to see the local postmaster unlock the red brick building. At least it would only be a half day. Anatole might not come to town for a week. Beadles was prepared for that. Anatole had to come sometime to pick up his check. The university. Social Security. Maybe a check from the Ute Nation, residuals from their casinos.

There was no internet service in the park. Beadles tentatively began to write a monograph on the Azuma intertwined with his personal history. He pissed in the bushes, afraid to leave his spot. They could add public indecency to his jacket.

Shortly after eleven, a battered, sand-colored Chevy pick-up pulled up in front of the Post Office and parked diagonally to the curb. An Indian kid with a shock of crow black hair got out and bounded into the PO holding his keys in his hand.

Rory? Beadles had only seen his picture once. Boy on a pony. A wave of recognition flowed through. Beadles hustled to his Jeep which was parked around the corner on 2nd, and had barely pulled up to the stop sign when Rory bounded down the steps, got in his truck and headed south out of town. Beadles saw boxes and grocery bags jouncing in the bed. The PO must have been the kid's last stop.

Beadles waited until the truck was two blocks ahead before pulling out. Traffic was light. Twelve miles south of town on 550, they entered the Southern Ute Reservation. A brown Toyota separated the pick-up from Beadles. The Toyota turned east on 160 and now it was just the two of them. There was no place to hide on the twisting mountain highway. The curves prevented Beadles from being seen in Rory's rear-view but sooner or later the road would straighten out. Beadles' luck would end when the boy turned off the highway.

If he hung back out of sight he might get lost. Who knew how many homesteads there were up those winding dirt roads? Two miles before the New Mexico border, the truck turned west onto Deer Canyon Road. Beadles drove on a half mile before turning around in the middle of the highway and following Rory up the canyon.

Dust from the Chevy hovered over the rutted path. Beadles switched to four-wheel-drive and wallowed up the rutted road passing turn-offs sporting clusters of mailboxes affixed to four-by-six planks. There was a name affixed to each mailbox. No Cerveros. Six miles from the highway there were no more mailboxes.

Sage and Spanish bayonet dotted the arid landscape. A big buck bounded across the trail in front of him. The road dipped and staggered between the hills until it finally dead-ended at a ranch carved out of a little plateau, one story ranch house in need of paint with a satellite dish, three horses in a corral, a horse barn, and the Chevy pick-up ticking in the front yard.

Rory leaned against the pick-up's tailgate, arms crossed as if he were expecting someone. Beadles parked the Jeep and got out. An old border collie ran up to him, sniffed his pants and retreated to under the pick-up.

"Rory?" he said, "I'm…"

"I've been expecting you, Professor Beadles."

The kid came away from the truck and stuck out his hand. He looked impossibly young although he had to be eighteen. His grip was firm and strong.

"Your father home?" Beadles said.

"You're too late. My father killed himself two days ago."

CHAPTER THIRTY-SIX

THE PAST

Beadles felt the color drain from his face. The kid looked at him as if he were a scientific specimen.

"Come in the house and have some iced tea." Rory headed for the house not looking to see if Beadles followed. The interior was cool and dark and neat. Rory went into the kitchen.

"Have a seat," he said. "I'll be right there."

Beadles sat on the cloth sofa beneath the picture window looking out on the yard facing a big flat screen TV. A stack of video games and DVDs sat on the low coffee table along with the game yoke. The stacks were neatly divided. Games on the left, movies on the right. The movies included *The Dark Knight Rises* and *Watchmen*. The games included *Grand Theft Auto Palm Springs* and *Assassin's Creed 1776*.

Rory reentered the living room carrying two tall plastic glasses filled with iced tea. He handed one to Beadles and sat on a Barcalounger facing him. It creaked when the kid leaned back.

"My father said you'd come. He wanted you to know he was sorry for what he did."

"Did he say he saw me take something?"

Rory stared straight into his eyes, an unusually forward and confident young man. "No, he never did. He never told me what it was but Liggett held something over him. I think it was a sexual assault charge from his early days there. Dad had a problem with the ladies. Or girls, I should say."

The kid had a punctilious way of speaking.

Beadles' mind churned. Here was his accuser's kid telling him it was a put-up job. Blackmail. But it was just hearsay, not admissible in a court of law. Maybe in a civil suit. He could hire Panny. He could seek proof of Liggett's collusion. He could depose Rory. It would all cost a fortune and get kicked down the road for years to come. The university would muster public opinion against him, claiming he was bitter and vengeful.

Something about it didn't make sense.

"Rory. Why would he kill himself because he cost me my job? Why not just come clean? Did he not want to hurt your mother?"

"Mom died two years ago. Drunk crossed the center-line and hit her head on," he said with no discernible emotion.

"I'm sorry. You mean you're living here alone?"

"That's right. Pop signed his power of attorney over to me so I can cash the checks."

"Was there a funeral?"

"No. I just buried him out back next to the dogs."

"I wish I'd got to know him better," Beadles said. "Was he a religious man?"

"My father was very old-fashioned. Although he was raised Baptist it didn't take and he always fell back on the old ways."

"Do you mean shamanism and Native American religion?"

"Yes," Rory said. He seemed poised, ready and intense. Beadles thought he might have a touch of Asperger's. "In other ways not so much. He understood I had to have a computer and internet access and spent a small fortune to bring it. But he never learned to use a computer."

"Are you his only child?"

Rory shook his head. "No. I have an older brother who's an attorney in Chicago. Brad got him the job with the university. It was far from home but he needed the money. My older sister Janet was here until yesterday. She works for a Kia dealership in Phoenix."

Rory looked at Beadles with an unsettling intensity, as if he were examining some rare artifact. "My father left a message for you."

Beadles felt his blood accelerate. "May I see it?"

"Like I said, Dad was old-fashioned. He didn't write things down. He told it to me so I could tell it to you."

Beadles pulled a spiral pad and a pen from his pants. "Go ahead."

"In the beginning there was the sun and the moon. There was no earth. Then the sun said I am lonely so he created the earth and all its peoples and animals. All the people were Indians. There were thirteen tribes. Twelve of them were good but one was bad. They made war for no reason and ate the flesh of their enemies. Their leader was a great warrior. The sun warned him not to eat the flesh of his enemies but he wouldn't listen. To punish him, the sun took his wife. This made the warrior angry. He vowed to do everything in his power to affront the sun. He savagely attacked other tribes, often enduring great hardship to do so. He killed animals and left them to rot in the sun.

"Then the Spaniards came. The leader believed the sun sent them to crush his tribe. The leader attacked them but a traitor spoke to the Spaniards and told them how to trick the leader. The Spaniards said they could bring back the leader's wife, and because the Spaniards appeared to be gods—no one had ever seen a horse before—the leader believed them. The Spaniards found a young woman who resembled the leader's wife from a distance. When the leader went to meet her they seized him, gouged out his eyes, tied him to a wagon wheel and left him to die in the sun.

"But the leader had made a deal with the moon. The moon covered the face of the sun and in darkness the leader escaped.

This made the sun mad. The sun caused the thirteenth tribe to scatter and die out and he cursed the leader to walk the earth for all eternity beneath a blazing sun accompanied by the lowliest of creatures, the scorpion and the snake. If any were to discover this tribe and seek to restore them to their rightful place in history, a scorpion would strike them down and the leader would walk again."

Beadles looked up from his pad in distress. "But I'm the one who sought to restore the Azuma! Why did the scorpion sting Rob?"

Rory shrugged. "I'm only telling you what Dad told me."

"What was this leader's name?"

Shrug. "He didn't say."

"Was the tribe the Azuma?"

Shrug.

"Why did Anatole tell you this? What does he expect me to do with the knowledge?"

"He said it would be better if you let the past stay buried."

CHAPTER THIRTY-SEVEN

EARL

The room smelled of Pine-sol but it was cheap. Get your kicks on Route 66 the song said, but all Summer got was a cheap motel room with a window looking out on a baking sheet parking lot. The old highway lay parallel to the Interstate a half mile away. But oh, what a difference a half mile made.

Summer had headed south from Grampa's with no particular destination in mind, looking for a place to hole up and get her bearings, try to make sense of what the old man told her. Modern Summer said Grampa was full of shit. All that Native American mumbo jumbo. Good for tourists, not good in the real world. If Ned Lead were such a great medicine man why wasn't he rich? She knew for a fact that at one time he'd been quite the ladies' man, that he liked fast cars and fine living.

He'd lived up that box canyon as long as Summer had known him.

Old Summer was not so sure. Grampa was the only one offering advice and encouragement. She'd seen some strange things in her life, not the least of which was Grampa himself, who had to be in his nineties. She needed to sell Vince's shit, get a grubstake, and find her champion.

She took a shower and headed across the street to Cowboy Bob's Bar and Grill, with a thirty foot Cowboy Bob out front waving to the passing traffic with his articulated forearm. It was five-thirty. A Coors sign shined neon blue in Cowboy Bob's big front window. Pick-ups and choppers in the parking lot. Ol' Waylon was on the juke as she entered.

It was twenty degrees cooler in the bar. Behind a rustic podium a lithe Indian girl wearing a flannel cowboy shirt with the sleeves rolled up, her long black hair in a ponytail, smiled.

"Eatin'? Follow me."

The dining room was past the bar. Four burly bikers turned on their stools to watch them pass. The dining room was period Western with framed Hopalong Cassidy and Roy Rogers posters, the inevitable steer horns, old branding irons and a bragging wall with photos of celebrities who'd dined there. The waitress seated Summer beneath Clark Gable.

"My name's Fiona and I'm your waitress. Don't mind those fools at the bar. They're harmless. Want a drink?"

"Fiona, bring me a rum and coke, heavy on the rum."

"I hear ya, hon. One Cuba Libre coming up."

Summer looked at the rustic menu. She was famished. Fiona returned with her drink and a glass of water. Summer ordered the barbecued pulled pork sandwich. She sank the drink and ordered a second one when her order came.

She had almost finished her sandwich when a bulky object filled the door to the dining room. One of the bikers, hair exploding from his head, black leather vest, blue-tatted arms. He stopped a few feet away, hands at sides like a repentant schoolboy.

Summer slid her hand into her front pants pocket and fingered the Beretta.

"Excuse me, ma'am. Weren't you dancing at Dante's last week?"

Summer experienced relief and even happiness. "Why bless your soul, yes, I was."

Now he didn't know what to say.

"What's your name, sweetheart?"

"Earl." He brushed his massive beard aside to show her the word Earl stitched on the black leather in red thread. "Me and the boys are cruisin' the southwest. Spent a week in Vegas losing money."

"Sit down, Earl. What's your club?"

Earl pulled out a chair and carefully lowered his 300 lbs. into it. Fiona came over. "Get you somethin', Earl?"

"I'll take another Guinness, Fi." He turned back. "Big Wheels. Back home got my own construction company. Pour concrete."

"Gotta card?"

Earl grunted and reached behind him, seizing the outsized Harley wallet and hauling it in by the chain. He handed her his card. Fitzroy Concrete. Earl Fitzroy, Fernando, MO.

"Do you have a card?" Earl said. Summer noticed his buddies craning their necks, sick with jealousy.

Of what, boys? Talking to a pretty woman?

"You got a boyfriend?" Earl said immediately coloring. "I mean a card! Do you have a card!"

Summer trilled with delight. As if. "I'm fresh out."

"I mean if I was to come back this way again would you have dinner with me?"

"I might. Now's not a real good time for me. I got an ex-boyfriend on my tail's meaner than a rattlesnake."

Earl puffed up. "Oh, yeah? I'd like to see how mean he is."

"You are a sweetheart."

"Can't stand to see a man bully a woman. That's what we're all about, the Wheels. People think we're a bunch of violent drug-dealing savages. Because of Hollywood. But we're just a bunch of decent, hard-working guys who like to ride bikes. It's nuts."

"I know what you mean. A lot of people think that because I dance at a place like Dante's, that makes me something else."

Earl shook his head. "I would never think that."

"You're a gentleman."

Earl cleared his throat. "Well, sorry to interrupt. I just had to say hello. You need any help, that fool shows up and you want some protection, don't you hesitate to call. I mean that. We're gonna be rattling around the Four Corners for awhile."

Suddenly, Summer rose, stepped up to Earl and kissed him on the cheek. "You take care now."

Embarrassed but pleased Earl rumbled back to his buddies.

My champion.

Fiona brought the bill. "Was he hittin' on you?"

"Naw. He's cute."

Summer left a generous tip, went out through the side door to the parking lot so as to skip the boys and returned to her motel room. The black satchel from the Camaro lay on her bed. She opened it up. She took out the map. She moved the satchel and spread the map out on her bed. It was made from some kind of animal skin, very thin with a fine but strong texture. The ink was faded along the folds. The map was almost three feet square and hand-painted but not crude.

Whoever had drawn the wadis, the mountains, the flats and certain geological formations was a skilled artist. She aligned the map with north at twelve o-clock. She was unfamiliar with the landmarks. In the northeast quadrant was a drawing of an unusual butte surrounded by a radiant pattern of squiggly lines.

It was labeled "Shipapu."

CHAPTER THIRTY-EIGHT

LUCA

Luca Bonamici ran Luca's Limos. He also owned Fernando's out by the airport. Vince had bounced for him and driven limo. He'd never got in the deeper stuff although Luca offered. He was about to get in the deep stuff now.

Vince pulled the gray Hummer into Fernando's parking lot at three in the afternoon. The strip joint looked drab in the merciless sun, its neon stilled, windows dark. Vince went around the back where Luca parked his Corvette. The delivery door was open. Vince stepped inside. It smelled of booze, sawdust and stale jism. There were several private rooms in the back which Luca used for all sorts of things.

Luca was expecting him. Vince waved to the dude stocking the bar and went through the main room to Luca's office in the back, up three steps.

Luca sat in his black leather and teak chair, hands behind his head, thick black hair smoothed slick with brilliantine, a Costa Rican guitar the size of a toilet paper tube jutting from his mouth.

Vince thought Luca watched *The Godfather* too much. Real hoods looking to Hollywood to learn how to behave.

"What I can do you for, Vince? Have a seat. Want a cool one?"

"Yeah, sure. Why not?"

Luca pressed on the intercom. "Manny, bring us a couple of that new whatchamacallit, that new micro beer."

"Odell's?" chirped the intercom.

"That's it." Luca waited patiently, puffing.

"My girl ran out on me. She stole some shit."

Luca's thick monobrow arched. "A good-lookin' guy like you? Why would she do that?"

"Maybe I hit her too hard. I don't know."

Luca shook his head. "Vinnie, Vinnie, Vinnie. What's with you and the ladies? You've got to treat 'em nice!"

"I know. But look, Luca. I need some help finding her. She don't know what she took. She took my car and the shit was in the trunk."

"Wha'd she take?" Puff puff.

"An old map. Like seventeenth century or something. I got a buyer lined up and everything. I need help finding her."

"So you say."

"Map's worth a hundred gees."

The eyebrow humped. "So you say."

"Come on, Luca. You know I'm a stand-up guy! Help me find her and I'll cut you in for twenty percent."

"Fifty."

"Come on, Luca! This is my one chance to score big. You've already made it. All I'm asking for is a little help finding her. You're plugged into those hackers, right? Face recognition hardware and all that shit?" Vince reached into his jacket pocket and withdrew a series of photographs of Summer. Some were from her dance portfolio. Others were personal.

Luca picked them up and puffed. "Beautiful girl. I think I seen her before. This the one dancing at Dante's?"

"Yeah."

"Fucking Dante didn't know what he had. Forty."

"Thirty," Vince said. Luca stuck out his hand.

"You got a rifle?" Vince said.

"You don't ask much, do you?"

"C'mon. No blowback. I promise."

Luca stood and walked to a closet door at the back of the room, opened it, rummaged around. Vince heard dull clanking. Luca returned with a Remington 30.06. "Sorta fell into my hands. Of unknown provenance."

"Perfect," Vince said, taking the rifle and sighting through the window at the passing traffic.

Luca turned back to the cabinet, withdrew a black windbreaker, tossed it to Vince. "Check this shit."

Vince looked at the windbreaker. It was XXL. It said Zobel's on the breast in white script. "What?"

"Check the zipper pull."

Vince found the molded plastic zipper pull and started playing with it. A tiny black nylon key popped out. "What the fuck?"

"It's a handcuff key! Ain't that the shits? I bought a couple dozen to give away. That's for you. Hope you don't need it. You got to get your own scope, though."

"No prob. Thanks, Luca."

Luca sat and puffed. "Just remember. We got your picture too."

CHAPTER THIRTY-NINE

AN OFFER

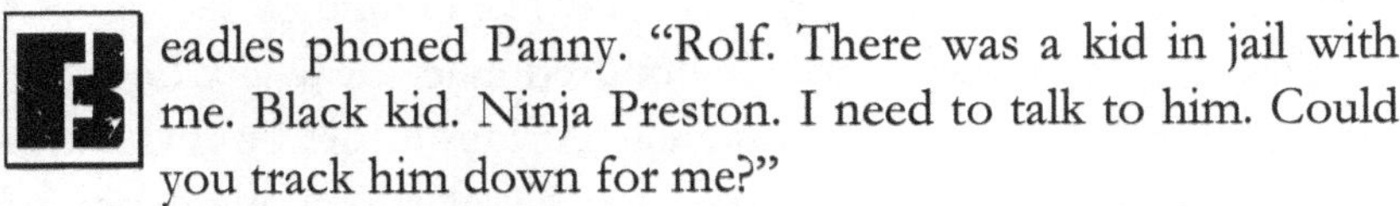

eadles phoned Panny. "Rolf. There was a kid in jail with me. Black kid. Ninja Preston. I need to talk to him. Could you track him down for me?"

"Not difficult. I can just check the jail records. They're public. You find Cerveros?"

"I found his kid. Cerveros killed himself." Beadles brought Panny up to speed.

"Wow," the PI said. "Looks like you've uncovered a snake pit. You got any money to pay me with?"

Beadles fingered the gold medallion in is pocket. "No, of course not."

"Do you expect to have any money down the road?"

"Rolf, I'm more convinced than ever that the Azuma existed and that I can prove it. When that happens I'll be able to write my own ticket."

"I'll do this one thing for you, Vaughan, because I believe you were framed. But that's it. I have a family to support."

"I understand. And thanks."

Beadles thought about the five grand. Panny would run through that in a week. Beadles was ready to start camping to save money. His only other expenses included food, internet service, and insurance. He'd converted Potts' check into cash and that was what he lived on. He thought others might be after the Azuma. Mainly Liggett. Beadles was getting paranoid, signing motel registers with a made-up name and paying cash for everything.

Beadles was close. He could feel it. Maybe getting fired was the kick in the ass he needed to get out in the field and do his job. Sure. So it had cost him his marriage. That was going to blow up anyway. There were structural flaws. Betty had always kept her own checking account into which she deposited her earnings. Occasionally for no apparent reason she would give Beadles money or pay for something like a vacation.

There were weeks, sometimes months, when she shunned physical intimacy. That didn't excuse the affair. Obviously there were trust issues. Beadles looked at other smiling couples and wondered what their marriage was really like behind closed doors.

Salvation lay within a couple hundred miles of where he sat in the Durango Public Library, studying ley lines in the Four Corners Region. Most significant Anasazi sites lay at the convergence of the ley lines. These had been tracked and quantified by scores if not hundreds of scholars over the years and virtually all major intersections had been thoroughly explored.

But still. It was like staring at one of those trick pop-art posters that initially appears to be a jumble of nonsense when suddenly the hidden message appears. Beadles hated optical illusions. He wasn't good at them and never saw the message even when others pointed it out.

The library closed at six. Beadles set up shop in a booth at Mel's Diner and ordered a cheeseburger. The waitress looked like a Will Elder drawing of an old woman. His phone rang as she plunked the burger down. Beadles thanked her and picked up his phone.

"Beadles."

"Panny here. The man with whom you shared a cell, his actual name is Arcel Preston and he has done time for hacking. I got in touch with him through his parole officer and gave him your number."

"Thanks, Rolf. How did they let him go if he was on parole when he was arrested?"

"The reasoning of the judicial system escapes me. This is the last favor I can do for you, Professor."

"Do you have his number?"

Panny gave him a number. "But it's probably no-good. This guy changes phones as often as most people change underwear. Don't worry. I told him there was money involved."

"Thanks, Rolf."

Five minutes later Beadles' phone rang again.

"This the cat I shared a cell with?" Ninja Preston said.

"Yes. Yes it is. Thanks for getting back to me. I wonder if you'd help me out with a scientific problem."

"A Sci-in-tif-ic problem? What that? Whatchoo got that I want?"

"I'm searching for an ancient civilization in the Southwest. I think maybe you can help me. As for what I can do for you, I can give you a stake in my enterprise. Sort of like investing in sunken treasure only the odds are better. I know what I'm doing. Google me."

"Done dat. Says you was fired from the u-ni-VER-sity for stealing that pot."

"I was framed!"

"Sure you were. All my friends be framed. They frame me!" Ninja sounded less manic than he had in jail. Maybe he was lucid.

Beadles laughed. Ninja chuckled. "Whatchoo likely to find?"

"Gold."

"Now you got my attention. Whatchoo need?"

"You mentioned hacking into a surveillance satellite. I'm trying to locate ancient ruins in the desert. Could you use spy satellites to look beneath the surface? Could you find ley lines?"

"Ley lines? Dat when you tell some hoochie you love her?"
Beadles explained.

"I can do dat for sure. Where you at, man?"

"I'm in Colorado."

"Well I'm in Springfield. You gots to come here. My la-BOR-a-tory here."

"I can be there in 24 hours. How do I find you?"

"Man, this better not be a set-up or you wish you never met me."

"It's not."

Preston gave him an address and a phone number. "You ain't here in twenty-four you find no one home."

CHAPTER FORTY

BLANKET AMNESTY

ince knocked on the double-wide's tinny door. Shreds of plastic whipped through the scrub brush as a harsh wind blew through the desolate trailer park on the edge of nowhere. Hava hadn't been hard to find. Nothing was in the internet age. Vince had googled it and come up with "a mobile home park seeking township status on the fringes of the Navajo Nation."

Four brown boys were doing skate stunts on a bare concrete apron—foundation for a missing trailer—on which they'd set up a plywood ramp. Three of them had buzz cuts as seen in *Skate!* magazine while the fourth favored the traditional long-haired savage route. It cost Vince five for them to point out the Funderburk manse. He thought of offering them meth but he didn't want to leave a footprint.

The door opened. A stupid young Indian with glazed eyes and a big nose stared at him smelling of weed. "What?"

"Summer here?" Vince said pushing his way inside.

The kid stepped back. "You must be the boyfriend. No she ain't here and I don't know where she went."

Vince looked around the trailer. What a shit hole. The TV was the nicest piece of furniture. Paid for with our tax dollars. "Where's my Camaro?"

"What Camaro?" asked stupid face.

Vince smacked him across the face and he went down like the little bitch he was. "You know what Camaro."

"Hey, chill out, dude! She took it down to Bosselman's and sold it to some bangers!"

"Get up," Vince said. "Sit down over there." He indicated the sofa. He walked over to the refrigerator, opened it and found two Dos Equis. He took out one and cracked it. The kid looked stressed. He'd been looking forward to those beers. Vince saw the baggie and works on the table. Not smart enough to hide his shit when a stranger comes to the door.

That baggie looked familiar. Vince scooped it up and got a whiff. He must have made a face because the kid cringed like a whipped dog.

"She gave it to me! I didn't know it was yours!"

Vince stuffed the baggie in his pocket. "What happened after she sold my car?"

"I don't know, man," the kid whined. "She came back here, talked to the old lady and took off again."

"In what?"

"An old Ford pick-up!"

"What year?"

"Fuck if I know! I don't even have a driver's license!"

Vince turned toward the bedrooms. "What old lady?" But he was already back there. He opened the door and saw the old lady sitting up in bed, one hand to her throat in a stricken posture, staring at him. But of course she'd heard every word. The trailer was made of cardboard.

"You Summer's mother?" he said going in.

The old woman hunched back in the corner. "I don't know anything."

Vince sat on the bed. "Bullshit."

Ten minutes later he was on the road to Ned Lead's place. Summer had mentioned him. Some kind of shaman/grandfather figure. But of course the Injuns loved their mystic mumbo jumbo. It gave them something to hold onto after they'd failed at every other aspect of life. Vince was surprised the old geezer was still alive. To hear Summer tell it, he'd been ancient when she was a little girl.

A pair of bony cattle looked up from a stock enclosure as the big gray Humvee jounced down the box canyon. Vince was surprised at the dome but the property was as unlovely as he'd imagined, surrounded by junk, a couple beaters, rusting appliances and wood pallets. An old man sat in front of the dome beneath a makeshift awning. He wore those geezer shades that fit over regular glasses and his lap was covered with an Indian blanket despite the heat. A mangy dog lay at his feet.

Vince parked the car, drained a bottle of NOS, and laid out a line on the center console. He hoovered it up and was good to go.

The old man removed a pair of ear buds as Vince exited his vehicle. Vince opened the passenger door on the driver's side and grabbed a bottle of Cabo Wabo. Trading goods. He probably could have got away with the cheap stuff but what the hell. Vince was a good tipper.

The dog raised its muzzle and growled. The old man remained motionless behind the wraparound sunglasses.

"Hey there," Vince said. "You must be Grampa Ned."

"You must be the boyfriend," the old man replied.

"So she was here. Brought you some tequila." He held out the bottle. The old man didn't move.

Vince stood directly in front of him, the dog off to the side a little bit. "You are going to tell me what I want to know."

"Git off my property. Go on. Git."

"How'd you like me to smash this bottle over your head?"

The dog's hackles rose and it showed its teeth. Vince's right leg lashed out and kicked it under the muzzle. The old dog yelped.

An erection rose beneath the blanket on the old man's lap. "You got 'bout two seconds to get the hell out of here before I blow out your brains."

Vince pivoted on his left leg and roundhouse kicked the old Indian in the head. Ned Lead went down sideways like a slamming door. With a snarl, the old dog attached itself to Vince's left calf, sharp fangs half-gripping the Tony Lama boots, sinking deep into the flesh.

Vince brought his right leg up and stomped straight down on the old dog's head, smashing it into the earth and busting its skull. It died without a sound. The old man grunted and struggled with the twisted blanket trying to free his pistol. Vince kicked him in the head so hard it bounced off the concrete base of the house.

The old man lay still. Breathing heavily, Vince knelt and put his fingers to the old man's neck. He was dead. Useless.

USELESS! The whole fucking trip wasted because the old fool had to act the hero. Vince reflected way back in the brain's root cellar maybe he was doing too much meth but fuck it, he needed the energy to track the bitch down and reclaim what was his. He'd dry out later.

Well fuck. Maybe the old fool had something of value in the house. The interior of the dome was neat and well-arranged, in contrast to the grounds. Motes of dust hung in sunny beams coming in through the skylights. The ceiling fan was inert. Vince found the switch and turned it on. In fact there was a lot of worthwhile stuff. If Vince had paid a hundred bucks for an auctioned storage locker he would have been well pleased.

There were hand-carved animals. Soapstone with turquoise eyes. There was an exquisite Kachina doll with handmade clothes. Numerous Native American pots and some framed sandstone paintings.

Vince spent twenty minutes going through the place as only a meth addict can. He emptied boxes of Quaker Oats and graham crackers into the sink. He cleaned out the refrigerator and freezer. He upended the old box spring and mattress lying on the floor. He found $125.76 in cash. On the way out he grabbed the old man's 1911 Colt .45. He couldn't have asked for a nicer handgun.

As to the bitch's whereabouts, nada. He would just have to be patient. Sooner or later she'd turn up and Luca would send him a blip.

His phone buzzed.

It was Luca.

CHAPTER FORTY-ONE

BINGO

It was an eighteen hour drive. Beadles drove straight through, downing shots of 5 Hour Energy Drink every four hours, stopping only to eat and piss. He was wide-awake at two a.m. when Art Bell assured him that the UFOs were real and that the Air Force had been hiding definitive proof since 1954.

The address Ninja had given, 1442 K Street, was in an industrial district separated from the river by a broad swath of railroad tracks. It belonged to a three-story red brick warehouse housing a half dozen businesses. Beadles parked directly in front of the building around six-fifteen, as the sun was rising. Carrying his laptop in a backpack he entered the foyer and consulted the listings. A vid cam stared from the ceiling. He pushed the button for Global Consulting. A second later the inner door buzzed and he went in. He took the staircase to the third floor. As he exited the well, Ninja poked his head out of a door halfway down the hall.

"Yo."

He went back in. Beadles followed, finding himself in a broad loft with a steel beam ceiling crisscrossed with air ducts and filled with hard drives, monitors, routers and storage systems. Ceiling fans stirred the marijuana-scented air. An enormous black man wearing shades and a black skull cap lounged on a sofa. Ninja stood with hands in pockets.

"That my man Gregorio. Say hello to the professor, Gregorio."

"Hello," Gregorio rumbled in sub-bass frequency.

"You know what Beadles means, Professor?" Ninja said.

"No."

"A parish officer having various subordinate duties, as keeping order during services."

"I did not know that."

"Tell me bout the gold," Ninja said.

Beadles sat at a long table holding printers and scanners. He opened his lap top, plugged it into a power bar on the table, and brought up his notes from Balmora's diary. Ninja sat, pulled the laptop in front of him, and read through the diary entries.

"Mm-hmm. How I know you didn't just make all this shit up?"

Beadles stared at him in astonishment. "That would make me batshit crazy."

"I do my research, professor. You was just fired by Creighton University for stealing ancient artifacts."

"I was framed!" Beadles said, surprised at his own vehemence.

"Mm-hmm," Ninja said with a knowing look. "Me too."

"Me three," Gregorio rumbled.

Ninja smiled, revealing perfect teeth. "Twelve pounds of gold, huh? Well that beats a poke in the eye. Gregorio! How much twelve pounds of gold worth?"

"At today's prices," Gregorio rumbled, "320 thou."

"Mm-MM," Ninja said. "That sound good to me!"

"If they're in the form of Anasazi artifacts they could be priceless," Beadles said.

"So what we talkin' bout," Ninja said. "Spanish conquistadors rippin' off the gold from Native Americans? And how they not bring that out with them?"

"Because they all died," Beadles said. "The Azuma killed them. That's who we're looking for. The Azuma."

"I be looking for gollld. You want a NOS or somethin'? You want to get mellow, do a line?" Ninja held up a pinkie. "Imbibe an adult beverage?"

Beadles noticed the slick under Ninja's nose. Looked like they had both pulled all-nighters. Beadles was too excited about his work to even entertain the idea of sleep, although he had been up for 24 hours. Best to push it through, then crash.

"Could satellite technology locate twelve pounds of gold in the desert?"

Ninja got up and walked among the work stations, sitting at a monitor mounted on an industrial cafeteria table. "Maybe. You gots to know where to look. We start with the National Recon. They the guys that launch the satellites. Spy satellites. They all kinds of shit up there now. HBO, weather, Sirius XM. We got to go where the money is which mean slipping into DARPA. We can't leave no fingerprints. That why they come to the ninja man."

"What's DARPA?"

"Defense Advanced Research Projects Agency. Dat where dey got de good stuff!"

Beadles wondered if Ninja was putting on an act. The screen morphed beneath Ninja's hands. Numbers and warnings appeared and disappeared like carp surfacing in a pond.

"They launched these cubesats last summer, each one with a special focus. One tracks maritime shipping. Another tracks weather. They got one that can see beneath the surface for certain geological concentrations. That's how they found that Mayan pyramid in Guatemala—by zeroing in on certain limestone composites the Mayan used to build. Lime seeped into the earth, turned the trees funny."

"Where zackly we lookin'?" Ninja said.

"Four corners region. Most likely north central Arizona."

"That's a big place."

"I can narrow it down some," Beadles said. "I'm pretty familiar with all the known sites, and which areas have resisted exploration. Can you draw up a map of that area?"

"Sheeit. You just want Google maps! Hang on."

Ninja saved his screen and brought up a satellite photograph of the Four Corners region overlaid with counties, towns and roads. Beadles directed him to the area he thought most likely to be the site of the Azuma civilization. Even in the twenty-first century with the internet and global communication, there were places that had never been completely explored. Places right here in the United States. Oh, they'd been mapped, platted and photographed, but they all said the same thing. Nothing there. A barren desert where the only things that lived were rattlers and scorpions.

Ninja worked in silence for twenty minutes, got up, went to the john, got two Mountain Dews from the fridge, tossed one to Beadles, sat at the long table, rolled a doobie, lit it, offered it to Beadles who declined and Gregorio who took it. Ninja returned to the computer. A bewildering series of numbers scrolled across the screen followed by a warning in red letters. He restarted the computer and began anew.

"Ain't this a bitch," he muttered.

Fifteen minutes later he said, "We're in."

Beadles looked over his shoulder at a view from space of the southwestern United States. Ninja typed in commands and the view magnified a hundred times encompassing an area of approximately twelve square kilometers.

"This here shit goes beneath the surface to find ancient roads which are usually made of a particular type of stone. They find them pyramids in Mexico by lookin' for the limestone signature. The limestone leaches into the ground and affects the forest— they chemical composition changes and they ain't the same color as the surrounding forest.

"But we ain't got no forest. This here program sees fault lines, roads, anything ain't consistent with the surrounding shit. Uses an extreme low alpha waves to look beneath the surface."

Beadles thought Ninja had to work at appearing stupid. Ninja hummed to himself while he worked, adding a little rhythm with his fingers and toes. The focus on screen shifted as Ninja worked the area like a forensic scientist. The area was located in North Central Arizona on the Carson Mesa some fifty miles from Monument Valley.

Fatigue washed over Beadles. He was light headed and needed to rest. He wondered if he could safely drive to a motel.

"I need to crash," he said.

"Hold on, hold on," Ninja said. "I got somethin'."

Under his hands the screen changed color several times. Ninja zoomed in a blank spot on the map. "Lookit here," he said.

Beadles blinked. He didn't see it. And then he did. Ninja put his finger right on the screen. A series of squiggly lines in a sunburst pattern.

CHAPTER FORTY-TWO

AND SO TO BED

Beadles felt the blood frothing in his chest. His heart played paradiddles. He'd tried using satellite imagery before to locate the Azuma through the university. But he hadn't know for what he was looking. It only became apparent now that he had the amulet in his possession.

"Can you give me the GPS coordinates?"

Ninja stroked the keys and the printer chattered. "Already done, son. You need a place to crib? You lookin' 'bout baked."

"Yeah."

Ninja pointed to the far end of the loft, separated by a series of incongruously beige and institutional acoustic dividers. "Go crib over there. I got to catch some too. Can't keep doin' crystal."

"No you can't," Gregorio rumbled from the sofa.

"My heart beatin' like a tom tom. You want some valium?"

Beadles was so exhausted he knew he would sleep through the bounce valium provided. "Sure."

Ninja gave him one of the pink tablets. He washed it down with Mountain Dew, went outside, got his overnight bag out of the Jeep and returned. "Can I park out front?"

"No prob," Ninja said. "They a bathroom off the side back there."

Beadles walked behind the screens and found four military-style bunk beds made up with tight sheets and khaki blankets. Some personal items were scattered on one. Beadles took the one at the other end of the line. The bathroom had a sloping concrete floor with a drain in the middle and a shower head protruding from the wall. He stripped and took a hot shower. He put on his skivvies and slipped beneath the clean sheets. It never occurred to him that Ninja would take off and seek the stronghold himself. Nor did he worry how vulnerable he was, sleeping under a jailbird's roof. The vibe he got off Ninja was a very intelligent young man trying to hide it.

Beadles shut it all off. He was asleep within minutes. He slept dreamlessly for some hours, got up in late afternoon to visit the bathroom and when he returned he saw that Ninja was sawing logs on the far cot. Beadles instantly went back to sleep.

Desert. A cookie sheet in an oven with an intolerable incandescence beating down like a KGB interrogator. Hot. So hot. And thirsty. Beadles could not, dare not raise his head to that awful light. It would sear his eyes and burn out his brain. His mouth was mired in muck. He scooped it out with his fingers like bailing a boat. It was a thick rubbery substance. No matter how much he scooped it kept pouring into his mouth.

He tried shielding his eyes with his hands. He could barely see—just his shadow in front of him as he trudged east toward a distant butte. It was afternoon. He looked down and saw eggs and pancakes sizzling on the desert floor. He trudged on, dying for a drink.

He was at the butte. He scrambled up the scree apron and began climbing a lava chimney, searching blindly for hand and toe holds. He opened his eyes. A rattlesnake stared at him from six inches, jaws wide, teeth aching, maracas shaking.

Beadles climbed on. He opened his eyes. A nest of milk-colored scorpions danced on a tiny shelf. He climbed on.

He emerged at the top. It was dark.

Beadles woke with a start, sweating, wrapped in the khaki wool blanket and sheet. He peeled them off and sat on the edge of the cot breathing heavily. It was dark out. He looked at his watch. Nine-thirty. He'd slept twelve hours.

Beadles went into the bathroom and took another shower. A cold one. When he stepped back into the big room Ninja was seated on his cot pulling on an XXXL Bulls T-shirt.

"Give me a half hour to get my shit together and we'll hit the road, Jack," he said.

Beadles stared. "What?"

"'At's right. Omma come with you. Protect my investment."

"What investment? All you did was twist dials for an hour."

Ninja flashed a slash of white. "People pay me big bucks to do that. Been thinkin' bout applying to the CIA, get on that sweet gummint gravy train."

Beadles adopted his best professorial tone. "I'm afraid it wouldn't work, Ninja. People are watching me. You'd attract too much attention."

Ninja stood and puffed. "Whatchoo sayin? No respectable college professor be travelin' with a nigger?"

"I'm not a racist," Beadles declared despising himself.

Ninja grinned. "See? See? I gotchoo goin. I pay half the expenses we can take my donk stead of that peckerdick redneck wagon you got."

Beadles shook his head. "No can do. I'm not the only one looking. I can't attract any attention! Not until I have incontrovertible evidence that the Azuma existed."

"That be the gold?" Ninja headed around the partitions. "Le's get some coffee goin."

Beadles followed. "It could be the gold, it could be an authentic record of their civilization. Hieroglyphs. A temple or dwelling. Something that sets them apart from the other known civilizations of the Colorado Plateau."

"You want to see my donk?"

"Ninja, I'm fine. I'll give you a contract. I'm not looking to grab the gold and run. It's worth a hundred times more as authenticated artifacts. I'm trying to vindicate myself! I have nothing to gain and everything to lose by betraying you. But this is something I have to do alone."

Ninja poured Javatime ground coffee into the coffee machine. "Let me think on that."

CHAPTER FORTY-THREE

THE COPPER KETTLE

Summer checked into the Kayenta Hampton Inn under the name Alice Showers. She'd never been religious although she'd attended a Baptist Sunday School at Maria's insistence, a twenty-four mile round trip to Hanes Baptist. She had a hard time believing the old stuff but there was no denying Grampa Ned's power. It was an electro-magnetic field affecting anybody who came close. And she'd seen Ned and others do amazing things. Handle rattlesnakes. Walk on hot coals. Always, always they preached the gospel of the old ways, worship of the sun and moon, worship of the earth.

Summer was twenty-nine and desperate. What did she have to show for her hardscrabble life? No husband, no children, no future. She'd wanted to go to school and become a nurse but her grades weren't good enough even with affirmative action. Twenty-nine, broke, a pole dancer.

"I must be stupid," she said softly.

She had no choice but to believe in the old ways. What else did she have left? She was uncertain exactly what awaited her at

Shipapu but she had to find it. Along the way she would find a champion. She came to Kayenta because of the search.

After showering she went out through the lobby and walked across the baking highway to the Copper Kettle Lounge. It was six o'clock. The Copper Kettle was a family-friendly stucco joint, parking lot filled with cars from half the States come to visit Monument Valley. She went in through the front. A Navajo girl seated her at a small table in the big dining room, with a view of the highway and the hotel. She'd ditched her cell phone in Hava, fearing that Vince would somehow track her using his mob connections.

Maybe taking the Camaro was a dumb idea. He might have let her go if she'd left his ride. No. Not after she slipped him the roofies. She'd seen Vince break a guy's arm for looking at him crosswise. She shrugged it off.

Come on, girl! Get some balls! She touched the Beretta in her pocket.

Her waitress came. She was young and Indian. "Would you like something to drink before ordering?"

"I'll have an Absolut martini straight up with an olive."

"Perfect." The waitress handed her a menu advertising "authentic Native American cuisine." She passed on the rabbit and rattlesnake and when the waitress returned with her drink, she ordered the meatloaf and a salad.

"Perfect," the waitress said.

Summer was in a good position in the corner to see the whole room, which was three quarters full. Four families traveling with young children. Some long-necked college boys on vacation, their tanned, lean physiques suggesting they were mountain bikers or climbers. A couple truckers in caps. The pleasant murmur of conversation and clinking silverware filled the room. On the walls were framed photographs including a couple Ansel Adams, two Georgia O'Keefe prints, and paintings by local artists depicting the landscape, daily life and spirituality.

The waitress made her rounds. "How is everything?"

"It's good."

"Perfect."

The waitress turned to go. "Ma'am," Summer said, "would you bring me another martini?" She gestured toward the window. "What's out there?"

The waitress looked at her quizzically. "Excuse me?"

"To the northwest. Is there anything out there between us and the Utah border? I mean apart from Monument Valley."

The waitress scrunched up her nose. "Just Gap."

"Gap? What's that?"

"Basically, just a bar and a gas station trying to be a town. Kids like to go out there and ride dune buggies or trip in the desert. It's a good way to die. People pass through there and go out in the desert and you never hear from them again."

"How far?"

"Sixty miles or so. Why? There's nothing out there."

Summer smiled. "I like out of the way places."

"Well it doesn't get much more out of the way! I'll be right back with your drink."

Something tugged at her. Tugged her northwest. Sixty miles. She could be there tonight but then the waitress returned with her martini. She already felt the effects of the first. She'd acquired the taste from a guy she'd dated, a high-roller from Palm Springs twenty years her senior. Decent guy, treated her well, probably better than any other boyfriend. But not for her.

She gazed into the martini's oily depths before tilting the glass to her lips and feeling its shivery contents. Stupid glass though. She would have preferred it in a tumbler. Easier for the waitress, easier for her. But maybe that was the point. Make the glass as ungainly as possible and the glass would tell you when to stop drinking. Palm Springs had once told her that the "champagne coupe" had been modeled on Marie Antoinette's breasts. The martini glass must have been modeled on Madonna's.

The second martini hit. Summer felt a knot at the base of her neck start to loosen. God she couldn't wait to get back to her room and take a hot bath. The early evening sun turned western walls white. Summer turned and looked out the window at the hotel across the street. A gray Humvee slid beneath the porte cochère too fast. A knot coalesced in Summer's gut.

The driver opened his door and got out. He wore a cowboy hat. It was Vince.

With a bolus of dread in her stomach Summer searched through her backpack and found Earl's card.

CHAPTER FORTY-FOUR

THAT'S EARL, BROTHER

e're at the casino in Many Farms," Earl said. "We can be there in forty-five minutes."

"Please come," Summer said into the house phone as the maître d' seated a family of four. "I'm in the Copper Kettle directly across the street from the hotel."

"We're on our way."

Earl sounded excited. She hoped that the sight of four big bikers would discourage Vince. Maybe hand him a beating.

Maybe he wouldn't find her. After all, hotel policy forbade giving out information to strangers. Vince could be very persuasive when he wanted. Even charming. She'd seen him turn it on. He'd turned it on her once.

Shaken, she returned to her table. An inch remained of her martini. She badly wanted a smoke but she'd given it up a year ago and hadn't had a butt since. She thought about bumming one— she'd noticed a pack of Marlboros behind the entry dais, but then she'd have to go outside to smoke it. If she didn't want to be seen she'd have to go around back where she couldn't keep an eye on the hotel. She decided to stay where she was. He had no way of knowing.

She couldn't go to the cops, not after what she'd done. There was no stolen car report. But they'd pick her up on the roofie charge. She had a record. She'd been arrested for soliciting. It was all a misunderstanding. She was still paying off the lawyer.

She lingered. She couldn't stop herself from staring across the street willing Vince to get back in his Humvee and move on. Move on! The motel wouldn't give him any information. That was against policy. But what if he charmed the desk clerk? What if she were a young woman? Vince was an experienced pimp which meant he had a black belt in seduction. He could meet a woman and have her in bed an hour later. He'd told her so many times.

The waitress saw her change in mood and stayed away except to deliver her bill. The dining room peaked around seven-thirty and then began to thin. Still Summer sat with her half-finished martini staring across the street.

Oh, please, she prayed. Please Earl and your mighty Big Wheels, get here! Get here now! She stared at her watch like a kid in junior high willing the seconds to pass faster. She gulped water, went to the ladies' room.

By eight there was only one other family in the restaurant.

What was he doing over there?

The waitress came by. "Are you all right?"

Oh, my God, Summer realized. She thinks I can't pay the bill.

Summer opened her backpack, took out her wallet and laid a twenty in the black bill folder.

"I'll be right back."

Summer thought about fleeing into the desert out the back. But what good would that do? Vince would discover soon enough she'd been there.

The waitress returned with her change. Summer left twenty percent and looked out the window. The tall, broad-shouldered man in a cowboy hat walked across the highway toward the restaurant. Summer froze like a seized piston, torn between fleeing and pleading. Tell the management it was a jealous boyfriend. Call the cops. But those were short-term solutions at best.

He would be at the door in seconds. Summer grabbed her backpack and hurried down the little corridor to the ladies' room. She went inside, went into a booth and locked the door. She sat on the toilet rim shaking.

Stupid, she thought. She'd trapped herself. Summer never was any good at sneaking around. She should have fled into the desert, or at least hidden in the parking lot until the Big Wheels got there. The door opened. Summer's heart stuttered. She waited breathlessly her knees pulled up. A woman entered the other stall and relieved herself. Summer bent down and saw her Crocs. The woman washed her hands and left.

Please go away please go away please go away.

The lavatory door slammed open as no woman had ever pushed it. Summer trembled, awkwardly balanced on the porcelain doughnut. She willed herself to shrink to an infinitesimal size. She was a black hole disappearing into her own gravity. No air moved through her body.

The stall door exploded inward from the impact of Vince's boot. Summer scrunched up, her extremities drawn in like a spider. Vince grinned and stuck his thumbs in his belt.

"Well here you are, darlin'! Let's go."

He reached in, took a fistful of her hair and dragged her out like a kitten, her backpack dangling from one shoulder. He ripped open the lavatory door, gripped her bicep and marched her down the short corridor to the main dining room gripping her arm like a chimpanzee with a banana. There were no diners. Earl and three other big hairy guys in colors and boots formed a line between Vince and the door.

My champion.

"Let her go, dipshit," Earl said, fists balled. The guys behind him were just itching to get into it. Summer saw it in their eyes.

The perfect way to end their vacation—heroically stomping a woman beater. Living up to their own image. Summer had never been so grateful to see someone in her life. Summer saw the waitress cowering behind the front desk next to a man she assumed to be the manager. He was a short, slight Indian with a buzz cut and glasses.

"The police are on their way!" he said in a squeaky voice.

"You want to let her go now?" Earl repeated stepping forward.

Vince grinned, released his grip on Summer's arm, took two steps forward arms flying up to seize the back of Earl's neck pulling him into a vicious head butt that sounded like someone whacking a steer with a sledge. Earl let out a muffled cry and tottered back, blood erupting from his nose. Vince grabbed Earl again, this time by his black leather lapels and swung him into the path of the dude on the left, a linebacker sort with a G.I. Joe beard.

Two Big Wheels on the right closed in. Vince flicked his leg up and sidekicked one in the chest so hard he flew back and smashed into a table. Without pause, Vince turned the sidekick into a reverse spinning back kick and tagged the second guy in the crotch. The only Big Wheel still on his feet was G.I. Joe, suddenly reluctant. Vince grinned and closed in on him.

That's the last thing Summer saw before she fled the dining room out the front door racing blindly across the highway. A semi laid down the air horn as she sprinted in front of him, ten feet from the massive chrome grill. Tears filling her eyes Summer ran to her truck, got in, started the engine and pulled out onto the highway heading west. As she accelerated up through the gears a Sheriff's Deputy passed her going into town, lights flashing, siren blaring.

It wasn't until Kayenta was a faint glow in her rear view that she remembered the pistol she carried in her pocket.

CHAPTER FORTY-FIVE

INTO THE GAP

Beadles left Springfield alone. Ninja had offered him a gun but he declined. Beadles had always thought himself civilized and scoffed when friends told him they kept guns for personal protection. Not once in his life had Beadles ever felt he needed a gun and he guessed the same about most of the people he knew.

The news was full of lurid tales designed to convince people that guns only caused trouble, lingering on every school or workplace shooting. The media pumped this shit all the time. No wonder foreigners regarded the United States as an untamed frontier wilderness where anybody could gun down anybody at a moment's notice.

The drive back through Colorado seemed shorter, as drive backs always did. This time Beadles stopped in Colorado Springs after driving fourteen hours. He started out fresh in the morning for the drive through the mountains. He was through the San Juans by noon. Snow still gleamed from the fourteeners like a diamond necklace around the earth's neck.

Lunch in Durango and then through the mountains again, cutting across the SE corner of Utah and into Arizona by mid-afternoon. The land spoke to him. Even as a child growing up in Illinois, he'd been fascinated by the desert and tales of the southwest, devouring Westerns, books and magazines. He'd subscribed to *Old West* and *Treasure Hunter*, the back pages filled with ads for metal detectors and back country excursions. He'd dreamed of prospecting for gold himself, finding the Lost Dutchman Mine or traces of a previously unknown civilization.

Beadles devoured Edgar Rice Burroughs, Jules Verne and Arthur Conan Doyle—filling his head with dreams of adventure and exploration. He became fixated with Henry Morton Stanley and Sir Richard Burton, the explorer, and read all there was to find on the subjects. Even as a kid Beadles lamented the closing of the frontier, the spread of civilization and the loss of wilderness. He contributed to the Sierra Club and the Nature Conservancy and longed to explore his own wilderness before it was too late. Before the comsats mapped and charted every square centimeter on earth. But wilderness persisted in Alaska, Canada, the terrible frozen places, parts of the Amazon, and even in the American southwest.

There were places no one went because there was nothing there. The mountains and deserts took their toll. Death by dehydration, falls from cliffs, even the occasional mountain lion mauling. Beadles had been on a couple of digs so he knew what to expect. He'd outfitted the old Jeep with four five-gallon water jugs, the kind with spouts near the bottom. An old five gallon jerry can filled with regular was attached to the rear gate. The air conditioning either froze him or produced nothing. He turned it off, cracking all four windows, feeling the dry heat suck the moisture from his body.

It was eight-thirty when he entered Kayenta looking for a place to eat and catch his bearings. The Garmin GPS velcroed to the dash indicated he was within seventy miles of the epicenter of the Azuma civilization.

A county mounty talked to a short bald man outside the Copper Kettle, his car at the curb strobing blue and red. Beadles drove two blocks west to the John Ford, an adobe-style bar and grill, parking lot near to capacity with old pick-ups, choppers and badly aging cars. The type of spot where you could pick up scuttlebutt if you were clever.

Beadles prided himself on ignoring class barriers. He'd always been able to relate to blue collar guys. He'd worked construction all four summers while going through college. He spoke their language and wasn't afraid of hard. Beadles found a place at the curb and left it there without locking the doors. He went into the bar where the air conditioning immediately sent a chill through his sweat-stained shirt.

He wore faded blue jeans, a blue work shirt and had three days' stubble on his face. He found an empty stool near the end of the bar next to three Navajo bikers in blue jean vests sporting the Kemosabes patch. Beadles guessed they were being ironic. He ordered a shot and a beer. The TV screen in a corner above the bar broadcast a basketball game. The bar was dark and smoky, although no one was smoking. Old burnished wood and twinkly lights.

He did the shot and beer and turned to the grizzled homunculus on his right wearing a Vietnam Veteran ball cap. "Can I buy you a shot? For your service to our country."

The old guy, who looked like Mr. Heartburn in old antacid commercials, grinned, displaying a gold tooth. "Mighty kindly of ya. I'm drinking Buffalo Trace."

Beadles caught the bartender's attention and signaled for two more. The old guy stuck out a shovel-shaped hand. "Norm Hester."

"Vaughan Beadles. You from around here?"

"Born and bred in Flagstaff. You?"

"Illinois. I'm an anthropologist. Mostly southwest Indians, some Central American."

"You here to see the ruins?"

"In a way. I'm looking for some evidence of an ancient Anasazi culture. Is there anything northwest of here? Between here and the canyon."

"Keet Seel and Betatakin," the vet said tossing his shot. "They're pretty well known."

"No," Beadles said. "I mean are there any settlements? Is there anything out there?"

Norm shrugged. "Gap, population 118. The Last Chance Bar and Grill," he added wistfully. "Used to be a bauxite mine but that closed when I was a boy. I guess it's a jumping off place for people looking for a desert experience. I don't know why they want a desert experience. I sure as hell don't. Our boys fighting in Iraq and Afghanistan? They don't want a desert experience either but they got no choice."

Beadles pulled out a map of Arizona and worked it so it showed Kayenta. "Where's Gap?"

Norm put his finger on a blank spot.

"Why isn't it on the map?"

Norm shrugged. "Beats me. Never was incorporated. Wouldn't even be there if fool hippies didn't go out there to trip in the desert. You head west and take Keet Seel Road, and when you get to Keet Seel just keep on goin'. You can't miss it."

Beadles thanked the man, looked at his watch and stood. "They got a motel?"

"'S what I hear. And they always got a vacancy."

"Thanks, Norm."

The desert was bright beneath a globus moon. Beadles almost missed the turn off because some kids had knocked over the sign. He stopped, turned around, went back, pulled onto the dirt road, got out and turned the sign over.

GAP—25 MILES.

Forty five minutes later he pulled up to the Last Chance hitching post and parked next to an old Ford 150.

CHAPTER FORTY-SIX
THE DRAWING

It was a little after ten. An old guy sat at the end of the bar staring into a shot glass. The bartender was an old Apache woman, gray hair gathered in a ponytail, wearing a seersucker shirt with Muriel stitched on the breast. Beadles sat at the bar and looked the room over through the mirror behind the bottles. Four booths. At one end two middle-aged guys sat playing checkers. At the other all Beadles could see was a woman's ankles in sandals, her back to the rest of the room.

"What'll it be, honey?" Muriel said in a whiskey-soaked contralto.

Beadles felt nothing from the two shots earlier. "Shot of tequila and a beer. How's that motel down the street?"

"The linens are clean. They got vacancies. There's the owner sitting down at the bar." She gave him a funny look. What was he doing there at ten-thirty on a weekday?

She returned a minute later with the drinks. "You here for the eclipse? You know not to look at the sun, right?" she said. "Last time we had an eclipse..."

"I'm an anthropologist. I'm searching for evidence of a previously unknown Anasazi tribe. I think there might be something out there." He gestured vaguely toward the desert.

"Only thing out there are snakes and scorpions and a whole lotta sand," Muriel said. "Back in the seventies, we got a lotta college kids thought it would be a good idea to go trip in the desert. Some of 'em never came back. That desert's been so picked over and prospected ain't nothin' left to discover."

"That ain't exactly true, Muriel," said the old guy at the end of the bar. "That wind picks up you never know what it'll uncover."

Muriel looked at the old man. "That's true enough, Vern." She turned back to Beadles. "Vern Weatherill. Owns the gas station/general store and the motel."

Beadles picked up his beer and sat next to Weatherill. "Vaughan Beadles."

They shook.

"You ever been out there, Vern?"

The old guy turned toward him. He had a ruddy, lined rancher's face, straight white hair and a mustache. "We used to ride dirt bikes out there when I was a kid. Hit a rock once, broke my leg. Lord I thought I was gonna die of thirst before my friends come back with a truck to pick me up."

"Ever see any ruins or petroglyphs, anything like that?"

"Yeah, seen a few on them rock nobs across the canyon back when they had a bridge. County declared the bridge unsafe in '89. One night some kids got out there and burned what was left down. Now there ain't no way to get across the canyons. That wind starts up, it'll move half the landscape."

"What's this canyon?"

"Don't got a name. Runs northeast bout twenty mile from here. What're you lookin' for?"

Beadles repeated his spiel.

"I heard that before," Vern said. "Used to get some prospectors. There's an old story that there's a mess of gold out there somewhere that the Spaniards put together from the indigenous peoples they slaughtered. We used to look for it when I was a kid. Back before they burned the bridge."

"Why was there a bridge across the canyon in the first place?" Beadles said. "What's over there?"

"Good question. Prob'ly built by prospectors. Ain't nothin' there. We would have heard about it by now. The oil companies don't prospect on the ground any more. They use satellites to look for likely reserves. Nobody out here bidding for mineral rights and things are gettin' scarce."

"What other rumors have you heard about that place?" Beadles nodded toward the void beyond the walls.

"Oh there's the one about the blood-thirsty Indian warrior seeking revenge on the Spanish who killed him. Old Indian legend."

"Anything to it?"

Vern regarded him with wry humor. "Enough liquor in ya you'll start to believe it. Well listen. I got to get back and spell May who's been mindin' both the store and the motel. Nice meetin' you, Vaughan. Stop on over you need a place to stay."

The old man left. Vaughan faced the mirror, eyes straying to the stuffed coyote and coiled rattlesnake mounted on a shelf above the bar. Brown liquor gleamed seductively in the soft yellow light. Behind it someone had taped photos and news articles to the big mirror forming a patchy frame. Cartoons. Post cards.

Beadles' eyes stopped on a drawing. It showed the outline of a butte on an eight and a half by eleven inch sheet of white Bristol board. Whoever had drawn it had made the rock come alive so that there was no question that it was a real place, if only in the artist's imagination.

"Say, Muriel," Beadles said pointing at the drawing. "What is that? Can I see it?"

Muriel followed his finger. "That old drawing? Funny you should mention that. A college kid gave that to me back in 1985. Said he kept seeing it in his dreams. He and his buddy went out to look for it and neither was seen again. It was a terrible tragedy. I remember his father coming down here, staying for a week tramping through the wilderness when everybody knew his boy was a goner."

"They never found the body?"

Muriel shook her head. "That night we had a big blow-up. Sand just gets up and walks all over us, burying some places ten feet deep, digging up other places. Never did find their bodies."

Beadles held out his hand. "May I see it?"

Muriel shrugged. She carefully unpeeled the drawing from the mirror and handed it to the professor, using a fresh towel to make sure there was no moisture on the bar before she set it down. The drawing drew him like gravity. You could practically reach out and touch it. It had been rendered in colored pencil and black ball-point. You could feel the texture of the stone and the Spanish bayonet and saguaro around the base. A chimney ran to the top disappearing occasionally behind rock outcroppings. The drawing had an almost hallucinatory quality, the way the artist had edged it in yellow and orange, bathed in a divine light.

"Could I have this?" he said. "I'll pay."

Muriel snorted. "Take it. I need to clear some of this junk out anyway."

Beadles held the drawing in his hands trembling. He had seen the butte before! It was not a case of deja vu. He'd seen it in his dreams. He was certain.

He felt a light touch on his arm and the scent of sandalwood. A lovely Indian girl slipped onto the stool next to him, regarding him with vast brown eyes, a purple bruise coloring one cheek.

"Are you going out there? Are you searching for that butte?"

CHAPTER FORTY-SEVEN

BEADLES MEETS SUMMER

'm looking for that place too. That's why I'm here."

Beadles looked around for a guy. A woman like this wouldn't be without a guy. He didn't see anyone. No ring. That bruise on her cheek. Her teeth were preternaturally bright.

"I'm an anthropologist," he said. "I'm trying to locate the epicenter of a previously unknown tribe whom I call the Azuma."

Summer stared into his soul. "I am searching for Shipapu. It is the spiritual fountainhead of our culture and possibly a gate to other dimensions."

It figures, he thought. *No girl this beautiful would be out here trying to pick me up unless she was stone crazy. Crazier than a bag of scorpions.*

His pulse accelerated and little Vaughan raised his head. It had been that way since he was twelve. He stuck out his hand. "Vaughan Beadles."

She took it. "Summer Funderburk."

"You Navajo?" Beadles said.

Summer nodded. "I'm kinda on a spiritual quest. My mother's ill and the medicine man told me that if I found Shipapu and prayed for her, she would get better."

"Well I certainly hope she gets better," Vaughan said. "What's wrong with her?"

"She's an alcoholic." Summer looked him straight in the eye waiting for a reaction.

"That's too bad. Have you tried to get her into treatment?"

"We can't afford treatment. She's scraping by on social security. I mean what the hell. I might as well try it. It's non-traditional medicine, right?"

Beadles had his doubts. He was a non-believer despite the weekly church trips to which his parents dragged him. He kept his non-belief private. He didn't consider himself an atheist either—just someone who believed in what he could verify with his own five senses. Betty had been the same way. Agnostic if you will.

"Prayer is non-traditional medicine?"

Summer smiled radiantly. "What the hell, right?"

Beadles shrugged. "Couldn't hurt." He realized his behavior now was all geared toward getting her into bed.

"Where you from, Summer?"

"Little town called Hava, bout a hundred miles from here."

He tilted the drawing her way. "Recognize this?"

Frowning, Summer took the drawing and held it in front of her face. "I know this is going to sound funny but I've seen this in my dreams. Must have a little Azuma blood in me, huh?"

"Know anything about a ghost who only appears in the day?"

A ripple of anxiety crossed Summer's face. "You heard that too, huh? I doubt it. I mean that show Ghost Hunters? It's been on the air what, five, six years? They haven't found a single ghost."

"Maybe if they looked in the daytime," Beadles said.

Summer punched him in the arm sending an electric jolt through him.

She had to be crazy. And he was crazy for even entertaining the idea. Instead he found himself saying, "Can I buy you a drink?"

Summer turned to the bartender. "An Absolut martini straight up with an olive."

Muriel raised her eyebrows. "I think I still know how to make one," she said. Beadles had a glass of water.

"What happened to your eye?" Beadles said.

Summer didn't blink. "Boyfriend. Ex-boyfriend."

"Did you go to the police?"

Summer's laugh sounded like silver coins falling into his hand. "The cops really aren't good at that sort of thing."

"You running from something, Summer?"

"You got it. I'm running away from my life. What about you?" She regarded him with unblinking intensity and he felt something inside give a little. A tidal wave of regret began to build in his gut and he stifled a sob, acutely aware that she was watching him like an eagle.

"Yeah," he choked. And the whole sorry story tumbled out. Summer listened, occasionally touching his arm in sympathy.

"Wow," she said when he had finished. "Just wow. That really sucks, Vaughan. I'm so sorry about your marriage."

Beadles shrugged. "Don't be. The thing I'm sorry about is what it will do to Lars. I intend to be there for him. But I'm not going to have my son growing up thinking his father is a thief!"

He fingered the medallion in his pocket. It felt hot through the fabric of his pants.

"So that's why I'm here. Prove my thesis, write a best-selling book, become someone of whom my son can be proud, and regain my rightful place in society."

Summer laughed. "You sound so professorial!"

Beadles grinned. "That's how I think."

"So," Summer said.

"So what?"

"So can I come with you?"

The door to the Last Chance creaked open admitting two aliens in oversize hoodies. Ninja and Gregorio.

CHAPTER FORTY-EIGHT

STRANGE BREW

A chill descended on the room. Muriel looked as if she'd never seen a black man before. Maybe she hadn't.

"Professor!" Ninja sang. "Are we there yet?"

He and Gregorio took the two stools to Beadles' left bringing a wave of Acqua Di Gio that washed gently over Beadles and Summer like a Caribbean surf. Ninja wore a black leather hoodie the texture of silk and carried a backpack. Gregorio wore a black leather sports jacket over a gray hoodie. A pair of shadows in a dark room.

The two old guys playing checkers packed up their game and left.

Muriel shook herself like a wet dog, pasted a smile on her puss and walked down the bar.

"What'll it be, fellas?"

Ninja squinted at the tap beer handles. "I'll have a… what is that? A Cactus Jack Ale? Gimme that."

"Dewars on the rocks," Gregorio growled.

Vern Weatherill reentered the bar and sat at a table.

Ninja leaned forward and leered at Summer. "Well lookie here! The professor got hisself a girlfriend! A fellow person-of-color like his own bad self, ain't that right, Gregorio?" He turned and nudged the big man with his elbow.

"Dat right," Gregorio growled.

Ninja turned back with a world-class shit-eating grin. "Dat right, Pocahontas! Professor tell you he was part Cherokee? Says so right on his job application to be a professor at Creighton University! Ain't that right, Prof?"

Summer regarded Beadles with shock.

"Don't believe them," he said.

"Oh we gots proof, don't we Gregorio? I can download the document rightchere on my laptop!" He swung his backpack onto the bar. It was black and featured the Punisher logo. Ninja threw his arm around Beadles' shoulders.

"Don't worry, Prof! We ain't here to jack you up! We're partners, remember?"

Muriel brought the drinks. Ninja held up his frosted glass.

"Drink up, Professor! We're gonna make history."

Beadles dutifully raised his mug and clinked, first with Ninja then Gregorio. They drank.

"So when are we going after the gold?" Gregorio rumbled.

Ninja's elbow shot out like a skeet launcher thumping Gregorio in the chest hard enough to make him grunt.

"What Gregorio means is," Ninja said, "when are we going to track down the remnants and ruminants of the Azuma Civilization? I'm talkin' history. We bout to make history."

"Not tonight," Beadles said. "In the morning."

"That's fine. Been a long day. Started out in St. Louis bout twenty hours ago." Ninja stood and stepped out to form a triangle with Beadles and Summer. "Hello you sweet thing. We ain't been properly introduced! Professor?"

"This is Ninja and that's Gregorio," Beadles said. "This is Summer."

Summer's mouth made a perfect 'o.' "You know these people?"

"Lordy, Lordy!" Ninja sang. "Know us? We're his sponsors! We the money behind the Great Scientific Expedition to Discover the Azuma. Ain't that right, Professor?"

"Ninja provides tech support," Beadles said. "He helped me locate the likely site with satellite technology."

"We far more than that," Ninja said. "Omma even buy you a decent motel room. We can't stay in that roach motel across the street. Whatever's out there has been out there for thousands of years. Ain't goin' nowhere. I say we all go back to Kayenta and check into the Hyatt. My treat."

Summer shuddered. "There's no way I'm going back to Kayenta. That motel's fine with me."

Beadles watched Weatherill in the mirror. The old man bristled when Ninja said roach motel. Muriel winked at Weatherill.

"You go on if you want," Ninja said. "You'll miss the good part. Professor, you come with us. Got plenty of room in my donk."

"Mr. Weatherill," Beadles said. "You got a vacancy for me?"

"I sure do, son. If you boys are lookin' for roaches you're shit outta luck."

Beadles smiled at Ninja. "Mr. Weatherill owns the motel across the street."

Ninja held out his palms fingers up. "Excuse me, Mr. Weatherill! I did not mean to besmirch the reputation of your fine establishment. It's just that Gregorio and me have become accustomed to a certain level of luxury, you know what I'm sayin'?"

"Apology accepted. Might even find a couple rooms for you boys if you're interested."

"Well let me and Gregorio think on that. Maybe later we'll take a look."

Beadles figured that Ninja had planted a transmitter in his Jeep while he'd been sleeping. Stupid! Now they were here and he had to deal with it. There was no reason to involve Summer. But he liked her. He felt a mutual attraction. Maybe it was just little Vaughan rearing his ugly head.

Ninja resumed his stool and removed a paper-thin laptop from his backpack. He opened it on the bar. "Zis here a wi-fi hot spot?" he asked Muriel.

"'Fraid not, hon."

"Tha's okay. I got what I need rightchere." He poked and stroked. A map came up. He turned the softly glowing panel toward Beadles.

"This here Gap," he said, using a soda straw to point at a brick-shaped cluster on an aerial photograph. He moved the straw. "And this here the center of whatever it is we're lookin' for. Sixty-two miles but ain't no roads. May need that old Jeep of yours. Me and Gregorio bought some shit at REI. We ready. Figure in and out in one day. We transport the, ah, artifacts straight back to Keyanta and divvy it up there. Howzat sound?"

Beadles just looked at him.

"What?"

"I'm sorry," Beadles said, "but if you haven't worked an archaeological dig you'd just be in the way."

Ninja's smile fell like a man from a scaffold. "Well I'm sorry but we're comin'."

"Have either of you ever worked in the desert before?" Beadles said.

"Do two tours in Afghanistan count?" Gregorio said staring into his Scotch.

It went without saying that Ninja, and even more so Gregorio presented a physical challenge. Beadles' black belt meant little. He was a holy terror faced with lawyers and accountants. He might be able to take out Ninja but no way could he stop a bulldozer like Gregorio. Not without a gun. He regretted not bringing one.

Stupid! What was he going to do with a gun? Get in a shootout at the Last Chance Saloon? There was no way he could keep them from accompanying him, not without giving them the slip. And what was to stop them from murdering him in the desert once they found the gold?

If there was any gold.

The whole thing seemed ridiculous. His life tottered like a house of cards. A great weariness crept up on him. Whatever made him think he could be a star of academe, much less media? He produced nothing, he provided no valuable service. His one conceit was an obscure anthropological footnote. So he discovered a new tribe, so what? Whoop de do! It wouldn't save any children from the pox or provide shelter for the homeless or clean water for slum dwellers in Sao Paulo and Ghana.

A deep sense of useless and futility came over him. Squabbling with two gang bangers in a bar over "buried treasure." Like one of those cheap tabloid magazines that touted the Lost Dutchman, classifieds filled with metal detectors. Pathetic. Magical thinking. And two sharp inner city operators had bought in. Bought in so heavily they couldn't let go.

It was funny. Beadles was thinking of giving up but Ninja and Gregorio wouldn't let him.

Ninja touched him on the shoulder. "Get your stuff, Prof. You're coming with us."

"No, I'm not."

Ninja smirked at Gregorio. Gregorio got up and loomed over Beadles. The front door opened. In walked a tall man in a cowboy hat.

CHAPTER FORTY-NINE

THE UNWELCOME PATRON

Summer turned white and touched Beadles' wrist. "That's him," she half-whispered, half-croaked. "That's Vince."

Vince paused inside the entryway, stuck his thumbs in his belt and looked around. He wore a belt buckle the size of a dinner plate, tooled snakeskin boots and a black nylon windbreaker which hung loosely from his frame. His gaze swept by the three men unimpressed.

"Where's my car, you bitch?!" he declared, striding up to Summer. "Honey," he said to Muriel. "Give me a shot of Jack and a draft back."

Ninja fronted him. "Who the fuck are you?"

Vince looked bored as he placed his palm against Ninja's chest and shoved the smaller man to the floor. Gregorio got off his stool. Vince stepped out.

"You better think twice before you make your next move, Holmes."

Gregorio stopped, glaring. "Best you splain yourself."

Ninja got up and stood slightly behind Gregorio.

"I don't got to explain shit," Vince said. "It's none of your fucking business. But since I'm feeling in a charitable mood, this here bitch used to be my girlfriend until she slipped me a mickey and stole my brand new Camaro Z-1. I want it back. What's so hard to understand about that?"

"I sold it, Vince," Summer said, unconsciously leaning toward Beadles.

Vince grinned and looked around. "Now why ain't I surprised? I knew you were gonna say that."

Beadles watched Weatherill quietly take out his cell phone and move to an end booth. Muriel stood by the cash register, hands beneath the bar.

"How much you get for it?"

"Less than you paid for it."

Ninja said, "Why don't you take your sorry hillbilly ass outta here while you can still walk? You think we're playin'?"

Vince looked from Ninja to Summer with mock surprise. "What the fuck, girl. You bangin' the whole bunch? I mean, what's your interest in this woman? You gonna turn her out I might be able to give you some advice."

Gregorio stepped up like a weigh-in face-off. "We turnin' you out."

Vince lowered his head and butted Gregorio savagely on the bridge of the nose. The big man stumbled back. Ninja tried to kick Vince in the nuts but Vince turned a thigh, scooped Ninja's kick up into the air landing the hacker on his ass. Gregorio picked up a bar stool and brought it around like a billy club. Vince ducked under it and took Gregorio to the ground. There was a furious scramble. Vince ended up on top and rained down blows. Ninja grabbed the bar stool and brought it down with both hands on Vince's head. The hard wood seat bounced with a bonk. Vince looked dazed.

Beadles didn't know whether to run or join in. He looked at Muriel. "Call the cops."

"I called the sheriff," Vern Weatherill said, "but might be awhile. Muriel, where's that scatter gun?"

Muriel reached beneath the bar and brought out a Remington twelve gauge with a pistol grip. The sound of her ratcheting a shell into the chamber caused the combatants to freeze.

"Get up and get back!" she barked. "Christ almighty, you don't go causin' a ruckus in my establishment!"

Rubbing the back of his head Vince got off the battered Gregorio and stood. Gregorio got up and returned to the bar where he laid an elbow on Ninja's backpack. Beadles had a split-second adumbration of the inevitable. Gregorio pulled out a .357 magnum with a nine inch barrel but he wasn't fast enough. A .45 appeared in Vince's hands and barked deafening everyone. Gregorio's head snapped back as brain and blood splattered against the mirror. It ran down the mirror in driblets. The automatic swung on the white-faced Muriel who had forgotten the shotgun on the bar.

"Back off the gun," Vince shouted to hear himself over the tinnitus. Beadles knew what he said from watching his lips. Her mouth a lipless slash, Muriel backed into the bottles causing them to clink. Vince strode up, grabbed the shotgun by the barrel and tucked it under his arm. He shoved the .45 into the windbreaker's pocket and ratcheted the pump-action, ejecting a shell and bringing another into the chamber. He grinned.

"You all saw it. Nigger tried to draw down on me. It was self defense." He turned to Summer. "Let's go sweetie pie. You and me got lots to talk about."

Beadles stood causing Vince to stare at him with exaggerated wonder. "What? What are you gonna do about it tough guy?"

"Self-defense is one thing," Beadles said. "Kidnapping's something else."

Vince bit his lip. He pulled the auto from his pocket and held a gun in each hand. "You got a point." Vince quickly glanced around.

An icicle piercing his chest Beadles realized Vince was figuring the odds of killing everyone in the bar.

Weatherill was gone.

"What happened to the motel guy?" Vince said.

The door banged open admitting a big gun followed by a man hunkered down in a sheepskin coat with a badge wearing a white cowboy hat.

"Drop the weapons! Get down on the floor!"

Beadles watched Vince weigh his odds and in the split second Vince took his eyes off the patrons Beadles scooped up his bar stool and swung it like a Louisville Slugger into Vince's head. Vince staggered. The sheriff ran forward and clubbed him behind the ear with the barrel of his automatic. Vince sank to his knees and dropped the guns.

The sheriff got behind him and kicked Vince between the shoulder blades so he went down face first on the hardwood floor.

CHAPTER FIFTY

ONGOING INVESTIGATION

The sheriff planted a knee in the center of Vince's back and got the cuffs on. He removed Vince's wallet, stood, stuck the toe of his boot beneath Vince's shoulder and said, "Turn over."

Vince turned over.

"Sit up," the sheriff said.

Vince sat up. The sheriff took in the scene, starting with Gregorio, slumped on the floor next to the bar, a red hole in the middle of his forehead.

"Who shot him and with what?"

"It was that guy on the floor, Rupe," Muriel said. "The black dude pulled a gun outta that backpack but Slick there was too fast for him."

The room smelled of cordite. Beadles' hearing was almost back to normal. The door swung open and Vern came in.

The sheriff walked to a booth and tore a napkin out of the holder. He stooped and picked up Vince's discarded automatic by the trigger guard. "Are you telling me it was self-defense?"

Muriel shrugged. "You could call it that. Slick there was being mighty aggressive."

"Muriel, would you bring me a couple plastic bags? Folks, I'm Sheriff Rupert Conway. We're a little understaffed on accounta a big pile-up out to the highway so I'm all there is tonight. Now ahmina have to talk to each of you one by one to figure out what the hell happened. I surely would appreciate it if you all cooperate."

Conway turned to Vince. "You got any nasty surprises in your pockets? Any needles or razor blades or shit like that?"

"No," Vince sighed like he'd been through this before.

"Stand up."

Vince got to his feet. The Sheriff went through his pockets removing a fat wad of cash in a gold clip, a wallet thick with cash and credit cards, not all Vince's, some change and a folding knife. The Sheriff walked Vince over to a booth and sat him down.

"Don't move," he said.

"Vern call you?" Muriel said.

"Ahuh. Who should I start with?"

"Well nothing was happening 'til those two black gentlemen came in here looking for this here fella." She indicated Beadles. "They called him Professor. Something about gold out on the shifting sands, damn fools."

Conway rounded on Beadles. "May I see some identification?"

Beadles produced his Illinois driver's license. Muriel returned with a box of large Ziploc bags into which the sheriff dropped the automatic and the contents of Vince's pockets.

"What are you doing here, Mr. Beadles?"

"I'm a professor of anthropology. I'm looking for ruins."

Conway turned to Ninja. "ID, son?"

Silent now, Ninja produced his driver's license. Conway looked from Ninja to Beadles and back. "What you doing out here?"

"I'm with the professor," Ninja said.

The sheriff turned to Beadles.

"Mr. Preston provided invaluable technical assistance but now he wants to come on the dig. And as I explained, you can't have amateurs on a dig."

"Ahuh," the sheriff said, stooping next to Gregorio and retrieving his wallet from inside the black leather jacket. The sheriff flipped it open and looked. "Gregorio Haines, St. Louis."

"Me and him were helping the professor," Ninja said. "We're his tech support."

"But he says he doesn't want you here, Mr. Preston," the sheriff said.

"You need some help you can deputize me, Rupe," Weatherill said.

The sheriff thought about it. "I appreciate that, Vern. Here's what I'm gonna do. I'm gonna put Mr. …" He removed Vince's wallet from the Ziploc and flipped it open. "Mr. Sealy here in the back of my car, then I'm gonna come back in here and get a quick statement from each of you people. Then I'm gonna ask you to wait here for other officers. Om get someone out here as soon as we can free 'em up."

The sheriff put a hand beneath Vince's arm. "Let's go."

Vince stood. The sheriff scooped up Vern's cowboy hat, planted it on his head and steered him out the door. The room was dead silent. Beadles and Summer looked at each other and saw the same things: fear and hope.

"This is bullshit," Ninja said. "Ohmma call my lawyer, Mr. Arthur Feldstein. I don't know nothin' 'bout that gun."

Beadles refrained from mentioning it appeared to be Ninja's backpack. As far as he was concerned he didn't see a thing. He just wanted out.

Ninja took out his cell phone and walked to the end booth. Weatherill picked up Muriel's shotgun off the floor and set it on the bar. "I called 911 bout five minutes after those two gentlemen came in. I just knew there was going to be trouble."

"'Cause they were colored, right?" Summer said.

Weatherill feigned indignation. "Not at all! They just looked like trouble."

Muriel poured herself a shot of Jack, looked around. "Who else wants one?"

Summer, Weatherill and Beadles raised their hands. Muriel poured shots. Ninja was still on the phone to his lawyer. The sheriff came back in. His eyes took in the drinks and his mouth twitched a little.

"Folks, looks like they won't get anyone out here for hours. Ahmina have to ask you all to stay here for the night so we can ask questions in the morning. Where's that other fella?"

Ninja stuck his head out of the booth still on the phone. The sheriff motioned him over. Ninja said something, hung up and complied.

"Need you to stay put for the night so you'll be here when the other deputies arrive. Anybody got a problem with that?"

"We under arrest?" Ninja said.

"No, but this is an ongoing investigation. I'm asking you as a courtesy."

"Sure, no prob, officer," Ninja said. "Guess I'll be looking at your rooms after all, Mr. Motel Man."

The sheriff stared at him a beat before nodding. The sheriff scooped up the Punisher back-pack. "I'm taking this as evidence."

Ninja swallowed.

One by one Conway took them to the corner booth and asked them what happened, making notes in a spiral pad. He questioned Beadles last.

Beadles faced the sheriff in the darkened booth. The sheriff smelled of sage. He removed a card from his breast pocket and slid it across the table. Beadles took it.

"Like I said, I'm out here looking for ancient ruins. I was let go from my university position two weeks ago. You might as well know, they accused me of stealing some artifacts and I agreed to resign to avoid prosecution."

The sheriff stared at him from beneath hedgerow brows.

"I was framed. I can't prove anything, but if I were a thief, would I be out here in the middle of nowhere searching for ruins?"

The sheriff shrugged. "Maybe you're an antiquities thief. Seen a few."

Beadles smiled mirthlessly. "Of course." He explained how he'd met Ninja and asked for his help. "They must have planted a transmitter in my vehicle. I was opposed to their coming."

The sheriff made notes and looked at Beadles skeptically.

"No doubt." He closed the notepad and eased out of the booth. He turned to the room. "See you folks tomorrow. Thank you for your cooperation."

Muriel pointed to the corpse. "You ain't gonna just leave it there?!"

The sheriff looked at the corpse. "Yes I am. Keep the air conditioning on."

CHAPTER FIFTY-ONE

LIKE A DOG

Folks," Muriel said, "I'm closing up. Anybody needs a place to stay, see Vern."

Ninja, Summer and Beadles followed the motelier out the door. For the first time Beadles saw Ninja's donk: a green and silver Chrysler 300 with suicide doors and huge, almost comical wheels and tires scraping against the underside of the body. It was wrapped in yellow plastic police tape with a neon orange sticker affixed to the windshield.

CRIME SCENE DO NOT TOUCH.

"Fuck y'all!" Ninja spat tearing off the tape and ripping the tag off the windshield. He removed a fob from his pocket and beeped the car unlocked. He got in the driver's seat and started the engine with a snarl. The passenger side window zipped down.

"Catch you later, Professor! Good luck!"

The big car zipped backwards into the middle of Main Street, the headlights flicked on and it rocked on down the road. When it was about twenty yards away booming bass shattered the night.

"Sheriff isn't gonna like this," Weatherill said.

They followed Weatherill up the slight incline beneath the flat port roof over the cracked asphalt. The motel was an L-shaped flat-top with the office and living quarters at the bottom and fourteen units. Weatherill led Beadles and Summer into the brightly lit office. A naugahyde sofa faced the small counter with a peeling coffee table in-between. There was a coffee maker on a sideboard and a soda machine.

Weatherill went behind the desk. "Who's stayin'?"

Beadles gave him his credit card. Rooms were $45.00. Weatherill gave him a key attached to brass fob with the room number. He pulled out his cell phone and the sheriff's card.

"I guess I'll see you in the morning," Summer said.

Beadles nodded, went outside and returned to his dirt-encrusted Jeep. He unlocked the tailgate, grabbed his overnighter, shut the gate and walked back up the hill. A faint light emanated from the unit next to his. He went inside, tossed his bag on the bed and went straight into the bathroom where he stripped off his clothes and took a hot shower. He dried off and put his jeans and shirt back on. It was almost midnight but he wasn't sleepy and didn't think he would be able to sleep.

Beadles sat on the bed, finished in a brown and turquoise Navajo pattern. He wished the bar hadn't closed. He needed a drink. His plans didn't include hanging around for a police investigation. If the news got out it would only come back and bite him on the ass—one more arrow in Liggett's quiver.

Christ, how did he get in this mess?

Soft rapping at the door. Beadles rose, inserted the chain and opened it. It was Summer. He took the chain off the hook and let her in. She carried her own bulging backpack.

"I'm sorry," she said. "I didn't feel like being alone and I've got something I think you should see."

Beadles sat in the chair next to the little round table, indicated for her to have a seat. "What's on your mind?"

Summer set the backpack on the table, opened it and removed a quart bottle of bourbon. "Would you like a drink?"

Beadles grinned. "You read my mind."

She poured a couple fingers into two plastic glasses. "You want ice?"

"Neat is fine."

Summer handed Beadles a glass and sat in the other chair beneath a framed black and white Ansel Adams.

"You're gonna need another set of hands," she said, holding up her cup. They touched and drank.

"Ever been on a dig?" Beadles said.

"No. But I make jewelry and I'm good with my hands."

She looked damned good for midnight. "You said you had something I ought to see."

Summer reached into the backpack and withdrew what looked like the Shroud of Turin, folded. It was made from some animal skin and creaked as she unfolded it on the table. Beadles switched on the overhead lamp and stood to look at it. It took him mere seconds to realize what it is.

"Holy shit," he said almost reverently. "This is it, isn't it? This is the map! Where'd you get it?"

"It was in Vince's car. He thinks he's an antiquarian dealer among his many other talents."

For some minutes, Beadles regarded the map in silence, his finger hovering like a plumb line. It found the butte. Beadles leaned until his nose was inches from the map. He could barely discern a series of squiggly lines radiating from the butte but they were there.

"Do you see these lines?"

Summer stood next to him and looked. Her scent drove him mad. "What lines?"

His finger traced the pattern. "These squiggly lines radiating from the butte."

"No."

Beadles reached into his pocket and withdrew the gold medallion. He held it out to her. Summer cradled it in her palm. "This is gold."

"Yes."

She reached beneath her shirt and withdrew the medallion Grampa had given her. "Mine's ceramic."

Beadles fingered the ceramic. "Where did you get this?"

"An old friend of the family. A medicine man. He said it would keep me safe."

She looked up, lips parted. Beadles cupped her head in his hand and kissed her. They came together like magnetic dogs. There was an awkward dance to the bed. Summer knelt and pulled off her shirt revealing high, firm breasts. She had a tat on her ass of a butterfly. Pants and shirts hit the floor.

Just before he inserted himself Beadles said, "Are you practicing any form of birth control?"

"I've been spayed," Summer said guiding him in. "Like a dog."

CHAPTER FIFTY-TWO

CHAMPION

She lay in the crook of his arm, black hair fanned across the pillow.

"Holy fuck," he said.

"I'm not a whore," she said, more to herself than him.

Beadles turned his head. "Who said you were?"

Summer sighed and trailed her fingers across his chest. "Sorry. I have a self-image problem."

"Not with me."

"I was working at a topless joint. Vince turned me out but I only did two tricks for him. Because I was afraid of him and I thought I loved him. How fucked up is that?"

"Don't beat yourself up," Beadles said. "We all make mistakes. We're all flawed human beings."

"Is it true you're part Indian?"

Shame flushed through his veins. "No. I lied because I thought it would help my career. I didn't think they'd ever check it out and they never did. They're so desperate for fucking diversity, excuse my French."

Summer laughed. "I bet I can out-curse you."

"I'll bet you can."

"I may have slept with a couple guys out of desperation but I was never a whore."

"No one said you were."

"Vince said it. All the time. Everyone expected it of me where I come from. Even my folks. You know what they used to call me in high school? Princess Thunderfuck."

"They used to call me The Beetle 'til I beat the crap out of them."

"So," she said wrapping her fingers around his arm. "What's the plan?"

"What plan?"

"For tomorrow, y'know? What are we going to do? I think we should hit the road early."

There was that "we" again. Once again Beadles found himself in bed with a strange woman only this time he couldn't sneak out on her. She had the map and she was far too street-wise to let him rip her off. Just beneath the luscious curves lurked hard edges. Well maybe she should come along. He could use another pair of hands and she was more than agreeable as a bed warmer. He hadn't asked her if she had any STDs. *Too late for that, you old horndog.*

She would have told him, right?

Summer was right. There was no point hanging around for more trouble. Beadles had nothing to do with the shooting and he'd told the sheriff all there was to say.

"Have you hiked before?"

Summer gave him the stiff arm. "I grew up on the res. I used to race the boys to school—four miles on foot. I've been hitting the gym four times a week for the last six years. I'm in better shape than you are! And my physiology is probably better-suited to the desert, white man."

"All right. Ninja was crazy to think we could get in and out in one day. We don't know if there are even any roads back there.

We'll see how far we get. I've got the site dialed in on the GPS. We can always take it with us if we have to walk."

Summer shivered. "People die out there. You heard that story about the two college kids. Isn't that creepy?"

"People die all the time. I can carry twenty-five gallons of water in the Jeep. Shoulda brought two mountain bikes. Think we can get any around here?"

"In this shit hole?" Summer said. "I doubt it. Where'd you get that amulet? Think there's any gold out there?"

"It was part of the collection I was cataloging when they fired me. I didn't have a chance to return it."

"And now it's too late, huh?" Summer said. "May I see it again?"

Beadles leaned over, snagged his jeans and dug out the medallion, feeling its weight in his hand. Had to be an ounce. He handed it to Summer who held it up and examined it with childish glee.

"Wow. Real gold. Wow. Grampa told me I have Azuma blood."

Beadles looked at her surprised. "You know about the Azuma?"

"Only from Grampa. He's not really my grampa. He's a very old medicine man. I went to see him before coming here. He said I had to find Shipapu. He said I would find a champion. I thought it was this other guy but it wasn't. Maybe it's you. I'm hoping it's you."

Beadles barked. "Sorry to break it to you, kid. I ain't no champion." There was that time in college, a bunch of jocks hassling an androgynous hippy. Beadles surprised himself by breaking it up. He and the hippie became friends and later the guy tutored Beadles in geometry. He'd done it without expectation of reward. He'd never liked those jocks. Maybe that was his reward. But as he gazed back at the map of his life there were few incidents of altruism and a great deal of opportunism. The cupboard was bare. Oh sure, the generous tip, helping a girlfriend change a tire, helping friends move. Any sociopath would have done the same.

"You're my champion," she sighed, her hand trailing across his chest. They slept. As was always the case when he had to share a bed, Beadles did not sleep well. He fell into a shallow sleep in which he was stumbling across the baking desert shielding his eyes from the merciless sun.

Summer was in it too.

CHAPTER FIFTY-THREE

DEAD BURRO

A ballistic nylon mesh separated the front of Sheriff Conway's cruiser from the rear seat. The rear doors lacked lock and window buttons. A laminated ID of the sheriff was affixed to the dash board like a cab license. A shotgun jutted up butt first in the passenger foot well. Vince sat on the right side testing the amount of play he had in his wrists and arms. He had to get the cuffs around to the front in order to get them off.

"Sheriff Rupe," the radio squawked. "We got multiple collisions out here by Saguaro Corner. Some tourist didn't slow down and ran into the rear of that semi. We sure could use a hand out here."

"No can do, Charlie," the sheriff replied. "I'm transporting a suspect to the jail. We had a homicide at The Last Chance. Ahmina need some help with this one."

"Well shit, Rupe," the radio said. "Looks like we'll be pulling another all-nighter."

"Do me a favor, Charlie. See what you got on Vince Sealy, got a Nevada license number…" He picked up the notepad while driving, flipped on the overhead lamp. He read the number.

"Roger wilco," Charlie said. "Maybe you can get out there after you get this guy booked?"

"I will advise once the prisoner is secured. Adios."

They rode in silence through the desert beneath the light of a million stars.

"I had no choice, sheriff. That dude pulled a gun on me."

"Son, anything you say can and will be used against you in a court of law."

"I know that. But I'm pretty confident they're gonna throw this out. And maybe you get a black mark for making a bad call."

"Won't be the first time," the sheriff said. "But since you're in a loquacious mood, mind telling me what you were doing out there in the first place?"

"Summer Funderburk stole my car. She used to be my girlfriend. I want my car back, that's all."

"Did you file a police report?"

Vince looked out the window at the undulating darkness. "No."

"Why not?"

"I love her. I don't want her to go to jail."

"How many times you been arrested, son? Might as well tell me. Ahmina find out anyway."

"Three times. Once for disturbing the peace and twice for assault. Both assault cases were thrown out. They both came from bitter patrons I ejected from various establishments when I worked as a bouncer."

"You never served jail time?"

Vince bit his lip.

"Might as well tell me. Ahmina find out anyway."

"I did a week for assaulting an officer."

"Okay, I'm sorry I asked. You'd better shut up now. What in Sam Hill is this?"

The sheriff slowed and pulled off the dirt road. Vince strained his neck and saw a dark bulk in the middle of the road. The sheriff left his headlights on, grabbed a big cell flash and got out. The object rested about ten feet in front of the car. The sheriff walked around it shining the light. All Vince saw was an indistinct shape as he rocked on his haunches and worked the cuffs to the front.

From there it was a cinch to deploy the zipper/key. The cuffs came off. Vince stuffed them between the seat cushions.

The sheriff walked back to the car. "Now why a burro would choose that as his final resting place is beyond me. I'd better set out a flare. No telling who'll come along."

"Say sheriff! I got to take a piss."

The sheriff looked at Vince, off toward town and back again. He came around and opened the rear door. Vince had his hands behind him.

"Here's what we're gonna do. Ahmina put on a pair of gloves and free your dick from your drawers. You don't like it you can pee in your pants. Ain't nothin' to me. And it don't mean I like ya."

Vince grinned gratefully. "No prob, sheriff." He swung his legs out, corkscrewed up and punched the sheriff on the mouth hard enough to break his jaw.

Spitting, the sheriff went down fumbling for his Glock. Vince brought his boot up and smashed the sheriff's nuts into gravy. The man curled up like a carpet worm and began to breath high and reedy and fast. Vince thought maybe he was having a heart attack.

Vince watched the sheriff go bug-eyed and wheeze. He gasped like a gaffed fish. It was taking too long. Vince reached out and removed the Glock from its holster, tossing it onto the open back seat of the cruiser. Vince planted his right knee on the sheriff's throat leaning down with all his weight. It was over pretty quick.

Vince looked around. The road was deserted. Vince got his legs under him, lifted the sheriff beneath the arms and dumped him in the back of the cruiser. Vince got behind the wheel and drove off the road across the gently undulating desert to a ridge a quarter mile in. He drove around the ridge until he found what he was looking for. He unloaded the sheriff in a dried-up wadi. He thought of covering the body with brush and rocks but what would that accomplish?

Once the sun rose the birds would come whether he was buried or not. Vince looked down at the lifeless khaki-clad form. He'd neglected to mention he'd served nine months in prison for assaulting a police officer. He'd always hated pigs. He went through the Sheriff's pockets and found ninety bucks. He unzipped his pants and pissed on the body.

Singing "I Shot the Sheriff" in a surprising falsetto Vince got in the cruiser and headed back toward The Last Chance.

CHAPTER FIFTY-FOUR

FATE OR FREE WILL

Beadles rose with the sun just after five. He showered, packed and was ready to jam before Summer woke. She was blinky and slow like a woodchuck dragged prematurely from her den but Beadles got her going and they were on the road by six. He'd gassed up the night before.

With the sun in their faces they both wore sunglasses and caps with the bills pulled down. Both sun visors were flat up against the glass. The air was dry and still and Beadles could see for miles. They followed a dirt trail east into the desert. Off-road tire tracks crisscrossed the road. In the distance hazy purple mountains hovered over the baking flats. They passed some modest hills topped with a sparse green stubble like a two day beard. Some lichen or succulent that could survive in the arid conditions.

Beadles thought of Evan Tanner, the UFC champion who rode his motorcycle into the desert and died of thirst. There ought to be a monument for all the forgotten souls who died of thirst in the desert. Beadles felt the weight of the water he carried every time the old Jeep hit a dip or a rock, which was often. Had they not been strapped in their heads would have bounced off the sky liner. By seven they had run out of road and rolled across the undulating hard-packed sand. Even with the AC cranked they could feel the heat through the windows. The glass was warm to the touch.

"What are you going to do if this doesn't pan out?" Summer said.

"It's got to. This is my only chance to clear my name and get back to academia."

"I took a class in hair-dressing," Summer said. "That's about as close to college as I ever got. Then I started doing blow and I kinda lost interest."

"Yeah, blow will suck you in," Beadles said. "I did some in college but fortunately I had the good sense to quit. I don't know what I'd do if my kid started doing blow."

"You have a kid?"

Beadles nodded. "Lars is two. He's with his mother."

Summer took time to digest this. "I used to dream of being a good little housewife living in the suburbs with two point three kids, y'know? By the time I was sixteen I realized that wasn't for me."

"Why not?"

"I don't know. Sometimes I feel like I was born bad, y'know? I like to party. I liked drugs. I liked having that power over men when they look at you and their throats go dry. The only reason I stopped doing blow was I couldn't afford it. Vince said I was snorting all his profits. He'd parcel out a line when he wanted to fuck."

Beadles cringed inside. He'd done the same thing. He'd treated women badly.

Not Betty. She wouldn't stand for it. She had an exaggerated sense of entitlement. And why not? She brought in more money than Beadles. He never said anything because he brought in enough. But it bothered him. He was a typical testosterone-loaded male in that respect. He prided himself on fulfilling his family's needs and paid most of the bills. He'd often wondered what Betty did with the bulk of her earnings. He guessed he'd find out, if he survived.

Fatherhood had changed him. He surprised himself by the depth of his love for Lars and vowed to be there for his kid every step of the way. His own dad had been benevolent but distant. They used to play catch in the yard when he was a boy but by the time he'd entered high school those days were gone. His father managed to make it to two basketball and three football games. His mother came more often but both were careerists.

Beadles and Betty had discussed having another child but agreed to hold off until Lars was five. Beadles had narrowly avoided fatherhood during college. He'd paid for two abortions. His feelings changed after he became a father and realized how precious life was. He didn't beat himself up over it.

Summer reached out and switched on the radio, twisting the dial until she found a classic rock station.

"A Horse With No Name" issued from the speakers.

"You know what I think?" Summer said. "I believe there is a higher power who watches over us and that everything happens for a reason. I probably wouldn't have left Vince if he hadn't beat me. I never would have gone to see Grampa Ned and I probably wouldn't have met you."

This made Beadles nervous because he didn't want to commit to some woman he'd barely known for sixteen hours. He'd shagged women on shorter notice, but not by much. She was along because she was a good fuck and he needed another set of hands.

"Predestination, huh?" he said. "That's the essential question—are we masters of our fates or do we unwittingly act at the behest of some higher power."

"Yeah. Not so much traditional religion, y'know? Like, I believe Jesus lived and was a great prophet but I don't think he was the son of God. My higher power comes from a different place. My father always used to bless the sun and the moon. He said the sun was father to us all and the moon our mother. Not that I subscribe to some animism or something. It would be sacrilege for me to speculate on the nature of my Supreme Being. I just accept that he's there. Or she."

"You're pretty well spoken for someone who didn't go to college," Beadles said.

Summer grinned. "I hung out with a lot of big shots who were trying to impress me. I guess I picked up some new words, y'know?"

Beadles was thirsty. "Reach back there and grab one of those water bottles, wouldja? And grab one of those cracker/peanut butter deals."

Summer turned and stretched back between the seats, her callipygian rump pointed toward the windshield and drawing Beadles' attention. She came back with the water bottle and the cracker. She uncapped the bottle and handed it to Beadles in his line of sight, then opened the cracker and placed it on a flat spot on the dash where he could see it like a good surgical assistant.

Beadles drank thirstily and handed the bottle to Summer who screwed the cap back on and set it at her feet. The Jeep was so old it didn't have cup holders. Beadles ate the cracker.

"Do you think there's any gold?" Summer said.

"I don't know. Maybe."

"Do I get a cut if there is?"

"Summer, that's a tricky question. Universities frown on tomb raiding. So does everyone else. I'm doing this to redeem my career, not to get rich. Well let me amend that. I do plan to get rich but not from any gold I find. Any gold we find will be part of an archaeological expedition. All I want is to regain my rightful place at the college. Doesn't have to be Creighton. If I'm right I'll be able to write my own ticket. There will be a book. I'll be on television."

"What about me?" Summer said. "Will I be on television?"

Beadles didn't answer. His gaze was fixed on an anomaly standing in the desert. At first he thought it was some freak cactus but as they approached it became the figure of an old woman wearing a shawl and carrying a basket.

"Oh my God!" Summer said. "There's someone out here!"

CHAPTER FIFTY-FIVE

CLOUD OF DUST

The sun was up by the time Vince reached Gap in the stolen police car but the streets were still deserted. Even at this early hour he could feel the heat gathering momentum like an avalanche or a freight train. His Hummer was where he had left it. He drove down Main and parked the police cruiser behind the dumpster enclosure behind the hardware store and walked back to his car which was parked in front of the Last Chance.

He pulled the keys he'd taken from Conway's pocket from his own pocket. As he got into the car Vern emerged from the motel office behind him. Couldn't be helped and what could they do about it anyway? Conduct an aerial search? Those were costly. That wouldn't happen until they found the sheriff's body—by which time Vince hoped to be over the horizon and gone. He had a rough idea where Beadles was headed because he had spent many hours puzzling over the stolen map. He'd considered using the map to find the peculiar butte, driven by man's atavistic lust for gold. But in the end Vince decided to sell the map to a rich collector. He thought he could get six figures.

The Hummer's twenty-gallon gas tank was filled with premium. Vince had enough gas to drive to Durango, as the crow flies, but who knew what conditions lay ahead? Like many uninformed consumers Vince figured the Hummer was a go-all do-all sort of vehicle. He could switch into 4X4 on the fly, but that took more gas. He headed out of town into the sun, pulling wrap-around Gargoyles from the center console and putting them on.

Vince waited until Gap was a smudge on the horizon before pulling over, pulling out the vial of coke he kept beneath the seat and laying out a line on the console. He snorked up. Ahhh. Breakfast of champions. He popped a NOS energy drink from the ice chest in the rear seat and hydrated. He pulled a zip-lock full of jerky from the ice chest and chewed. He followed the tire tracks east. They made him nervous. If they led to the butte there would be nothing to find.

He still wanted Summer. Wanted to possess her and fuck her and beat her for what she'd done to him. That map was going to be his fuck you money. He was going to take the proceeds and move to Puerto Vallarta. If he could recover the map at least he could sell it.

Back on the road. He twisted the FM dial but all he found was C&W and Come to Jesus meetings so he ran his finger along the CD holder in the sun visor and found the Li'l Wayne jam, shoved it into the player and settled back to the dulcet tones blasting from his Harmon Kardon speakers at 85 decibels.

Vince never got a fair shake. The world owed him. The son of a Boston meat cutter who left when he was nine, he never really knew his father. His mother was a drunken slut. She just couldn't get her shit together. She died from a heroin overdose when Vince was sixteen. His siblings were already gone. He bounced from foster home to foster home using his size and brains to outwit the jackals who opposed him at every turn. Family after family threw up their hands and he was eventually raised by the state in a facility for minor offenders.

The counselors urged him to get his GED and pursue a vocational career but Vince had always been a hustler. He knew from day one he was smarter and stronger than most people and had spent most his adult life running one scam or another.

The first time he saw MMA in a Vegas lounge he was hooked. The *Pride Fighting Championships* on PPV from Japan. *Yes!* Vince thought. To be a fighter, beat the shit out of other dudes and get paid for it. For the first time in his life Vince had a concrete goal. He enrolled in a karate school and obtained his black belt within a year. He was a natural. Everybody told him so. He moved onto Brazilian jujitsu.

Within two years, at the age of twenty-six, he was ready for his first fight. He entered the *International Kumite Competition*, a low-rent fight card at the Silver Saloon Hotel and Casino at the north end of town. The certification process was a joke. They never tested him for drugs. If they had they would have found traces of cocaine and human growth serum.

At six two and two twenty-five, Vince was a heavyweight. He had cauliflower ears. His first opponent looked like a cigar-store Indian with a massive chin and shoulders. When the bell rang Vince ran across the ring and cold-cocked the dude with a flying right hand. He set a record at four seconds for the IKC that still stood.

He won his next three fights but then he moved up the slightly less seedy *International Fight League* and they did test for drugs. Vince was barred from competition in Nevada for twelve months. He fought in "tough man" competitions in Wyoming and Montana and got a reputation for being a dirty fighter. Even without a manager he wasn't making any money.

He took a job bouncing at Lucifer's and that's when he met Summer. Lucifer's was down the road from Dante's. Even among the dancers she stood out with her exotic good looks and long straight crow black hair. Most of the dancers were on the downward spiral. Vince never got that impression from Summer. She held herself to a higher standard, didn't turn tricks, hardly touched blow until she hooked up with him.

She didn't even look at him the first time he approached her. He pulled that stunt with the comic book.

After that he had her eating out of his hand.

Until a couple days ago. Maybe he shouldn't have hit her so hard. He never was one to let sentimentality interfere with a buck.

Ahead on the horizon he spied a cloud of dust as of a vehicle driving fast. Vince stepped on the accelerator, coaxing the big black SUV to ninety mph.

CHAPTER FIFTY-SIX

MISMATCHED EYES

The old woman stood by the side of the road wrapped in a Navajo blanket and carrying a wicker basket with a zigzag motif. Beadles stopped the Jeep. He and Summer got out and walked up to the old woman. Her walnut-colored face had more wrinkles than a Shar-pei. Beadles wondered why she wasn't dying from the heat.

Summer stooped to look before the old woman's shawl. "Are you all right, ma'am? Do you need help?"

"Have you seen my son?" she said in halting diction that made Beadles think English wasn't her first language.

"How did you get out here?" he said.

The woman pointed east at the purple mountains. "He's out there somewhere. I'm afraid some bad men got hold of him and hurt him. I warned him. I warned him about that woman."

"What woman?" Summer said.

"He never had much sense when it came to women," the old woman said. She did not seem distressed. Beadles wondered how she got there. They hadn't seen another living being since leaving

Gap. If they had to rescue her it was going to interfere with his plans. Better to bring her along. He did a quick calculation on their resources. Beadles had always erred on the side of caution and figured he had more than enough food and water for the three of them, at least for a couple days. It was better than turning around and driving her back to Gap.

"How did you get out here?" he said again.

The woman looked at him and blinked revealing a brown eye and a white eye. "I live here," she said.

"Where's your home?" Summer said.

The old woman gestured vaguely to the southeast. "Over there."

"Do you need a ride?" Beadles said.

"I would like you to help me find my son."

We don't have time for this.

"If he's missing, let's notify the police. They can do a better job finding him than we can. We're sort of busy."

Summer shot him a warning glance.

"What does he look like?" she said.

The old woman reached upward. "He's very tall. Very strong. What woman wouldn't want him?"

Beadles suspected she might be a little crazy. How had she come to this desolate place? There was no shade for miles in any direction. He sighed deeply.

"Do you want to come with us? If you stay out here you may die of dehydration."

The old woman shook her head. "No. This is my home. I know how to survive in the desert."

Summer reached into the jeep, into her backpack for her phone. "I'm going to call 911. We can't leave her out here."

Beadles shrugged. He didn't know what else to do. Summer looked at her phone in consternation. It was one of those smart phones from which you could buy stocks or watch movies.

"I'm not getting a signal. Really? Really, Verizon? We're only a hundred miles from Kayenta!"

Beadles looked at Summer. "We're going to have to take her with us."

He opened the rear passenger side door. Summer put her hand on the old woman's arm and tried to steer her to the Jeep but the old woman shrugged free with a surprisingly forceful gesture.

"I am waiting here for my son."

"What if he doesn't come?" Summer said.

"He will come."

"Do you have anything to drink?" Summer said. The wicker basket had a wicker lid. Summer removed the lid and looked inside. A series of leather pouches, bones and what appeared to be a collection of rattles from rattlesnakes. Instinctively she shrank back.

"Eyuck."

"Well we can't kidnap her," Beadles said looking in the Jeep for a plastic water bottle. He pulled one from its yoke, placed it in the wicker basket, took the cover from Summer and replaced it.

"If we have any luck we'll be in and out in a day and we can pick her up on the way back if she's still here."

Summer turned to the old woman. "Ma'am, what's your name?"

The old woman looked at her with a hint of panic. "My name?" she said like someone waking from a coma.

Summer bent down to look the old woman in the eye and the amulet fell out of her shirt. The old woman stared at it. Fast as a rattlesnake the old woman's hand shot out and gripped the amulet. Summer's forehead bumped the old woman's. Her mismatched eyes stared with a frightening intensity. The white eye looked like a Comanche moon. Summer felt a twinge of vertigo.

"Where did you get this?" she said so softly only Summer could hear.

"An elder of my tribe gave it to me. A medicine man."

"You are one of us," she hissed.

"One of who?" Summer said.

"The Azuma."

"Where is Shipapu?" Summer said with equal intensity.

The old woman gestured east. "Look for the rock."

Beadles tapped his watch. "Summer."

With a glance back at the old woman, Summer got in the Jeep.

CHAPTER FIFTY-SIX

NAVAJO CASINOS

eadles was silent, worrying about the old woman. But what could they do? Force her into the vehicle?

"Don't worry," Summer said. "She'll survive."

"How can you be so sure?"

"Because I grew up around people like her. I have it too. Survivability."

"Good," Beadles said. "Maybe some of it will rub off on me."

Summer put her hand on the back of his neck. "It already has."

"So what are you gonna do if this pans out?"

Summer gave him a look and withdrew a little. "When I was a little girl I wanted to be a doctor. Crazy, huh? I never liked school. The only classes I liked were gym and English lit. Wouldn't get me into college never mind medical school."

"You're young," Beadles said. "You have plenty of time to do whatever."

Summer looked out the window. "Yeah right." The land morphed from pancake flat to rumpled sheets. Strange rock formations appeared in the distance distorted by heat rising from the desert floor. Like the ground was a stage with trapdoors.

"Seriously. You're a bright woman. I know a couple of scholarships you could snag, with your background."

"What?" Summer said. "You mean that I'm an Indian?"

Beadles grinned. "Don't knock it. It worked for me."

"For awhile."

"What did the old woman tell you? I couldn't hear."

"She said," Summer said slowly, "that I was one of them. The Azuma."

Beadles' knuckles tightened on the steering wheel as energy zinged through his nerves. He'd never been spiritual but he couldn't help but think that he was fated to do this. Summer was confirmation. Never before had he encountered anyone who claimed Azuma blood. Most Indians had never heard of them.

What was so terrible that Cerveros had killed himself?

"She was Azuma?" he said.

"Yes."

"Do you know about the Azuma?"

"I know they were feared by all other tribes. That their leader was a great medicine man and a giant, and that the Spanish wiped them out."

"Yes, hard to believe, but at that time during the sixteenth century, there were literally dozens if not hundreds of tribes competing for scarce resources on the Colorado plateau. The Four Corners area. Used to be you could just go down there and put a limb in each state and snap a picture. That was before the Navajo realized they could charge admission. Now the whole thing's surrounded by a chain link fence and you enter through a turnstile."

"Can't blame the red man for cashing in," Summer said. "I would if I could figure how."

"Isn't there a tribal council doling out goodies from gambling revenue?"

Summer shook her head. "Ain't seen a dime. Lo, the Noble Red Man is just as crooked as a Chicago ward-heeler once he gets in the high clover, y'know?"

"Are there many Navajo casinos?"

Summer shrugged. "Twin Rivers. Fire Rock. I went to Twin Rivers. They offered me a job. They said I could be a cocktail waitress or they would train me to deal blackjack."

"What's wrong with that?"

"Nothing, I suppose. I've considered it, but I can't go there right now. I went there with Vince and it's one of the places he'd look for me."

Beadles realized that unless Vince had outstanding warrants, he was likely to walk on the Gregorio shooting. Self-defense. Beadles knew the type. Big, sure of themselves, think they're smarter than they really are, and forever condemned to fuck up bad. Beadles saw the disgust on the sheriff's face. Vince looked like someone begging to be busted. That greaser look might fly in Vegas but out here it was an invitation for scrutiny. With any luck he'd have outstanding warrants. Guys like him left a trail.

"Dig around in that cardboard box behind the seat, wouldja?" Beadles said, "and grab me another one of those peanut butter cracker deals." He'd laid down the two rear seats and the entire back of the jeep was crammed with equipment and water containers, including a small two-man tent, sleeping bag, air mattress, and a tool box filled with picks, trowels, brushes and bottles for delicate work.

Summer turned around. That butt again. He couldn't help but stare. He wanted to reach out and touch it. She shifted things around, grunting.

"You really pack tight!"

"You betcha!" he said, slapping her butt.

She found the crackers, removed them from their plastic wrapper and handed them to Beadles. He was famished. He crammed the entire cracker into his mouth and masticated. The food zigged when it should have zagged. Beadles started coughing and couldn't stop. He was coughing so hard he couldn't keep his eyes open to see where he was going so he brought the Jeep to a halt, put it into neutral and sat there leaning over the wheel coughing his lungs up.

Summer pounded him on the back with the flat of her hand. Beadles wondered if it ever did any good or was just an old wives' tale. With a massive hiccup he got himself under control, both hands draped on the wheel breathing heavy.

Suddenly Summer was in his face holding on to his ears. "Were you really choking or just playing?"

"I was choking! Thanks for helping."

"Listen," she said, staring into his eyes with intensity, "Don't start coughing on me. I had an uncle died of emphysema. I care what happens to you."

She kissed him hard. Right on his cracker barrel mouth. He reacted as any man would. He thought about maggots and rat pie to make the boner go away. It worked. "Grab me a bottled water, wouldja?" he said.

Summer let go and turned. She wiggled around and freed the ice chest lid. Her butt went still. They drove for ten seconds like this.

"What?" Beadles said.

"Someone's following us."

CHAPTER FIFTY-SEVEN

OVER THE EDGE

ith a hollow feeling in his gut Beadles looked in the rearview. It took him a minute to find the minute smudge marring the endless blue horizon.

"Maybe it's a dust devil," he said.

Summer crawled back into the front seat, opened the bottled water, handed it to Beadles, and looked over the back of her seat on her knees. "You got binoculars?"

"In the khaki duffel," Beadles said stopping the car. He opened the door and got out. He put on a gimme cap from the inside door pocket, pulled the brim low over his eyes. The smudge moved around but did not appear to grow. Distances were deceiving out here with heat distortion from the ground. The clear air enabled you to see much further than you could in most cities.

Summer found the binocs, got out and climbed up on the old Jeep's hood, from there to the roof. She stood on the roof, feet braced against the package side rails, and trained the binocs to the west. She looked in silence.

"Shit!" she said, leaping from the roof to the ground. She handed the binocs to Beadles. "It's Vince!"

Beadles put the binocs to his eyes. "No way. He was in custody. They're not gonna cut someone loose on a manslaughter charge that quickly!" He adjusted the knobs to bring the image into focus. A cloud of beige dust formed a nimbus around a broad black grill. It was the Humvee.

Beadles got behind the wheel and slammed the door. "Get in!"

Summer joined him. Beadles put the vehicle into gear, accelerating rapidly, eyes roaming the horizon for shelter, shade, some redoubt, some place they could hide. The fact that Vince was now on their trail could only mean he'd escaped custody. And if he'd escaped custody it was because there was more at stake than the manslaughter charge. It meant Conway was most likely dead.

Beadles' heart whirred like a hamster on a wheel. Why had he so stupidly neglected to bring a gun? Was it because most of his colleagues and friends were anti-gun? Did he, in his hubris, think this was going to be a stroll to the bank? The sheriff had been the only law within a hundred miles.

Beadles glanced at Summer. She gripped the passenger bar on the 'A' pillar with both hands, white-knuckled. She looked at him.

"You got a gun?" she said.

Beadles gritted his teeth. "No."

"I do," she said reaching into her pocket and pulling out a small black automatic.

Beadles almost laughed. It looked like a toy. You could fire the whole clip into Vince and it wouldn't stop him. That's what his gun-savvy friends said, speaking of stopping power and the importance of a large grain bullet.

He realized he was letting fear get the best of him. The automatic may not be a howitzer, but it was still a lethal weapon. Hit him in the eye or the nuts to slow him down, put it to his ear and pump in the rest.

Beadles barked mirthlessly at his Dirty Harry reverie.

"What?" Summer said.

"We're going to have a showdown!" Beadles said with a hint of hysteria. "Shootout at the Double V Corral!"

Summer punched him on the arm. Hard. "Keep your eyes on the road!"

"What road?"

"Look," she said pointing right. "Over there—see those rocks?"

Beadles turned the car southeast. All he saw was a dark knobby ridge hovering over a beige furze. He looked in the rearview. The black rectangle was bigger. Beadles stepped on the gas. The old Jeep shook like a wet dog as it flew at seventy across the rough surface of the desert. The black shapes ahead firmed into a series of overlapping buttes. They approached some sort of canyonland.

Summer jacked a shell into the chamber.

"What are you doing?" Beadles said.

"I'm going to try and shoot out his tires if he gets close enough."

Like TV or a video game. Beadles could hardly believe it. A month previously he'd been a respected tenured professor on the verge of his greatest career triumph—cataloging the Azuma Collection. And here he was fleeing across the desert.

After two days in the desert sun my skin began to turn red.

"What?" Summer said.

The Jeep hit a gully-whumper. Beadles' body lurched up and down in a split second, shoulder strap cutting into his body.

"What?" Beadles said.

"What were you singing?"

Beadles giggled. "'Horse With No Name.' I can't get it out of my head."

"You can't sing," Summer said.

The big Humvee ineluctably closed the distance until it was within a quarter mile. The only thing that prevented it from overtaking the less powerful Jeep was that the big Hummer jounced and rocked on its suspension wildly, often affecting its direction.

Beadles gripped the wheel in both hands frantically searching for a place to hide. He saw the yawning gap opening before them and yanked the wheel so hard the Jeep nearly tipped over. He succeeded in altering their course and avoided flying into a vast chasm that had snuck up on them.

Vince adjusted course away from the gap. They raced east adjacent to a canyon whose bottom Beadles couldn't see from the driver's seat. Even five feet would be enough to stop them but he had a feeling it was deeper than that.

"What is it?" he said.

Summer looked out the window. "I don't know! I've never seen it before."

Sand raced across the desert at ankle level. The wind picked up and howled eerily through the open windows. Through the pitted windshield Beadles saw a great haze rising and pushing forward.

The sand storm would not reach them quickly enough. Vince would be on them within minutes. There had to be something. A road down into the canyon. Beadles desperately searched ahead for salvation. There was no sign of civilization—no tire tracks, no wires. The wind brought sand to windshield level. They closed the windows and turned on the AC.

Summer twisted in her seat. "Here he comes," she said tensely. She lowered the window and leaned out with the pistol in her left hand. Beadles noticed she was left-handed for the first time.

The tiny pops disappeared immediately in the wind like little firecrackers. Vince surged forward until he was almost at their rear bumper. Summer fired some shots. Vince pulled out to the left and accelerated. Beadles steered right so that he was now racing along ten feet from the edge of the chasm.

With a metallic bang Vince steered his vehicle savagely into Beadles' front fender. The old Jeep bucked and Beadles lost control of the wheel. He pulled his foot off the accelerator and jammed the brake but it was too late.

The Jeep rolled over the edge of the chasm.

CHAPTER FIFTY-EIGHT

THE CANYON

The world became a series of blurs and bone-jarring jolts. Beadles and Summer spun like kittens in a dryer, only their seatbelts preventing them from hurtling out the doors like depth charges. They tumbled forever, accompanied by sickening impacts and the sound of breaking glass. The view through the windshield was of sand and sky all mixed together. Beadles feared he might throw up before they came to a stop. Astonishingly the Jeep landed on its wheels but the fenders were stove in and a dense gray cloud issued from beneath the wrinkled hood. The engine died.

Beadles was sick to his stomach. A gash on his forehead leaked blood into his eyes. He wiped the blood away with his hands, then with a napkin from the center console as the wind whipped through the broken side windows peppering them with sand. He inhaled deeply and let it out slowly through his nostrils trying to damp down his rising gorge. In out. In out. He had it under control. He wasn't going to puke. He looked over at

Summer. She slumped in her seat with her head against the glass frame.

Time stopped as he reached for her. *God let her live* he thought, stunned by the very idea of prayer. How long had it been? He touched her shoulder. She opened her eyes and looked at him.

"Are you all right?" he said.

Summer put her hand to her head. She had a nasty goose egg over her right ear. "I think so," she said, testing herself. She released the seatbelt.

Thank God.

Beadles released his own seatbelt and tried to open the door. It was crimped shut. "Try your door," he said.

Summer opened the passenger door and stepped hesitantly out, hanging onto the door frame. Beadles eased himself across the console and out the door. He ached all over. Even his hair ached. They hugged one another hardly believing they were alive. Beadles looked up.

The top of the chasm was hidden by the blowing sands like a model's tawny hair whipped by a fan. Hair that went on and on and on. He couldn't see the rim and Vince could not see them. He put a hand up to shade his eyes. Where were his sunglasses? He found them wedged against the gas pedal and put them on. It was better but the flying sand still peppered his exposed skin and got in his mouth. The wind was picking up.

"We'd better get back in until this blows over," he said, leading the way. The passenger window behind Summer had been shattered. Glass lay all over the back of the car, water bottles, ice chests, boxes, tool kits mixed in a jumble. Water leaked from the upended ice chest. Beadles struggled with the boxes and blankets trying to return the ice chest to an upright position, feeling bruised up and down his arms and legs.

At least there was no way Vince could get to them without risking his neck. If there were a road down into the canyon they hadn't seen it. It wasn't marked on any map. Beadles estimated it was at least a hundred feet to the rim. Their fall seemed to go on forever but that was just his subjective reaction to being tossed around like a doll.

The wind howled. Sand flew.

"We have to seal these windows," Beadles said, reaching for a blanket.

Summer sprang into action. She opened the tool box and found Gorilla tape. She used a pocket knife to cut the blanket to size, Gorilla tape to fix it to the rim. It was a poor fit but at least it kept most of the sand out. With the windows up it was hot as a stove. Beadles found he still had electricity and ran the blower. It offered some relief.

They bent the seatbacks back as far as they could go and tried to make sense out of the mess. There was that ass again. Beadles reached out and cupped Summer's unshod breast. She looked at him. She kissed him and pulled him over to the passenger side.

Then she was on top tearing at his belt.

The sandstorm went away for several minutes.

They put their pants back on and the sandstorm was back, blowing grit in through tiny openings around the blanket. Beadles could barely see farther than the hood, which was covered with sand. He worried that they might actually be buried. But that wasn't possible, was it? It had to be much worse up top where Vince waited.

Maybe the sandstorm would cause Vince to turn around.

Probably not. Vince didn't get his rap sheet by playing it smart. Like most thugs payback was more important than living well.

Beadles checked the GPS. There was no signal. He'd brought extra batteries just in case.

"Let's eat," Beadles said delving into the heap in the back seat. It was dim inside the Jeep due to the storm even though the sun shined straight down. Beadles found beef jerky, individually wrapped string cheese, apples and bottled water. They ate in companionable silence. They napped.

When they woke the storm was over. Dim sun shined in the cabin through the layer of sand covering the windshield.

"See if you can open your door," Beadles said.

Summer had to use her legs to push the door open with a hair-raising shriek against a pile of sand. They eased out. The landscape had changed. Whereas before it had been rock, the ground was now covered with sand to a one foot depth. It wasn't as hot as it had been before the storm but it was hot. Beadles opened the rear hatch and unloaded backpacks and supplies.

Beadles took out the GPS and four military-style canteens filled with water. He retrieved the ancient map from its folder and opened it on the hood. The map showed the canyons and to the east, the strange rock. Beadles checked his Boy Scout compass. The canyon ran east/west.

Beadles handed two of the canteens to Summer. "We're going to have to hoof it. I don't think it's more than twelve miles to this butte but we won't know until we're out of these canyons or find a way to the rim."

He put on his ball cap, handed an extra to Summer. They put on their sunglasses. "How much can you carry?"

Summer puffed up. "Me strong squaw! Carry wood all day!"

They spent several minutes sorting through supplies. He found a tube of sun lotion and smeared it over his face and arms. He handed the tube to Summer. Beadles left the tent and the sleeping bag. He was already toting fifty pounds and Summer thirty. Water was heavy but they had to carry as much as they could for the chances of discovering any were slim. By now the sun had edged over so that the north wall of the canyon lay in shadow. They stood close to the wall staying in the shade, heads gyrating like bobbleheads, stunned by the sere beauty of the canyons. The rock rose in multicolored striations. Beadles took pictures with his phone.

Beadles returned to the cargo area for his Bowie knife. He saw the pommel sticking out from under a towel and pulled out the towel. Something brown and chitinous scurried up over his hand

and leaped to the sand. Beadles recoiled and fell on his ass, his face white.

Summer looked at him with alarm. "What is it?"

"Scorpion," he croaked. Jesus Fuck. Why couldn't they leave him alone? He used a stick to retrieve his knife.

They walked in silence for an hour, pausing from time to time to sip water. In addition to two canteens, Beadles had put six water bottles in his ruck. He felt the weight in his shoulders and legs and was grateful he liked to run. The next time they paused Summer took the lead. The canyon walls closed in as the canyon zigzagged, following the path of some antediluvian river. The sand receded exposing the rocky canyon floor. Summer was spry as a springbok. Beadles followed her rump like a donkey after a carrot. She rounded a corner.

"Vaughan!" she said.

Beadles stepped around the corner and stopped dead behind Summer. The canyon had opened up into a broad wadi. A hundred yards ahead hulked a massive toadstool-shaped butte. Beneath the overhang, sand over the rocker panels, lay an ancient VW bus.

CHAPTER FIFTY-NINE

THE BUS

Sand had drifted up over the wheels but the roof was swept clean. A coarse patina of sand adhered to the windows. The bus was old school with four tiny windows above the doors. Beadles and Summer stared in silence. As a boy Beadles became fascinated with the story of WW II B-24 bomber *Lady Be Good*. Returning at night from a bombing run over Italy to her base in Tunisia, the plane overshot the African coast and flew a thousand miles inland before running out of fuel. From 10,000 feet at night the desert looked just like the Mediterranean.

The desiccated remains weren't discovered until 1959 when an aerial surveyor searching for oil spotted the ghost plane sitting in the desert. Ground patrols found the bodies of the nine airmen as they had tried to walk to safety. All had died of thirst. One made it thirty miles. They had set off in all directions hoping one of them would find help. Stunned and dehydrated, they often meandered. A map showing their paths would resemble the Azuma symbol.

The bus radiated crazy. A jarring juxtaposition, a relic washed up by the Sea of Time. It didn't belong there any more than a B-24 sitting in the middle of a desert. Or a scorpion in Illinois.

Beadles and Summer approached the ghost in reverent silence. Beadles took several pictures. The sun had baked its once brick exterior a pale orange/pink. All that remained of numerous window decals and bumper stickers were bleached-white markers. Only by looking very closely could you see the Grateful Dead symbol. Sand had drifted up against the windshield so that the bus seemed to be emerging from the ground.

The bus faced east. The driver's side window was missing. Beadles set down his rucksack, walked up the dune and knelt to see inside. After the blazing sun it took his eyes a minute to adjust to the shade.

"Ho - ley shit," he said.

A jumble of ribs and arm bones slumped in the seat. The arm bones remained connected by leathery tissue but there was no skull. Sand filled the interior to knee level. The other seat was empty. Sand had frosted the remaining window glass so that it was impossible to see.

"Skeleton," Beadles said.

Summer came up and crouched on her knees. "Let me see."

Beadles moved aside so Summer could look in the window.

"Wow," she said. "That's so creepy, y'know?"

Beadles noted the coordinates on his Garmin and dialed them in. They'd have to inform the police when they got out. He walked around to the opposite side, the side closest to the oddly-shaped butte. He opened the rear door with a horrendous screech and leaped back as a half dozen pale brown scorpions leaped to the sand and skittered away.

Beadles shivered despite the heat. He hated them. He'd always hated bugs. He'd hated standing in left field as a Little Leaguer feeding the mosquitoes. He hated flies so much he would stand in the parking lot of the A&P for hours smashing them with a copy of *Sports Illustrated* as they landed on the warm outer wall.

But the scorpion. The scorpion was the worst. What god would create such a thing and why? Well, his not to question the Almighty. If the scorpion had a constructive function he couldn't see it. Likewise rattlesnakes.

"UGH!" Summer exclaimed. "Be careful! Do you have an anti-venom kit?"

"Yes, I do but it won't help against a scorpion sting." What had they used on Rob?

"They're rarely fatal," Summer said.

"I knew a guy died of one," Beadles said, using his twelve-inch Bowie to poke around in the back of the bus. The sand was lower here and he saw the top of an old ice chest. When they finally found the *Lady Be Good* the coffee in the thermos was still drinkable.

A small camp shovel poured out. Beadles picked it up. It was about two feet long with an adjustable steel spade head. He used it to shovel sand out of the back. Several scorpions joined the exodus, disappearing beneath the van. Beadles uncovered a shoe. He shoveled. The shoe was connected to a leg in ancient faded denim. Beadles stepped back. Summer looked inside.

"Jesus!" she said.

Carefully, Beadles removed sand from around the body. The upper torso was a shriveled mummy in an Electric Flag T-shirt. It lay face up. Its feet were encased in leather hiking boots. Beadles pulled on them gently to shake off the sand. The corpse had no more weight than a satchel. The skeleton had frozen in position. It's left hand had shrunk to fused bones gripping something white, ribbed, and delicate. A rattlesnake skeleton. Beadles saw the scimitar-shaped fangs and the rattle.

Beadles delicately eased the brittle wallet from the skeleton's hip pocket. He opened it and found the well-preserved driver's license.

Curt Mayweather, Evanston, IL. He knew the name from somewhere.

Something shiny tumbled out and slid down the sloping sand. Summer picked it up. It was an aluminum cigarette case decorated with an Indian in a war bonnet. It rattled. She pried it open. Inside were three rolled doobies and a strip of blotter acid. She handed it to Beadles who put the two halves back together and tossed it in the back of the bus. Exposing the side handle of the old Thermos cooler Beadles rotated the spade's head ninety degrees, hooked the chest and dragged it out.

Another scorpion abandoned ship.

Beadles used the shovel to open the chest. There was a green sandwich in a frosted Ziploc, some shrunken apples and a bag of trail mix. There was something beneath the detritus. Beadles reached in and carefully removed the layer of ancient plastic bags.

Beadles and Summer lurched back and repulsion.

"What is it?" Summer wailed in a tinny voice.

A desiccated diamondback, jaws wide open, body twisted like a pretzel.

Beadles shut the chest. He opened the front passenger door, causing a small sand slide around his shoes. From the passenger side he saw that the jumble of bones lay atop a waist-sized hole surrounded by thread-bare denim. Sand must have covered the lower portion of the body preserving it. He looked down. The skull lay in the passenger foot well.

There was a large hole in the windshield directly over the steering wheel as if someone had hurled a softball-sized rock.

He had to get the driver's ID but he feared putting his hand anywhere near the sand-filled cavity of the waist. Straightening the shovel, he gently prodded the bottom half of the corpse. Nothing emerged. He used the shovel to move the sand away from the right hip pocket. Ever so gingerly he slipped his fingers between the threadbare cotton and snagged the wallet. It was made of some exotic leather, perhaps ostrich skin. He opened it up and removed the driver's license

That's when he realized where he'd heard the name Mayweather.

CHAPTER SIXTY

THE WHEEL

onald Potts," Beadles said.

"Do you know him?"

"His dad gave me five thou to finance this expedition. Actually he gave me the five thou to go away. He'll be happy to get some closure at least."

Fifty thousand for information leading to the discovery of his son's body.

He snapped a picture of the remains.

It was cooler in the shade with the slight breeze. Summer leaned on Beadles' shoulder. "What do you think happened to them?"

Beadles gestured toward Mayweather. "Looks like he was bit by a rattlesnake. I wouldn't know how Potts died. You'd need a coroner and even he might not be able to tell. It's been thirty years. It must have laid under the sand all these years and that storm uncovered it."

"They call these places the walking hills," Summer said. "Because of the wind. Hey do you mind if I grab that reefer?"

Beadles shrugged. "Be my guest."

What the hell. It wasn't like he'd never smoked dope. In college he'd tried it all: coke, acid, meth. Everything but smack. You had to draw the line somewhere. It all stopped after graduation. No chemical high could compete with academic success. He'd shared the occasional toke at parties over the years but he could take it or leave it. Thank God he wasn't what they called an addictive personality.

He wondered about Summer though. She'd as much as said she was a coke head. Working at a strip club, living with a dealer. It went with the territory. But she hadn't been twitchy. Never mentioned drugs or craving. What harm could a couple of joints do? He might partake himself, but not before they reached their destination.

He pulled out his cell phone. Zippo. He put it back. "Let's get going. We've got about eight hours of daylight left."

They headed east down the zigzagging canyon which now lay mostly in shadow. Twenty minutes later while negotiating a narrow defile they came upon hieroglyphs on the canyon wall. A tall man leading an army of scorpions against conquistadores, accurately depicted in their double-prowed helms riding surreal horses. These would have been the first horses the Indians saw. The satanic, mummified horses were larger in proportion to the men than they would have been in reality.

Had they seen the horses as demonic invaders and scorpions as their saviors? Beadles photographed the images. He carried extra batteries in his backpack. Maybe if they got up high he could get a signal. At least the GPS still functioned. According to the GPS they were ten miles from ground zero.

It was the perfect place for an ambush. Beadles looked up. He could practically hear the warriors chanting from the rim as they fired arrows and hurled rocks on the invaders.

They walked in eerie silence through the canyon mesmerized by the different strata. A multi-colored layer cake of rust, beige, brick, charcoal and dozens of infinite variations. At one time the Mojave had been the bottom of a vast inland sea. Beadles was not surprised to discover a trilobite fossil close to the ground. He took a picture.

An hour later the canyon debouched into a broad alluvial plain. And there, hovering in the distance, shimmering over waves of heat was an odd-looking butte.

Beadles felt his pulse quicken. Yes! They weren't there yet but it looked like the butte in Mayweather's drawing and the one on the map. He pulled the map out and opened it on a flat rock. Summer leaned on the rock next to him and looked at the map.

"You think that's it?" she said.

"I'm hoping."

They had entered a hallucinatory landscape out of a Sergio Leone film. There was no sign of man in any direction. Beadles looked up. The faint after print of a contrail was the only thing indicating modernity. They walked with the sun at their back. The wind had died down and the heat was intense. Gradually the weight of their canteens transferred into their bodies. Beadles feared they would run out of water before reaching the butte but he still had several bottles in the ruck.

And what if they reached the butte and there was no water? He prayed he could find some cell reception. He opened his phone. No signal. The sun evaporated their sweat as soon as it appeared. Side by side they walked toward the distant butte which never seemed to get any closer. Beadles turned around. They had come at least two miles from the canyon lands. He looked down. The desert floor was covered with obsidian chips. Tiny stunted cacti struggled for survival. A gliding rattlesnake was the only movement.

The cerulean sky was cloudless. They walked in silence to save their energy. A low parabolic shape appeared before them. As they approached they saw it was the top of an ancient wagon wheel protruding from the sand, occupying a slight depression. They arrived. The wood was bleached white. If there had been a metal strip around the perimeter it had long since corroded. The top of the wheel protruded perhaps six inches above the sand revealing two wooden spokes through which a rattlesnake twined. The rattlesnake escaped the depression and disappeared in the sand.

Beadles and Summer looked at the wheel.

"Storm must have uncovered it," Beadles said.

"Oh God," Summer said.

"What?"

She pointed to a tiny white tip protruding perhaps a half inch from the sand at the edge where the wheel emerged. "Is that a bone?"

Beadles stared at the tip with a sense of foreboding. The sky seemed to darken as if a shadow has crossed the sun. He shivered. He knew what it was. He blinked. The brightness returned. It was overwhelming. He felt light-headed. His mouth forced a rictus grin.

"What?" Summer said.

Very carefully Beadles used the blade of the Bowie to draw sand away from the tip revealing a finger bone, then another. "Distal phalange. Finger bone."

Summer's face drained of color. She stepped back and grabbed Beadles' arm. "Skorpio," she whispered.

"What?"

"They tied him to a wagon wheel and left him to die in the sun."

"Skorpio? Is that what they called him?"

"Don't say it. It's bad medicine."

A rock lodged in Beadles' throat, a thrill of terror and triumph. What if he clipped the digit and tested the DNA? Would that constitute proof of an Azuma identity? If Summer were truly part Azuma, would it not match hers in some capacity?

Was it desecration? One phalangeal. The thing was over 400 years dead. There was no one to see. Yet standing beneath the baking sun were not his actions open to the sky?

Like a child maliciously spitting in the holy water.

The southwestern tribes believed that if you disturbed the graves of the dead their ghosts would rise to take revenge.

Summer sensed his distress. "What is it?"

"Nothing," he croaked. "We'd better get moving."

He marked the coordinates on his GPS. Let the university sort it out. He wasn't about to disturb the creature's final rest. He also felt a fierce surge of exhilaration. If it was the legendary Azuma warlord, he'd just scored the brass ring.

Summer's fingers sank into Beadles' bicep. She stared west. Beadles followed her gaze.

There was a cloud of dust on the horizon.

CHAPTER SIXTY-ONE

CUT TO THE CHASE

eadles stared, dry-swallowing. He took a swig of water. The tiny cloud vibrated representing furious activity. Was it a hallucination?

"It's getting closer!" Summer said, picking up her ruck. "Come on!"

Her fear was contagious. Beadles shouldered his heavy pack and chased after her. They jogged toward the butte, each jarring step causing their backpacks to dig cruelly into their shoulders.

Vince had found a way down.

Summer bounded ahead, her elegant calf muscles flexing. Beadles struggled to keep pace. The butte seemed close but it was difficult to judge distances. He thought it was no more than a mile away. On the flats the Hummer was easily capable of 90 mph. Maybe it would hit a pothole. Maybe it would run over a rock.

Beadles prayed as he ran. He prayed to whomever would listen: God, Buddha, Allah, Wankantanka, Our Father the Sun, Our Mother the Moon and Aleister Crowley. Water sloshed. The heavy Bowie banged against his leg. Their breaths came in gasps as they pounded east running right over a nest of rattlesnakes so fast they were gone by the time the snakes reacted. The afterimage of the viper pit blazed in Beadles' mind and faded.

The butte was getting closer. It wasn't his imagination. He felt a cramp drive like a tiny wedge into his ribs. Ignoring it, he forced himself to place one foot in front of the other, grateful that he'd always been a runner and that he wore light, Saucony over-the-ankle shoes.

Now they could hear the vehicle, a faint whine like a Junebug hovering too close to the ear—or was it his own breath whistling through his nose? No. There was a fluctuation in the buzzing, a sudden rise and then a fall to silence.

Panting, Beadles turned around. He pulled the binocs from the rucksack and dialed in. It was the Humvee, Vince getting out and walking around to the front. Staring at something. Walking to the back and opening up the gate. A flat tire? A rock? Beadles thanked all his gods for this reprieve and picked up the pace. Summer had stopped to look.

"Come on! Maybe he's got a flat tire!"

Every step sent a jolt up his spine. But they were getting closer. Details began to emerge—vertical striations where volcanic rock had forced its way to the surface millennia ago. It was the butte of his dreams, the butte in the picture, the butte on the map. The epicenter of the Azuma universe—Shipapu. The Great Road. The gateway between this world and the next.

Now Beadles could see the scree of rock surrounding the base, the faint green furze indicating moisture. They ran in silence until the pulse of their blood rushing through their heads became the loudest thing in the universe.

They reached the bottom of the butte and collapsed on a flat rock gasping. Beadles weighed his water. There was no point hoarding if they couldn't reach safety. Fuck it. He tilted back the canteen and drained it in six big gulps. He still had a couple bottles in the ruck.

Summer drank too, stood and looked for a route up. She walked counter-clockwise around the base until she disappeared from sight. With the sun in the western sky all the shade was on the east—too far for Beadles to go. He saved his strength for the climb, if they could find a way. The sun beat down.

From the slight advantage of the scree he trained his eyes to the west. The cloud was back. Whatever problem Vince had encountered was solved. He could hear the engine's roar. Summer appeared, breathless.

"There's a way up!" she said. "Follow me!"

Beadles hoisted his pack and followed her a quarter of a way around the butte to a chimney accessible between two massive boulders tilted together at the top to form a crude arch. Beadles crouched to get through the arch. The chimney, one side open, was approximately three feet in diameter although its width varied as it followed a crooked path up. Crude hand and footholds had been carved into the rock. Exultation blossomed in Beadles' chest—here was proof that the butte had been occupied. Gleefully, almost triumphantly, he followed Summer up the butte, his backpack occasionally snagging on a rock outcropping.

Halfway up Summer stopped. "Oh fuck."

"What is it?" Beadles said.

"There's a fucking rattlesnake sleeping on a ledge." She resumed climbing with a renewed sense of urgency until she was well above the spot.

"Wait!" she said. "Maybe I can get it to move." She grabbed a stone off a ledge and pitched it at a downward angle. Then another.

"Great. Now it's awake. Wait a minute." She pitched a couple more rocks "It's gone."

"Where did it go?"

"I don't know—deeper into the ledge."

Well fuck, Beadles thought. Now it was pissed off. Rattlesnakes could leap amazing distances. Might it not have been better to let the snake sleep? He couldn't go back. He had to go up. Carefully he boosted himself to the snake's level. No snake. The ledge on which it had been sleeping seemed to tunnel into the rock. Beadles didn't wait for it to come back. With renewed effort he climbed past the spot, urging Summer upward.

Some of the handholds had eroded to nothing but they were sharper near the top and at last Summer heaved herself out of the chimney to find herself in a bubble-shaped depression with a slight incline to the plateau. Seconds later Beadles joined her. They walked up the incline to the top of the butte and froze, slack-jawed.

A grove of cottonwood sprouted from the center of the island. Behind them to the east was an odd structure that looked like a decaying castle keep, natural rock smoothly blended with hand-carved stones to form a cliff-dwelling in the sky. Three small vertical windows punctuated the inner wall. The top of the butte was about 100 feet in diameter.

Vince laid on the horn announcing his arrival with a wail that increased as he approached. Beadles and Summer went to the western rim and looked down. The black Hummer roared up trailing a cloud of dust and jerked to a stop at the foot of the scree 200 feet below. Vince shut off the engine and sat there.

Summer pulled out her tiny automatic. "If he tries to climb up here I'll shoot him."

Beadles doubted whether the tiny caliber weapon would stop the clavigerous thug. They would have to ascertain whether there was another path to the top but Beadles doubted it. They could always prevent Vince from climbing by rolling boulders down the chute. The top of the butte was filled with scattered boulders of various size.

Maybe a snake would bite him. Maybe a scorpion.

The silence was deafening.

Vince opened the car door and got out. He wore his cowboy hat and stretched leisurely in the sun, holding a water bottle in one hand. He uncapped the bottle, drank and tossed it aside. He cupped his hands.

"Professor! How y'all doin'? Summer honey, you done good work."

Beadles checked his phone. No signal. That was wrong. It was the latest Razr and was supposed to have pick-up virtually anywhere in the world via satellite. He checked the power level. Still good.

"What happened to the sheriff?" Beadles yelled.

"The sheriff? Oh him! He let me go. Knew damn well it was self-defense. This here's the place on the map, isn't it? What's up there? I know there ain't no water. Me, I got plenty. I got enough to sit here for a week while you die of thirst. Is that the way you want it?"

CHAPTER SIXTY-TWO

THE POND

Beadles dug around in his ruck and pulled out three plastic water bottles, all full. They could easily run through those in the next couple of hours. Summer did the same. She had three more bottles and half a canteen. They looked at each other. Without more water it was doubtful they would last another day.

Vince laid siege.

"Well I'm down here if you want to talk!" he said, sitting down with his back to the grill in the shade provided by the vehicle. The sun lowered in the western sky.

Wordlessly Beadles rose and walked counter-clockwise. Summer joined him. The top of the butte was a flat, flinty surface covered with rocks and sand, the occasional withered cactus struggling to survive. It was not entirely flat. There were numerous depressions and holes that might represent molten bubbles that had burst to the surface. Beadles watched where he stepped. He did not want to encounter any snakes. It took them ten minutes to reach the opposite side and the strange half-chimney thrusting from the rim. The tower-like protrusion rose another fifty feet above the butte top. Most of it appeared to be volcanic upthrust but it had been augmented with carefully fitted stones and white mortar to form a cliff-dwelling in the sky. The entrance formed a crude triangular arch. Mayan influence?

Every cell in Beadles' body leaned toward the door. His heart banged a Neil Peart solo. This was it. The Big Time. The gold at the end of the rainbow. He'd gambled and he'd won. It was a better high than coke. Than sex. The sun cast his shadow in stark relief on the ancient walls. Faintly he heard a car door slam.

He couldn't die now, not with success within his grasp. Nor could he indulge in the luxury of exploring this ruin while the thug lurked below. It was only a matter of time before Vince discovered the chimney. He wasn't stupid. He knew there had to be a route to the top. And the crooked chimney provided no clear shot. Nor would Vince attempt the climb, fully cognizant of the danger of falling rocks. All Vince had to do was sit back and wait them out.

He moved on. Aside from the chute there was no way to the top. He and Summer turned their attention to the center of the butte where six cottonwoods incongruously grew. Their lushness gave Beadles the creeps. They should not have existed.

They scrambled over a low berm of scattered rocks and approached the center. The six trees were as evenly spaced as clock numbers. In the center a brackish pool of water. What was it doing there? If it was rain, how did it exist? It hadn't rained in that part of the desert in months.

Beadles knelt, cupped pond water in his hands and brought it to his face. Odorless. He dipped his tongue. Aside from a slight mineral taste it seemed fine but it was still unsuitable for drinking. Who knew what bacteria festered in that pond? If snakes could get up here so could mice and insects. He had a water purifier but he'd left it in the Jeep.

Summer looked at him hopefully. "Can we drink it?"

"I don't know. We may have to." His eyes swept the surface of the pond. It was about ten feet across. On the opposite side a series of ripples radiated from a disturbance in surface tension. Beadles walked around to the pond and crouched. It was a spring. The water bubbling up from the bottom of the pond was clear, unlike the brownish pond water.

Geologically it was an impossibility. What source of water could possibly exist 150 feet above the desert floor? There wasn't another source of water for miles in any direction. It was a miracle. A bonnaroo medicine man miracle. A holy place. Only the divine could create such a miracle, and if it was a divine place, evil had no place. An invisible burden eased from Beadles' shoulders. It was going to be alright. God, Wankantanka, our Father the Sun, our Mother the Moon was watching over them.

Yeah right.

Beadles had no illusions. There were no miracles. There was some rational explanation for the spring. They were in a desperate situation but at least they had water, whatever the cause. Beadles looked around. There was plenty of fuel from the cottonwoods. They could always boil the water to rid it of bacteria.

If they could find something in which to boil it.

Repetitive honking ruptured the silence. Vince wanted their attention. They returned to the westernmost lip of the butte and looked down. Vince stood next to his vehicle and honked the horn through the window.

Beadles picked up small smooth stone and pitched it over the edge. It landed on the Hummer's roof with a faint crack. Vince laid off the horn and looked up.

"What?" Beadles yelled.

"I just wanted to give you a head's up, professor! About our little friend! Did she tell you she slipped me a mickey, stole my car and my money?"

"Wasn't that after you punched her out?" Beadles said.

It was hard to tell but he thought Vince grinned.

"Did you ask her about her record? Drug dealing and prostitution? She's got a rap sheet longer than the immigration bill. You think you can trust her? She's a scorpion, Professor! She's going to stab you in the back. She can't help it. It's her nature."

Summer put her hand on his shoulder. "He's lying."

"I know that!"

"Hey professor!" Vince continued. He had a good voice. Deep and rich. Would have made a terrific announcer. "Right now she's telling you I'm a liar and that she's a virtuous angel! I'm just warning you, one man to another, don't turn your back on her."

Beadles looked at Summer. Her eyes had closed to furious slits. Her mouth was a grim line. What did he know about her, really? She was very beautiful. What kind of woman goes to sleep with some guy she just met in a bar?

Wasn't he being hypocritical? How many women had he talked into one-night stands? Vince's warning had a disturbing undertone of truth. Maybe she wasn't the damsel in distress. How easily she had manipulated him.

"Well folks it's gonna be dark soon. I'll just settle in for the night. Or maybe I'll find that path to the top you took. Come to think about it, you can't be sure I won't come up there in the middle of the night and blow your fucking brains out. You'd better take turns guarding."

CHAPTER SIXTY-THREE

CHAMBER IN THE SKY

eadles and Summer huddled at the rim.

"Do you think he'll try and come up?" Beadles said.

"No. He knows we have no place to go. He'll just wait us out."

The burden was on them. What if Beadles were to descend in the middle of the night with Summer's pea-shooter and put one in Vince's ear while he slept? Beadles was no hero. He didn't relish the idea of approaching the well-armed Vince but they had little choice. Even with a water source if they stayed on top of the butte they would die from starvation. They'd only brought enough victuals for a couple days.

The sun sat atop the western peaks casting long shadows across the desert.

"Let's take a look at those ruins," Beadles said, cutting a path through the center of the butte. They skirted the pond keeping an eye out for scorpions and snakes. With the last rays of the sun striking the ruins horizontally every detail stood out in bas relief. The lintel above the arched entrance was a triangular rock with a carved motif: a circle radiating squiggly lines. Beadles had never seen it anywhere else. It was the symbol of the Azuma. The entrance itself was an astonishing seven feet tall—much taller than any other cliff dwellings of which he was aware. Taller than any temple entrance throughout Central America. This in itself constituted a startling archaeological discovery. Most Native Americans had been five and a half feet tall or less at the time of Columbus.

There were always exceptions. The great Navajo chief Narbona was six feet six inches. His son-in-law Manuelito was also well over six feet. Crazy Horse was said to be over six feet tall. But never before had anyone encountered archaeological evidence that tall Indians were anything other than anomalies.

Or had it been built for just one man?

Beadles entered and found himself in a shallow chamber, perhaps six feet front to back, approximately fifteen feet in length, with a flat, seven foot ceiling made of bleached timbers mounted crossways, woven branches atop them. The sun shown so brightly through the entrance Beadles did not need his flashlight. Two slot windows faced west. Ten feet away to the south lay the remnants of ancient ladder. Above them a round hole led to the next chamber. The back wall of the chamber bore petroglyphs similar to those they had seen in the canyon.

Beadles took out his cell phone and snapped pictures of those that lay in direct sunlight. He walked toward the nearest window. From the window he looked west across the butte to the distant mountains and the setting sun.

He was alone.

He walked back to the entrance and looked out. Summer stood with her arms wrapped around her shoulders shivering.

"What's the matter? Come inside."

"No," she said softly. "It's too old."

"What do you mean it's too old?"

Summer's eyes were round with fear. "The ancient—it frightens me. The earth is so old, this is so old, I'm afraid if I touch it, it will suck the life out of me like a sponge! That's why nothing lives around here."

Beadles stepped outside and held her. "Come on. You've been walking on the earth that's just as old and that hasn't sucked the life out of you. It's just an old building! Haven't you been inside a cliff dwelling before?"

"It's not just an old building. I can feel it! It hates us. It wants us dead."

Beadles barked and walked to the wall. He slapped his hand against it. "This? It's inanimate matter. It's a rock! It's not going to hurt anyone. Come on. You've got that gun."

"No. You go. I'll wait here."

Shaking his head Beadles reentered the cliff dwelling. He stood beneath the ceiling hole, leaped and caught the upper rim with his fingers. He hoisted himself up. The floor was formed of ancient timbers laid front to back. Beadles stood and walked north to another slot window facing west. Hieroglyphs clung to the back wall. Shards of pottery lay in one corner.

Beadles' pulse pushed *adelante*. This was it. The Big One. He was right and they were wrong. He saw the TV interviews, the book tour, the awards. The women. He stooped to examine the drawings. The tall man stood in the center radiating squiggly lines warding off the strange invaders with bow and arrow. The invaders rode monstrous four-legged beasts and wore peaked helmets. Arrayed against them, behind the tall man was an army of scorpions and snakes.

The Maya had worshiped the feathered serpent Quetzalcoatl.

Beadles stared at the display. And then it hit him.

The squiggly lines were snakes.

How had he failed to see it? The outer points consisted of rhomboids. The inner a series of perpendicular lines meant to indicate rattles.

The Empire of the Snakes.

A bone-dry rattling issued from the far end. Beadles backed toward the floor opening eyes riveted on the ground. It took a minute before he saw the rattler in the corner, eight feet away. It was coiled like a fat garden hose, thick as his wrist. A rattler can strike the length of its body. It that were a seven footer Beadles had nowhere to go but down.

He did so, lowering himself quickly through the vent and dropping to the stone ground. Beadles exited and found Summer seated on a rock hugging herself. Shadow had begun creeping up the rock face.

"Come on," he said, offering a hand. "There's a fucking rattler up there. We'll go back tomorrow. Maybe it will leave. Let's figure out how we're going to spend the night."

They'd left the tents and the sleeping bags in the Jeep. They'd expected to get in and out on the same day! They returned to the western rim and checked on Vince, who sat in the shade between the Hummer and the butte. Beadles looked around for a big rock. Maybe he could break the fucker's neck. Summer saw what he was doing and immediately ran off, returning with a boulder the size of a soccer ball. A series of tooth-like rocks formed a jagged crown around the butte.

The butte tapered toward the top. If Beadles were to drop the rock straight down it might strike a projection and go off course. It would be better if he heaved the rock six feet beyond the rim so that it came straight down on Vince's head.

If he could do it.

Beadles picked up the rock. It must have weighed forty pounds. He ran toward the rim and heaved the rock over like a free throw. He rushed to the edge in time to see the rock strike a protrusion and angle off to the SW. The rock landed with a thud.

Vince jumped, turned around and backed away from the butte.

"NICE ONE HEY!" he yelled through cupped hands. He got in the Hummer, started it up and backed fifty feet away from the butte. He got out of the truck. Shadow reached the desert floor.

CHAPTER SIXTY-FOUR

WITCHING HOUR

They gathered dead leaves and branches from the cottonwoods and made a sort of nest, laying out their two sweatshirts as bedding. The temperature could fall into the forties in the desert at night. Beadles pulled out his lightweight cookpot and suspended it from a branch stretched between two rocks. He built a fire beneath the pot in a natural stone kettle. He boiled enough water to fill their canteens and then made soup from dry mix. They ate from a bag of trail mix and a sack of peanuts.

Night fell. They clung together for warmth and that led to sex. They put their clothes back on and lay in each other's arms gazing at the sky. In Creighton on a clear night you might be able to see a couple dozen stars. Light pollution hid the rest. The desert sky looked as if God had tossed up a barrel of diamonds. The stars were uncountable and the half moon lit the desert floor like a stage set.

Summer burrowed in. "Do you think there's life on other planets?"

Beadles barked. It was unexpected. He liked this girl. "Speaking as a scientist, I gotta say yeah. I mean look at that. We can't even count the stars we can see. There must be a hundred thousand stars that we see tonight. All those stars, all those planets, how self-absorbed would we have to be to conclude that we're the only intelligent life in the universe?"

"Mr. Spaceman," Beadles sang in a spot-on falsetto, "won't you please take me along, I won't do anything wrong."

Summer giggled and snuggled closer. It was cool verging on cold. "Do you believe in God?"

"I don't know. My folks were Episcopalian and dragged me to church every Sunday but I don't think it took. I think maybe I'm part of a generation that's too sophisticated and self-aware to believe in God, which doesn't mean God doesn't exist! It just means I lack faith."

"You're smart enough to know what you don't know," Summer said.

"Exactly."

They lay in each other's arms swapping heat. "I believe in God," Summer said. "I don't know if it's that old white guy with the beard, but there's got to be a higher power in charge of all this. I mean, humanity, civilization, love, it can't just have sprung forth from the void! There's too much order—the seasons, the birds and the bees."

"The way the sunlight plays upon her hair..." Beadles sang.

"Huh?"

"'Good Vibrations.' The Beach Boys!"

"Oh. I couldn't tell. Do you believe the universe just happened? Like what do they call it, the Big Bang?"

"I try not to think too big."

"Well that's the beauty of God," Summer said. "You can trade your doubts in on faith."

Beadles shifted to relieve irritation from a stick that poked him in the back. "What kind of God created scorpions and rattlesnakes?"

"The same God who created violets and sunny days. We can't know His purpose."

"Or Hers."

Summer giggled. "That's right. Don't they derive some sort of serum from rattlesnakes?"

"Yeah. For rattlesnake bites. I might be able to see a case for the rattlesnake, but the scorpion? What possible purpose does it serve? Just looking at it makes most people queasy. What kind of god would make such a thing?"

"The Lord works in mysterious ways. We should try and get some sleep."

"I'm going to need your gun."

Summer got up on an elbow and looked at him. "Why?"

"I'm going to go down there in a couple hours and take care of Vince."

"Really? How are you going to do that?"

"I'm going to sneak up on him, stick the gun in his ear and blow his brains out."

Summer laughed. "Have you ever killed anyone before?"

"There's a first time for everything."

"Are you serious?"

"Of course I'm serious."

Summer turned away and rustled around in her backpack. She handed the tiny pistol to Beadles. It didn't even feel like a real gun, it was so light. "It's got a really hard loading mechanism but if you push this button the barrel pops open." She did so. "And you can load a cartridge directly into the firing chamber. After that it works just like any other automatic."

She handed the gun to Beadles who ratcheted one into the chamber, dropped the magazine, and ratcheted the cartridge out. "Got it."

"You sure you're up for this?"

"Do I have a choice?"

Summer sighed and laid down. "Try to get some sleep."

Gradually her breathing relaxed and she slept. But Beadles could not sleep. He was entirely focused on the task at hand. In a way he was pleased. Vince had left him no choice but to prove himself as a man. Most things in life came easy—his athletic prowess, women, the climb up academia. He didn't kid himself that he was special—no more than hundreds of thousands of other young men fortunate enough to be born into wealthy, white nuclear families. It was better to be lucky than good.

He would move as silently as the scorpion. He would catch the thug asleep and blow his brains out. They would avail themselves of Vince's largesse and when they had the proof he needed they would drive out in Vince's Hummer.

Beadles checked his watch. It was only eleven-thirty. He tried to sleep but it was no use. This was the place where his storylines and ambition converged. This was the nexus of all his ley lines. Shipapu. He reached into his pocket and withdrew the gold medallion, easily visible in the bright star light. He ran his finger over the embossed snakes. It might as well become his family crest. If he survived he would make it so.

A healthy fear prevented him from sleeping. He lay on his back and feasted on the galaxy of stars, spotting familiar constellations, wondering about those tiny stars that lay at the very edge of his sight. There must have been a million.

He thought about good things. The rewards, the book, the TV show, wealth, women. He told himself not to count his chickens. Beneath it all beat the steady pulse of healthy fear at what he had to do.

The hours dragged by like a garbage truck. Finally it was three a.m., The Witching Hour. The hour which studies showed most people were most deeply asleep. Careful not to disturb Summer, Beadles rose and headed for the rim.

CHAPTER SIXTY-FIVE

AT THE HOP

The chimney was black as pitch. Not even the half moon and a million stars penetrated its serpentine path. Wearing a hooded sweatshirt with the hood up Beadles shivered in the desert night. It was in the low fifties. He gripped his tiny halogen flashlight between his teeth and carefully lowered himself, sliding his feet along the rims from catch to catch. He turned the flashlight off as soon as he was confident that he could feel his way down. There were enough kinks in the tube for him to brace himself and rest from time to time. His eyes adjusted and he could make out the general contours.

Any snakes still in the tube would be asleep or sluggish. He'd brought the snakebite kit just in case. He didn't think about the scorpions. He didn't know whether they were diurnal or not.

He thought instead about the book deal, the tour, the fame, the fortune.

He would sue Betty for custody of Lars and he would win. She'd only emasculate the poor bastard like she'd tried to do to him.

Concentrate, you moron. He paused halfway down and realized he was only using the top third of his lungs, wheezing and panting like a Chihuahua. He got his breathing under control and listened. The desert was eerily silent. No crickets, no chirping birds, no gurgle of stream. If anything was moving out there, it was soundless.

He lowered himself the last twenty feet with the delicacy of a diamond cutter, landing silently on the rock. He waited and listened. Keeping his back to the rock he edged out of the chimney clockwise beneath the natural arch, staying in shadow cast by a series of tooth-like boulders. Within five minutes he came in sight of the Humvee which gleamed in starlight like some chitinous insect. Beadles froze, eyes trying to penetrate the opaque windshield. Useless. But the passenger side window was wide open. If he moved away from the butte he would at least be able to see if someone were sitting in the driver's seat.

To do that he would have to give up the safety of the rocks. He would stand out like a lead soldier on a paper plate.

Beadles pulled the pistol from his pocket. Stupid! There was no shell in the chamber. If he jacked one in the sound would carry like a cannon shot. Then he remembered the tilt-up feature. As silently as possible he released the magazine. It was tiny. The bullets were the size of pencil erasers. He squeezed one out, released the barrel and pushed the cartridge into the chamber. He slid the magazine back into place muffling the click with his body. He thumbed back the hammer.

Good to go.

Stealthy as a ninja, he edged out from the rock radially until he stood twenty feet from the vehicle, the stars casting his shadow to the east. Gun gripped in both hands he zeroed in on the Hummer.

Someone sat behind the wheel. In a second he could make out the cowboy hat.

Was he awake? A sleeping man made sounds. Was Vince wide awake waiting for him with a cannon in his lap?

Beadles stared. The figure was motionless. Beadles considered rushing the vehicle and simply emptying the automatic. But wait. What if it were a ruse? What if it was just a pile of sleeping bags and clothes with a hat on it? If so, hadn't it already served its purpose? Was Vince standing behind him chuckling?

Beadles turned around. No one. He scanned the rocks for movement.

He turned back to the Hummer. He felt like part of a museum diorama. The butte, the man, the car. He'd helped set them up.

He walked toward the vehicle aware of his shadow keeping pace. Ten feet from the window he stopped again. It couldn't be Vince. Whatever sat behind the wheel had a grotesquely swollen head that had snapped the hat band. Beadles walked around the back of the car and came up on the driver's side. He shone his flashlight on the thing behind the wheel.

It was a carbuncle of cancerous flesh. Orange like a misshapen pumpkin, more pig than man with mounds of swollen tissue surrounding the eyes. An eye bulged from its socket like a soft-boiled egg. Beadles felt his gorge rebel, turned, bent over with his hands on his knees and breathed rapidly. He stood and inhaled deeply letting it out in a controlled stream through his nose over and over until he had himself under control.

Gun in hand he grasped the door handle and pulled it open.

Beadles jerked back shouting as dozens of scorpions spilled from the open door, a river of pale shining poison. Scorpions leaped from the seat and the floor as Beadles ran shrieking, waving his arms wildly.

Twenty feet away he stopped. He looked. There were no scorpions on him. He watched the flow slow to a trickle as the scorpions fled west. West. Away from the butte.

He shook like a paint mixer. The heebies left him sweating and exhausted. Gun in hand he approached the Humvee. He shined his light on the thing behind the wheel. It had blown up to nearly twice size. Moist red spots covered the things face, arms and hands. Everyplace the scorpions could reach. Beadles didn't doubt that if he were to remove Vince's clothes his entire body would be covered in stings.

Beadles played his flashlight across the front seat. A .45 automatic lay on the passenger's seat next to a loaded clip. He shined his flashlight through the open rear passenger window.

Next to a pile of gear lay a misshapen human skull.

CHAPTER SIXTY-SIX

THE SNAKE

The skull seemed preternaturally long with an enormous dome and fang-like incisors. Patches of sand clung to it between the teeth on the lower jaw. The Indians considered it sacrilege to disturb a grave, even one dug by conquerors.

Beadles didn't know if it was the skull beneath the wagon wheel but he thought it was. What else could it be? Vince had followed their tracks closely, probably dug it up and tossed it in the back seat for his "collector's market."

A priceless curse.

Vince's death was beyond abnormal. It was freakish. Scorpions did not attack en masse. They were not hive animals and too elemental to train. At least a hundred scorpions had poured from the Hummer. How had they gotten in? Leaped through the open windows? Could scorpions leap that far?

Did they come up through the floorboards?

It defied nature.

Beadles opened the rear passenger door behind the driver and leaped back. Nothing came out. The interior was as still as the desert.

Beadles released the rear hatch via a lever next to the driver. He pulled out a loaded backpack. He opened the front passenger door and took the .45 and its clip. It already had one in the butt. Finally, he helped himself to full canteens that lay in the passenger foot well and shut the doors.

He looked at the skull. The skull grinned back.

He recalled a passage from Hampton Sides' study of Manifest Destiny, *Blood and Thunder*. Speaking of the Navajo, "But the ghosts of the dead were devilish enough. They were vexing and malicious and unimaginably frightening—and they were everywhere. They could even invade a person's dreams."

"No sir," he said. "Ain't gonna touch it."

He took a long drink and headed toward the pipe. The waning moon illuminated the butte a pale ivory. He mounted the backpack on his chest. Halfway up his muscles screamed and he longed to let go but the thought of that grinning skull and the leaping scorpions urged him on.

Dawn broke as he dragged himself up into the bowl, flopped on his back and lay there panting. He shrugged off the heavy pack and drank deeply from the canteen. He got to his knees, dragging the backpack behind him by the strap and trudged wearily back to the camp where Summer lay on her back, one arm across her forehead, sawing away.

He flopped down on the rocks and dug the pistol out of his back. Must have weighed a pound. Like most members of academia he'd always considered guns vulgar and faintly louche, and had gone along with all gun control measures. He didn't hate gun owners or wish them ill. He didn't have any guns. Like most people he knew he couldn't visualize a scenario in which he would ever need one.

And here they were. The gun felt heavy and reassuring in his grasp. He wondered if the same principles applied. He ratcheted the shell from? the chamber and Summer woke with a start.

"What?" she barked. She saw him.

"Are you all right? What happened?"

"Vince is dead. The scorpions got him."

Summer put a hand to her throat. "What do you mean?"

He told her. Summer stared with her mouth open. "What if they come up here?" she croaked.

Beadles handed her the canteen. She drank deeply. "I don't know why they would. There's nothing for them up here."

"There's us," she said.

Beadles pulled out the .25 and passed it over. "Here."

Summer looked at the .45. "That's Grampa Ned's gun. Aw shit."

She turned away and covered her face with her hands. Beadles put his arm around her shoulder and held her to him as she sobbed, gasping. The sobs gradually subsided into hiccups. She held her breath and the hiccups went away.

She pointed at the backpack. "What's that?"

"Let's see." Beadles unlatched the straps and pulled out the contents. There was a box of crackers and a summer sausage in its plastic skin. They cut the sausage and had that for breakfast along with the crackers. The backpack contained a black nylon windbreaker, medical kit, maps, socks, and a good Zeiss binocular.

Stuffing the .45 in his belt Beadles stood. "Let's go check out the ruins."

"I'm not going in there," Summer said.

"Well come with me anyway. What else you got to do?"

They crossed over to the ruins which lay in shadow, back to the sun. There was enough ambient light for Beadles to see the length of the ground-floor room, light shining down from the second floor. He was determined to take a closer look at the glyphs. The rock face was cool to the touch but that would soon change. They could already feel the promise of heat where the sun struck.

Again, Beadles boosted himself up and onto the second floor, scanning all around for snakes. It was still cool in the rocks and whatever snakes remained would be sluggish. Or so he hoped. He watched for a long time.

"Are you all right?" Summer called from below.

Beadles went to the vertical window, barely large enough for him to lean out. "I'm fine. Just looking for snakes."

"Be careful."

Beadles turned his attention to the far side of the room, too dark to see. He shined his flashlight in the corner and there was the damn snake, slowly uncoiling as if wakened by his light.

Beadles drew the pistol, ratcheted a round into the chamber and aimed with both hands. The report caused dust to fall from the ceiling and momentarily deafened him. The snake flew into two pieces splattering gore and ichor on the walls.

"WHAT'S WRONG?" Summer wailed.

Beadles stuck his head out the window. "It's okay. I got the snake."

Still holding the cocked pistol he approached the corner with his flashlight. The snake had been sleeping on a pile of rubble that had filled in the corner. Something dull and silver gleamed. Beadles used his foot to scrape away the rubble revealing an ancient blade embossed in Latin.

CHAPTER SIXTY-SEVEN

GOLD!

Beadles played his light all around the corner. No more snakes. He knelt in the soft dirt and brushed away the rubble. It was a Spanish saber with a two foot blade. Beadles believed it was from Toledo, the source of most Conquistador armor and weapons. The swords were tested by bending them into a full half-circle and attempting to shatter them against a steel helmet. No sword was released that did not meet these tests.

Holding the light in his teeth he played it across the tarnished steel until he read the letters.

Consilio et animis.

By wisdom and courage.

A fat crucifix engraved near the hilt.

Beneath where the sword lay, a rotting canvas sack. Beadles gripped it and tugged gently. The bag partially emerged before disintegrating in his hand spilling a pile of yellow ingots at his knees. They were the size of quarters, each with a turquoise in the center surrounded by radiating lines. Childish glee rose in his gullet. Every treasure hunter's dream—the end of the rainbow. Beadles picked one up and examined it beneath the flashlight. Was it possible the Azuma had developed a form of currency? It flew in the face of all accepted knowledge. It was so un-Indian! If it were true it would only add luster to his discovery. Beadles counted the coins. There were thirty-two of them and they were heavy.

Beadles had lied about the gold to entice Ninja. His lie had become the truth.

"Hey, Beadles!" Summer called anxiously from outside. "What's going on?"

Grinning, Beadles went to the window and tossed a coin at Summer's feet. She picked it up.

"Oh, my God," she said. "OH MY GOD!"

"There's a lot more where that came from!"

"I'm coming up!"

Summer entered the west-facing door.

"Over here," Beadles called through the skylight.

Summer stood beneath him. "How did you get up there?"

"I jumped."

"Well look out. Here I come."

Summer easily leaped up and caught the rim of the circular hole. Beadles leaned down and helped her up with a grip on her arm. He pointed to the corner with the saber. Summer knelt in the dirt and ran doubloons through her fingers laughing, a sound like hummingbirds hiccupping.

"We're rich!" she declared.

"Not so fast. The law says these belong to the state. It's possible they'll let us keep one or two as finders' fees, but the real money will come when we tell our story."

My story, he thought. Summer was just along for the ride. Sure he liked her. Given enough time it might grow into something more. But right now he was on a mission and it didn't include Summer.

"They won't miss a couple. They don't know what we found. I'll go get that backpack."

"Please leave it where it is, Summer. The entire site has to be preserved exactly as we found it."

"Says who?"

"That's the way we do things. And it's the law."

Summer frowned. "How are we going to make money again?"

"Books. Television appearances. Lectures."

She stared uncomprehending.

"Reality show."

Her entire face brightened.

"Look. Take one. Put it in your pocket. Don't tell anybody about it, okay?"

Summer rubbed the gold coin on her jeans and slipped it into her pocket.

"Come on," Beadles said. "We need to eat."

Summer hung from the lip of the hole and dropped two feet to the floor. Beadles followed. They walked back to their makeshift camp and found two Canadian geese paddling in the brackish water.

"Where in hell did they come from?" Beadles said. The geese were far off the beaten path.

Summer drew her little pistol. "Dinner."

Beadles said nothing as Summer knelt and aimed with both hands. She squeezed the trigger and drilled one goose through the neck. The other exploded in a paroxysm of wild honking, flapping its wings, only taking to the air when Summer waded into the pond after its mate.

Beadles felt bad. Geese mated for life. Another stone on his karma. He thought of the albatross from *The Rhyme of the Ancient Mariner*.

Summer expertly cleaned the goose, tossing the feathers and entrails over the edge. She rigged a fire from dead cottonwood limbs and spiked the goose on a sharpened stick. The goose sizzled on the stick, fat dropping into the fire with a crackle.

Summer turned the stick from time to time to cook it all the way through. It took over an hour. She cut it up with a hunting knife and served it to Beadles on a flat rock.

Beadles had never tasted anything so delicious in his life. They wiped themselves off with cottonwood leaves. Summer picked up the binoculars.

"I'm gonna take a look."

Beadles sat cross-legged by the fire and wrote in his notepad, detailing the morning's events. Later, he would go back and photograph what he'd found with the western sun shining straight in through the windows. He looked at his watch. It was almost noon.

Beadles stretched out in the shade of the cottonwoods noting that the sun was near its zenith and the only shade came straight down. He drifted. He dreamed he was on the desert, flat and hot as a chopper's straight pipes. Unable to see because of the glare of the sun when a stark shadow fell across his path. Mind-numbing fear seized his lizard brain, a mouse before an owl. He dared not lift his gaze to see what cast that terrible shadow. Acid ate his guts.

"BEADLES!" Summer cried.

He woke up with a start. She ran to him wild-eyed and grabbed his arm so hard it hurt.

"Please, you've got to come. You've got to see this."

"What?"

"You've got to see it."

She leaped up and ran toward the western rim.

CHAPTER SIXTY-EIGHT

GHOST WHO WALKS IN THE SUN

When he got to the rim Summer was already hunkered down behind one of the tooth-shaped rocks, balancing the binocs via her elbows. Beadles stared west into the blazing heat trying to discern what it was she saw. He thought he saw a flicker of motion but he couldn't be sure. It could be distortion rising from the desert floor.

"What?" he demanded.

She handed him the binoculars and pointed. "There."

It took him a minute to adjust the lenses and another to sweep them left to right across the barren landscape. He swept by a quavering parentheses. He swept back. He zeroed in. He couldn't believe his eyes.

There was a man out there walking toward the butte. He had to be at least five miles away. As Beadles zeroed in he saw that the man was tall with long hair, bone-thin, wearing only a loin cloth. No equipment. No water bottles. Just walking.

An iron burr enmeshed itself in his guts.

Maybe it just wants its skull back! He giggled.

"What is it?" Summer demanded.

"I don't know," Beadles said, afraid to speak his mind. He really didn't know. He was an anthropologist, a scientist trained in rational inquiry. There was no room in his portfolio for ghosts, demons, bugaboos and things that went bump in the night. The unreality of the landscape, so different from his regular habitat, gave rise to craziness. Beadles understood why many early pioneers went insane traveling through the vast, desolate landscape, terrified of unseen eyes and Indian attacks.

"It's him!" Summer said with a note of desperation and hopelessness.

"Don't be absurd. It's just some lunatic tripping in the desert. We'll probably have to go out there and rescue him when he collapses."

"Why isn't he carrying anything?" Summer said. "No hat, no water, no guns! What is he doing there?"

"Chill!" Beadles barked, irritated. She mirrored his misgivings and it made him mad. At himself, her, Liggett, Betty, Ninja, the press, the whole damned world.

It wasn't in the script!

Seriously. It had to be some lunatic. In fucking broad daylight. Maybe it was a hallucination. He turned on Summer.

"What did you do with those acid tabs?" he hissed.

Summer backed up, shocked. "Nothing! I still have them. Why?"

"You didn't put them in the drinking water? In the pond?"

Summer half guffawed in disbelief. "Come on! I would never do that!"

"How do I know you're not lying?"

"Because I love you!" she said, shocked.

Beadles tried to stop the words from coming out. "Love me?! We've only known each other for two days!"

Summer crossed her arms and cried. He never could tolerate a woman crying.

"I'm sorry!" He tried to take her in his arms but she twisted away and ran off.

"Go fuck yourself!"

Beadles panted, took a drink from the bottle clipped to his belt. Give her a little time to calm down. Give them both time. Surely she could see the absurdity in her declaration. What really troubled him was the weight. He wasn't ready for another serious relationship. Was it wrong to deny unconditional love?

Or was it? She could be an awfully good liar. Vince had said so. Summer didn't come straight from the convent. She'd been a stripper and a hooker. Everybody lied. Especially hookers.

But what did she have to gain from such a declaration? His trust? For what?

The gold, dummy.

The big score.

If they lived.

He was afraid to look. A ferret clawed at his heart. And yet he must. He looked up. The figure was still miles away, a tiny wavering line in the sand. The ground at its feet had darkened and seemed to ripple forward like time lapse creeping fungus. The figure strode at the head of a wavering darkish blob that spread in a delta behind him. With each step the blob seemed to grow.

Beadles brought the binocs to his eyes. For a minute he didn't understand. This writhing, rippling thing on the ground. He adjusted the focus.

"God, Jesus God," he said as the sun drilled into his skull.

Scorpions. Rattlesnakes. They followed the grim man like children after the Pied Piper.

Beadles stared, grinding his teeth. They would be at the butte in an hour. Beadles recalled seeing two gas canisters in the back of the Hummer. They had to prepare. He needed Summer.

He ran after her.

Summer sat cross-legged by the pond weeping. Beadles knelt next to her and put his arm around her.

"I'm sorry. I didn't know what to say. I need your help. They're coming here. We have to get down to Vince's car and back up again before they arrive."

"Who?" Summer said. "Who is coming here?"

"That thing and thousands of scorpions and rattlesnakes."

Summer stiffened into a leaf spring. "What?"

"Whatever it is, it commands the scorpions and rattlesnakes. That's how it got Vince in the middle of the night. It sent scorpions. We've got to get the two cans of gas in Vince's car to stop them from crawling up here."

CHAPTER SIXTY-NINE

THE FIRST ASSAULT

They shot the chute accompanied by rockslides and clouds of dust. Beadles' hands were raw from applying the brakes. From the ground they couldn't see the creature, hidden behind waves of diffraction.

They approached the Hummer, shadows clinging to their feet like ink blots.

"Don't look in the front seat," Beadles said.

Summer ignored him. She gazed over the sill and stared at the grotesquerie behind the wheel, a buffet for insects and snakes. A straw-colored centipede crawled out of Vince's open mouth. Summer turned away.

Beadles opened the tailgate and threw everything within reach on the ground. There were two five gallon gas canisters. Beadles also found a box of .45 cartridges and emptied the contents into his pockets. He cut up a rope for straps for the gas tanks. They slung the tanks across their backs and returned to the chimney.

It was almost noon.

The climb was much harder this time. The gas cans caught on rocks and banged against Beadles' ribs. The smell gave him a headache. Summer was above him climbing like a rhesus monkey. By the time she reached the top he was only halfway up, breathing in wheezing gasps. He stopped to catch his breath, balanced precariously on two jutting rocks. He twisted the can around so it hung on his chest.

"Hurry!" Summer called down the chimney.

Groaning Beadles resumed the climb. His arms screamed with pain. Sweat streamed into his eyes. Tiny insects hovered around his eyes and mouth. Each step was a titanic effort. One after the other. At last he heaved himself up into the bubble, Summer holding his arm. He unstrapped the gas tank and sat gasping. Summer handed him a bottled water. He twisted off the cap and drained it in nine gulps.

They stood, climbed out of the bubble. Beadles put his gas can next to the other on the flat next to the bubble. "If they come, they'll come this way. We'll pour gas down the tube and light it."

He headed back to the lookout perch, Summer right behind.

"What if there's another way up? What if they just climb right up the sides?"

"I don't know. I don't think they will. We went all the way around. There's no other way up." He put his hand on the gun butt. What if he shot that thing through the head?

Maybe it just wanted its skull. He retrained the binocs.

The glare coming off the desert floor was almost too much. The thing had a head surrounded by long, stringy flaxen-colored hair. Its face remained in shadow beneath the zenith sun. The weird pulsating wave followed, scorpions leaping like spawning salmon. The ground writhed and pulsed like an acid flashback.

They watched in dread silence. Five hundred yards. Three hundred. One hundred. The dark wave rippled and gleamed, a roiling sea of poison. The Giacometti-like creature advanced, thin, dark, tensile, its head tilted slightly forward so that its face remained in shadow. Fifty yards from the base of the butte it stopped, put its hand over its eyes and looked up. Beadles watched through the binoculars.

They stared at one another for ten seconds. Ten seconds in which neither Beadles nor Summer drew breath. The longest ten seconds of their lives.

The creature extended an insect-like arm and its venomous army surged forward. But not in a blind rush. They did not surround the butte and mindlessly attempt to scale it. They headed for the chimney.

"Let's go!" Beadles yelled racing back to where they'd left the gasoline. Timing was everything. At this height the gas would mostly evaporate by the time it reached the bottom. They only had ten gallons. They needed to wait until the snapping, clacking, clicking wave of vermin surged to within twenty feet of the top. He felt in his pocket. He still had matches from The Last Chance.

He grabbed a can, loosened the lid and got on his knees. Sound rose from the chimney— a filthy white noise like a hornet's nest. Chittering and slithering. It was something he could never unhear. It seared itself into his brain, an aural petroglyph on the inside of his skull.

Summer crouched opposite him on the bubble's rim, six feet away gripping a gas can, her lovely gray eyes in a warrior's squint.

"Come over here and take the can when I'm ready," Beadles said.

Summer came around and crouched next to him. Beadles removed the cap and handed it to her.

The hissing skittering sound grew louder, amplified by the tube. The soundtrack of hell. It filled the sky, that awful sound.

Beadles sloshed a gallon into the tube a split second before the first wave of vermin bubbled up. Beadles shoved the can at Summer, picked up the matches, lit the book and tossed.

The tube erupted with a satisfying whump, shoving Beadles and Summer back. Beadles' eyebrows crackled. He scrambled on his ass up and out of the bubble. He watched in astonishment as burning insect parts rose like soot from a chimney and wafted across the plateau. The wind shifted and the noxious black grit blew on them leaving a greasy, acidic deposit.

He half ran, half-stumbled back to his previous perch and grabbed the binocs. He looked down. The figure watched stoically arms at its sides. It raised an arm and made a circling motion. The tide of vermin receded, pouring around the gaunt man.

Beadles waited. Would the thing go after its skull? Was it even its skull? And if that was its skull in the back seat, what was that on its shoulders? Summer peered down next to him, tugging her hat down low.

"Is he leaving?" she whispered.

The creature turned and walked into the sun.

CHAPTER SEVENTY

RAIDING THE DEAD

They watched until it disappeared in the quavering heat.

"Oh God!" Summer cried. "What if it comes back?"

"Not today. Maybe we can drive out of here."

If we can dislodge that thing behind the wheel.

"What makes you so sure it won't come back?" Summer whined. It was an unattractive sound.

"It only appears in the sun! Its strength peaks at mid-day. It was killed in the sun and can only walk in the sun."

Summer slumped in despair. Beadles put his arm around her.

"Come on. If we move right now we can be back in Gap by sundown."

"How?" she wailed.

"Vince got down here. We can find our way back. I'll use the GPS."

"What if we go by it?"

"I don't know! How's it going to stop a two ton vehicle going sixty mph?"

Hurriedly they gathered their things, the guns, the canteens, the binoculars, packed them up and descended the chimney. A ten foot section near the top was covered with a greasy black soot which clung to their hands, feet and clothes. It had an acrid, acidic smell. They reached the desert floor shortly before one and headed for the Humvee.

Beadles opened the driver's door. The sack of putrescent flesh wedged behind the wheel looked immovable. Beadles got in the front passenger seat, closed the door, braced his back against it and tried to shove Vince out with his feet. The thing bulged with his efforts releasing a stench from hell's sewer. Drawing his feet back he lashed out, shoving with all his might. A yellow eye popped loose and dribbled down Vince's shirt. The thing budged. It had the consistency of a beanbag chair.

Struggling and sweating, Beadles strained with all his might, both feet up against the corpse's thigh, sweat streaming down into his eyes. Grunting, he ejected the horrendous corpse. It fell with a dull whump releasing a blast of ordure. Beadles used a cloth from the back seat to wipe a disturbing brackish fluid from the driver's seat. He tossed it, grabbed a towel and rubbed some more. Finally, when the seat was bone dry, he slid across. The key was in the ignition. He turned it.

No response. No lights came on, no dials budged. The electricals were dead. He reached down and found the hood release. It let go with a thunk. He got out the passenger door and opened the hood. The wiring was disconnected and stripped. Insects and snakes had chewed through everything. An electrocuted rattler hung from the battery, a streak of burnt black flesh running down its belly. The stench was unbearable. Beadles slammed the hood in disgust.

"We're fucked!" Summer said.

Beadles fell into a sinkhole of despair. But he was the man. He was the scientist. It was up to him to take charge and find a way out of this mess. There was no way they were walking out. Not today. They had to retreat and survive another day.

"We're going back up," he said.

"What's the point? We're going to die sooner or later."

"No we're not! I've got an idea. I'll come back down here tonight and torch the vehicle. With any luck someone will see the fire and investigate. Now let's go through the vehicle and salvage anything usable."

He went around to the back, both of them avoiding the mound of swollen flesh on the ground. It had burst its seams, spilling out of shirt and pants like some morbid fungus.

They took Vince's sleeping bag, knife, matches, an NDuR water purification system, a tiny camp stove with a propane cylinder, dehydrated food, trail mix, beef jerky, a box of Snickers bars. Beadles found an old copy of *Western and Eastern Treasures* dated July of the previous year and a metal detector. With a start he realized the date.

It was June 20.

Tomorrow was the summer solstice—the longest day of the year.

When the creature's power would peak.

He kept this fact to himself.

Muscles screaming in protest, burdened with straps that cut into his seared flesh, he followed Summer up the chute. Acid sweat stung his eyes. His mouth was as dry as the Sahara. The pain of reaching for the next handhold left him gasping. He had pushed himself too far but there was no place to stop, no time to rest. He came to the blackened throat. A slick patina of arachnid and snake parts clung to the rock, little flecks of snakeskin and bristle-like mandibles. His foot slipped and for a blind instant he was caught in a terrifying nanosecond of freefall. He struggled to find footing and slipped several times, each time saving himself at the last minute, finding purchase in one of the hand-hewn slots. An inert stinger penetrated his thumb, striking out in death. He strained every muscle wedging himself in place, unable to stop the sweat from streaming into his eyes. He clawed upward like a scorpion.

Summer reached down to help him with the final step.

Beadles staggered to the pond and put the water purification filter to work. It sucked water with a hand pump and passed it through a series of filters. Of course to be certain there were no harmful bacteria they would still have to boil it. He collapsed by the pond and fugued. When he sat up he had a splitting headache. Summer watched him with a crease of concern.

"Are you all right?"

"I think so," he croaked. "Can you get a fire going and boil this water?"

"Sure. What are you going to do?"

"I'm going to photograph what we found."

"How can you even think of that right now?"

"What else am I supposed to do?" he snapped. In a softer tone, "Don't worry. It's not coming back today. We're safe until tomorrow."

He set off toward the ruins. Summer watched him dully.

CHAPTER SEVENTY-ONE

A VISITOR

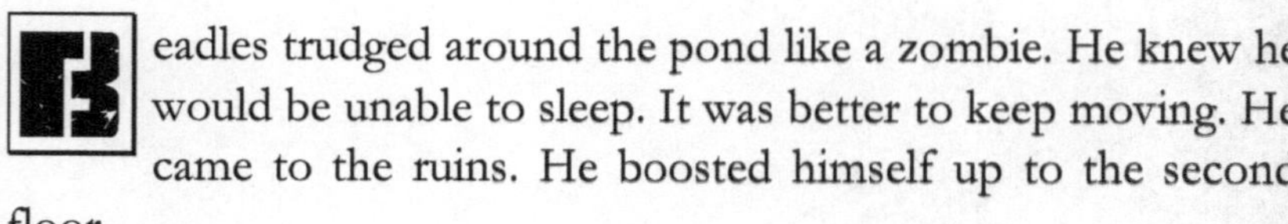

eadles trudged around the pond like a zombie. He knew he would be unable to sleep. It was better to keep moving. He came to the ruins. He boosted himself up to the second floor.

The sun slanted through the slots allowing enough light to photograph the petroglyphs and the pile of gold in the corner. Beadles sat on the hard-packed earth his back to the wall. He was enervated. He didn't look forward to the evening's climb but it had to be done if they had any chance of getting out of there.

It might make more sense to build a fire on top of the butte. It could be seen further. But there wasn't much left in the way of fuel. They'd used most of the dead wood to cook and the gasoline was for warding off the snakes and scorpions.

The Hummer, on the other hand, still contained fuel in the tank. Even if it was only fumes it would cause the car to explode. Now that they had a water source they could last for days. And with each passing day the creature's power waned.

Or so Beadles hoped.

He dozed off. When he woke the sun was slanting into the cliff dwelling almost horizontally. He felt old as if the walls' age had rubbed off on him. Or maybe it had sucked the youth out of him. He sloshed a little water on his face, dropped from the manhole in the floor and left the cliff-dwelling. The sun hung over the purple western mountains. It was past six.

The smell of marijuana drifted through the air. Summer lounged on the sleeping bag by the pond smoking a joint and wearing nothing but panties and an abbreviated T. Beadles was so exhausted and scared he couldn't summon a grain of lust. His mind took in her lithe body, the mane of black hair, the parted lips and duly registered her desirability. The flesh was inert.

Compulsion pulled him to the western brink where he once more put binoculars to eyes and scanned the horizon. All clear. Not a creature was stirring, not even a mouse.

He looked down. He wished he hadn't. The mound of putrescent flesh that had once been Vince roiled and throbbed with predators. A coyote growled as it worried off a hand. Six turkey buzzards hopped around the corpse, taking turns darting forward tearing off gibbets. The gray/blue skin pulsated with insects. An ant column so thick Beadles could see it without binoculars marched back and forth between butte and body.

Party time in the desert.

Beadles wanted to drop five gallons of gas on the obscenity and light it. The predators worked so fast the body would be gone in a day or two. Not fast enough. He caught a whiff of putrescence. Or was it his imagination?

He pulled the pistol, dropped the clip, checked the action. Ten in the clip. Twenty-two in his pockets, their weight like ballast in a high sea. Two to the head ought to stop that thing.

Unless it didn't.

Well there it was. The once proud scientist ceding ground to the heebie jeebies beneath the mambo sun. How low he had fallen.

All right. What if it were a ghost? And if it was a ghost, what if that was its skull sitting in the back seat? Obviously two to the head would accomplish nothing. Did the creature possess sinew and muscle, the ability to move things? Or was it insubstantial, evanescent, a mere image? Whatever it was, the things it controlled were all too real as the damaged Humvee and blackened chimney proved.

Scorpions and snakes were nocturnal. The only reason they didn't attack at night was because the thing did not exist at night. It gave him a throbbing headache.

He had to get out of the sun.

Beadles returned to the pond and sat in the shade, his bare feet in the brackish water, back against a cottonwood. He drifted. Summer's shriek cracked the air. Blinking and disoriented he watched uncomprehending as she rushed to his side and physically dragged his feet out of the pond.

"Shoot it!" she spat pointing. "Shoot it!"

Beadles scrambled to his feet and drew the pistol. He followed her finger to the undulating shape gliding through the water. Air coming in high hot gasps he jacked a shell into the chamber and fired four shots as fast as he could pull the trigger, blowing the sidewinder out of the water.

How did it get there? Were there more? A jackhammer went crazy in his head. He used his knuckles to dig into his temples.

"Do you have any ibuprofen?" he croaked.

"Yes!" Summer leaped toward her backpack. Beadles watched swirls of red describe arabesques in the brackish water. He compulsively checked all the canteens and water bottles. At least they'd laid in a supply. Enough to get them through the night. If they were unable to attract salvation within twenty-four hours at least he had the pistol.

Beadles swallowed three ibuprofen and tried to forget the images seared into his skull. He looked up. Turkey buzzards circled overhead. His headache pulsed like a quasar. He lay down in the shade drifting in and out of a shallow sleep, the kind where he knew he was asleep and struggled to wake like a surfacing whale trying to break the surface.

Several times, through sheer force of will, he woke himself, looked around, realized his circumstances and drifted off again. He thought about writing something for Lars in case he didn't make it. The more he thought about it the more certain he was it was the right thing to do. He hauled out his little spiral notepad.

What could he say? I'm sorry, Son? Sorry that your mother and I split and left you without a father? That your father was a great man who failed? That your father was a thief who gambled everything on a dream?

What if they died and no one ever learned what became of them, or what they'd discovered? Would the shifting sands hide the Humvee and their bodies turn to mummies beneath the baking sun, only to be discovered decades hence like the survivors of the *Lady be Good?*

With a yelp of despair he tossed the notebook aside. He'd need a rag to lower into the Hummer's gas tank. He would tear up one of the shirts Vince had left in the back. Matches, check. Pistol, check. Water, check. Time passed slower than a midtown train. The sun settled in the west like a geriatric lowering himself into a hot bath. It was past nine when dusk spread across the skies.

The temperature dropped. Beadles put on a Dethrone hoodie he'd salvaged from the Hummer. Summer walked with him to the top of the tube.

"Be careful," she said, hugging him. "I love you."

"I love you, too," Beadles said and lowered himself into the pipe.

CHAPTER SEVENTY-TWO

BONFIRE

s Beadles cautiously extended his foot he found a protrusion and shifted his weight. Suddenly he was in freefall, heart jammed in his throat like a potato in an exhaust pipe. It was the tumble into the canyon all over again. He yelped. In blind panic his hands flew out and found a juniper root extending from a crack in the stone and he grabbed hold as the root laid a bloody groove through his palm. He hung there for long seconds panting, fighting vertigo, savoring the pain in his hand for its focus.

"Are you all right?" Summer whispered.

"I'm good," he said, willing himself to calm down. Rivets of sweat popped on his forehead despite the chill. Down he went muscles shrieking. He used to get weekly massages at the University Club. Their memory was almost too painful to contemplate.

He hit the desert floor, crawled out between the slabs and headed for the Hummer. It was chilly. He put the hood up. Nocturnals mobbed Vince's corpse like freelancers at an open bar.

Coyote, buzzard, snakes and lizards darted and flowed in an endless game of musical chairs. A coyote snarled. A squall of growling before sound returned to the snap of gristle.

Beadles walked around the back of the vehicle and beheld Vince's remains in the moonlight. A purple pile of meat. Something half-glimpsed in a slaughter yard. The eyes, lips, and ears were gone, lupine teeth exposed. Three coyotes and five buzzards took turns hopping in like some macabre game of Maypole. The coyotes looked at Beadles, bared their teeth and went back to ripping. The gas cap was on the driver's side of the vehicle. Beadles had no choice but to stand within six feet of the swarming corpse. The tailgate was still open. Beadles found a dirty T-shirt, used his knife to rip it into strips which he tied together braided into a three foot lanyard as he'd been taught in the Boy Scouts.

He glanced in the rear seat. There sat the skull. Should he remove the skull as a courtesy? If the skull burned up did the thing go away? Dr. Samuel George Morton published a book in 1839 called *Crania Americana* in which he argued that the shape of Indian skulls proved they were intellectually inferior. He amassed a huge collection in Washington which were eventually redistributed to the tribes along with letters of apology.

Beadles returned to the tailgate and found a discarded T-shirt. With the shirt wrapped around his hand he reached in through the open rear window, grabbed the skull by its eyeholes and removed it. He walked toward the butte, looked around, found a shallow depression hidden by a rock against the base and left the skull there wrapped in the shirt. He returned to the vehicle.

Holding the lanyard in one hand and the pistol in the other, Beadles approached the driver's door where lay the gas release lever. The coyotes snarled and grudgingly gave ground, eyes watching with yellow malice. He leaned over and popped the panel. He unscrewed the cap and tossed it to the ground. He lowered the lanyard all the way into the tank, waited for it to soak up fuel, pulled it all the way out and lowered it in again from the opposite direction. The fuse was now soaked with gasoline. His headache came screaming back.

Stooping, Beadles lit the end of the fuse with a match, turned and ran into the desert expecting to be slammed in the back any second. He was still running when he heard a dull whump and concussion from the explosion knocked him flat on his face. He barely got his hands out in front of him. A wave of heat rolled over him. Beadles rolled over, got up on his elbows and looked. A fireball sent a column of flame twenty feet in the air. A series of repercussions followed like the last kernels of popcorn in the microwave—ammo left in the car.

Beadles laughed like a kid on Christmas morning. The fire surpassed his expectations. On a clear night such as this surely somebody would see it. Surely a passing plane or persons elevated above the desert floor would report this conflagration to the authorities. It was only a matter of time! Maybe even tomorrow.

They could easily send a plane out from Flagstaff or National Park HQ. He and Summer could do something to attract attention atop the butte—use rocks to spell out an SOS. Use the gold to catch the sun!

Beadles felt the heat as he circled the burning wreck twenty yards out. The flickering flames cast his shadow on the sand. He returned to the chimney and climbed, arms spasming. He paused to wedge himself against protuberances and let the pain subside. At least he was free from the burden of the gas cans. It took him twenty minutes to reach the bowl. Summer waited to pull him up.

She handed him a thermos. "Here," she said. "I made some hot cocoa for you."

Beadles took the thermos gratefully, unscrewed the cap and drank from the bottle. He had never tasted anything so delicious in his life. He stumbled back to their camp. Summer had moved it farther from the pond because of the snake. They hadn't seen any snakes in the pond since then but you never knew.

Exhausted from tension and the climb Beadles collapsed on the sleeping bag. Summer knelt and covered him with the hooded sweatshirt. "You try to sleep, honey. I'm going to watch the fire for awhile."

Beadles crashed like the Twin Towers. Dreaming. *The New York Times* reviewed his book, *The Azuma.* "An astonishing journey of discovery that adds immeasurably to our understanding of Native Americans," said in the reverent tones of NPR. All his friends were there. Betty, Liggett, and Tommy Lee Jones. Ninja said that he had written the review, hacked the NYT website and inserted it. Everyone was in the desert. The glare made vision difficult. Gradually they slipped away one by one until only Beadles remained.

He looked up. The sky swirled in purple and green paisleys. Acid flashback. Beadles trudged toward a distant tower. The paisleys swirled like a peacock flashing its feathers and disappeared leaving the glaring sun. Hot and bright. Sweat streamed down his face. His mouth was full of rubber. He scooped it out with two fingers. But like the Sorcerer's Apprentice, the rubber filled his mouth faster than he could scoop. It had a chemical taste.

Beadles woke. Sunlight slanted in through the trees. He was hot and damp with sweat. Groaning, he rolled over and looked at his watch. Almost noon.

His heart hammered like a bent piston. He sat up breathing rapidly and shallowly. He had to pee. He was desperately thirsty. He looked around. There was the thermos from last night. He hesitated.

He didn't feel right. It wasn't just a panic attack, although he had that too.

The paisleys were back. The ground swirled.

She'd put something in the drink.

Beadles stumbled to his feet and reached for his gun.

The gun was gone.

He looked around.

"Summer!" he yelled, cursing himself in the same instant. Don't be a fool!

I'm just warning you, one man to another, don't turn your back on her.

Dread poured into his gut like a load of shot. He found a canteen by the fire and drank deeply. He slung it over his shoulder and headed for the western perimeter.

CHAPTER SEVENTY-THREE

THE MOTHER OF ALL DIAMONDBACKS

The binoculars lay on red rock almost too hot to handle. Beadles picked them up and looked toward the distant mountains. Heat rose from the ground in wavering curtains—an optic mist, a diaphanous curtain. Beadles could conjure anything he wanted—the U.S. Cavalry. A thousand dinosaurs. The devil himself.

Nothing.

Beadles realized he had been staring at nothing for five minutes, slowly sweeping the binocs left to right and back again. His head hurt.

Was he tripping? Did she put the acid in his drink?

Beadles saw a ball cap lying on the ground. He put it on pulling the visor low. Where were his sunglasses? He couldn't think. Go back to the camp and look for them?

He felt something slip inside, a fault line. An enormous black word balloon burst from his jaws. He roared at the empty desert, turned and sprayed it on the cliffs. He screamed until his throat was raw and bent over with his hands on his knees, chest heaving.

He straightened up, uncapped the canteen and drank it dry. He leaned over the rock parapet panting. Below lay the black, twisted remains of the Hummer in the center of a carbon stain. Vince was down to twenty pounds of sinew and bones strewn across the landscape.

Beadles raised the binocs again. A vibrating bristle appeared in the shimmering heat. A cannonball of dread dropped in Beadles' gut. For a long time the quavering didn't seem to get bigger or smaller. Just a quavering line on the horizon, so small and insubstantial he wasn't sure he saw it.

His head was a pressure cooker. He had to get some shade. He set the binocs back on the rock and stumbled back toward the trees, the sun lasering through his skull. He sat in the shade rubbing his temples furiously. He rubbed his eyes. It helped a little. He dug through the backpack, found the first aid kit and emptied a couple Ibuprofen into his palm. He reached for a water bottle.

He washed it down. Once, in college, he'd been at a pot party at an old house off-campus, maybe eight people in the room stoned to the gills. Grooving on black lights and the Dead when some hipster in a fucking black beret for chrissake slipped into the room and started slapping palms.

His name was Beako and he was a dealer. Beako opened a big plastic Ziploc filled with hundreds of little pastel pills. "Anyone want some acid?" he said.

A kid named Grover jammed his hand into the bag, grabbed a fistful and swallowed them down with a Coors.

Grover was never the same after that. Years later Beadles learned that he'd died from a drug overdose.

Beadles stared at the brackish pond. The surface roiled and flowed. He leaped to his feet. He realized it was a hallucination. Or was it? He stared at the pond panting, trying to discern the snakes. He'd dropped LSD in college. He knew how it felt. It felt like this. The air filled with sparkles, a snow globe with firecrackers.

He sure could pick 'em.

Water. He needed water. One full canteen left. They'd need more soon. Have to use the filter. What if the pond contained alkali? Alkali had the same effect as acid. But that didn't explain Summer's absence.

He was not going to look for her. He wouldn't give her that satisfaction. Maybe she'd already left—grabbed the gold and as much water as she could carry, shinnied down the chute and headed east. She wouldn't get far. No way could she even carry all that gold plus the water down the chute without slipping and killing herself.

He lifted the binocs. The wire-hanger figure was barely identifiable as a man. Somewhat like a man. It strode at the head of a roiling delta, a tiny frigate with a huge wake. Beadles guessed they were ten miles out. Maybe three hours. They would arrive at noon.

High overhead a plane left a contrail headed toward the west coast.

Water. He needed more water to flush the toxins from his system, help him to think straight. But he couldn't think straight. He was tripping. He returned to the pond and use the NDuR filter. No time to boil. He drank straight from the canteen tasting the alkaline minerals.

Maybe it was the water. Please God let it be the water.

For all his success and good looks, Beadles felt unloved. Certainly Betty hadn't loved him. Maybe she thought she did when they first met but Beadles had known too many women like that. They were in love with being in love but never were. Minds rationalizing like cash registers, gears clicking, always on the lookout for a better deal. Looking to trade up.

Someday I will meet my soul mate and give up smoking.

Beadles wondered who the lucky guy was. Betty wouldn't jump ship without a lifeboat and despite being a self-proclaimed feminist she believed that a woman without a man was a woman without a man.

She would never quit smoking.

Beadles collapsed on his bed of straw. He laughed. He sobbed. If only he hadn't been an only child. If only he hadn't gone to Shimer. If only he'd never learned about the fucking Azuma.

Wiping his face on the discarded sweatshirt, Beadles looked around for a weapon. He seized Vince's Bowie Knife. It had a twelve-inch blade. Fat lot of good it would do him. A longer blade might delay the inevitable.

A longer blade like the Spanish sword. Yes!

He ran across the rising oven of the plateau and entered the ruins, so intent on his task that he forgot the snakes. He leaped up, grabbed the second tier and hauled himself up into the treasure room. He went to the corner and looked down. Ambient light softly illuminated the empty corner.

A buttress broke loose in his chest and crashed into his heart. He had nothing. No gun, no sword, a twelve-inch Bowie knife.

He saw himself struggling with the creature as in a lurid painting on the cover of a Robert E. Howard novel. Something by Joe Jusko. He knelt in the dirt and sifted his hands through the sand.

Whoops. She'd missed one—a tiny gold medallion similar to the one in his pocket. He left it there. What was the point.

Rapid clicking filled the chamber. Beadles turned. The Mother of all Diamondbacks had been asleep against the wall the whole time. Now she was up and shaking her maracas, body thick as a fire hose. It lay in loops like a hangman's rope, obsidian eyes fixed on Beadles' face with primordial hate.

Beadles laughed. Maybe it was Summer. Maybe she was a shape-shifter. Skinwalkers they called them.

"Go on" he sang. "Do it!"

CHAPTER SEVENTY-FOUR

HERE IT COMES AGAIN

The spade-shaped head bobbed, black tongue flickering in and out. It lowered its head, looped back in on itself and slithered away like some obscene earthworm. Beadles watched it leave a series of chevrons in the sand until it reached the hole and slipped over the rim. Beadles felt empty. Light-headed. He grabbed a handful of sand and squeezed tight, feeling the grit dribble through his fingers. He got up, scanning the room for more snakes. Thirsty again. He reached for the canteen strapped to his belt and emptied the lukewarm contents.

Beadles returned to the hole in the floor, got down on his belly and examined the first floor for snakes. Nothing moved. Beadles dropped down, out, cut around the pond and went to his vantage point. The figure was now clearly recognizable as a man— or at least manlike. It glided on boneless legs like Michael Jackson doing the "moon walk." The oily delta at its feet surged forward with every step, sometimes overshooting and drawing back.

Behind the shimmering delta faded into the sand and heat. Were there army ants? Why no flying insects? Where were the South American killer bees, the yellowjackets? Why only things that slithered or skittered?

Beadles trotted to the top of the tube every muscle aching. He felt like an old man. The gas cans were intact. He picked one up. All there. It was going to be a great show, too bad they couldn't do it at night for full effect. Beadles had to time it perfectly. He intended to dump both cans down the tube and catch them when they were about halfway up. This required him to remain on post watching their approach until the last possible minute.

Beyond that he didn't have a plan. That thing might even be boneless. A ghost. Insubstantial. Able to inflict harm only through its venomous minions. It this were true he had only to turn back the onslaught. Did he have enough gas?

"We'll soon find out," he muttered.

Through the glasses the quavering nightmare approached. Its indistinct features made it worse. Beadles dialed in on its enormous hands, out of proportion with the rest of the body. Its segmented fingers ended in stingers. Its feet were outsized too, the toes elongated and pointed down like claws.

Time ticked by. Heat crouched on him like a monkey. He reached into his pocket and applied lip balm. He thought about his past mistakes, the people he'd wronged. All those girls whose hearts he'd broken. Parents and instructors. Even Betty. Especially Betty.

The sun threw death rays. The sun hated him. Ironic because he'd always loved the sun. But not this sun. He'd loved a cooler, more distant and benign sun, not this ball of fury that bore down with the insupportable weight of its heat. He glanced at his watch. Almost noon. Beadles was drifting. He shook himself and looked down. The thing was a hundred yards out striding so smoothly it could have been riding a skateboard. Boneless legs. Snaky arms. An unusually limber tourist out for a stroll.

On it came. Across the fifty. It glided up to the Hummer, twenty yards from the base of the butte.

It stopped and looked in through the charred remains of the tailgate. It walked clockwise around the vehicle to where Vince's bones lay scattered. It stooped on its haunches and examined the bones, picking one up and smelling it.

Beadles dry-swallowed. The thing circumnavigated the vehicle returning to twelve o'clock. It looked up.

Rebar in his gut, Beadles lifted the binocs. For an instant he couldn't focus. He found its face. It was a crude metaphor for a face, something a boy would draw on a bathroom stall. Unfinished and inhuman. Mesmerized, Beadles searched the face for some sign of intelligence. Even from that distance Beadles could read its hostility. It shot death rays. Beadles felt a sick sort of vertigo insert itself needle-like behind one eye.

He was damned if he'd be the first to break it off. His hat kept the sun out of his face while the creature shaded its black sinkholes with a claw. Beadles lost track of time. He fugued unfocused and leaned forward with both forearms on the hot rock. He, the white interloper looking down from the heights, staring at the eidolon of native fury and resentment.

You have no more right to this land than I.

The Navajo came from Siberia around 1000 AD and displaced the Anasazi. The Anasazi likely took the same path a millennium earlier. This is the way it had always been—the more sophisticated civilization displacing the primitive, often in the most brutal manner.

Beadles had nothing to do with it. The thing had no right to hold him accountable. Beadles was the one trying to restore the thankless creature to its proper place in history! The thing ought to *thank* him. His own anger slammed down like a fire door.

He cupped his hands and leaned out. "WHAT DO YOU WANT?!"

There was no motion, no answer. After a ponderous pause its right arm raised as slowly as an RR crossing and pointed at

Beadles. With an abrupt twisting motion, the claw snapped shut and rotated. Its meaning was clear. The creature whirled its gruesome arm over its had and released an ear-splitting yell that struck Beadles like a hurtling truck.

"*KI YI YI YI YI YI!*"

The army of chitin and scales sizzled back like a wave withdrawing from the beach, bunched into a two foot ridge and surged forward, elongating as it raced toward the chimney. A giant's fist wrapped around Beadles' throat. He gasped, hearing his breath scrape like an anchor chain through a steel grommet. Panic attack. He bent over and put his hands on his knees gasping for breath.

Now. It was happening now. *Go to the chimney.* A goony bird in flight, he broke into a stumbling run with a keening whine of anxiety. Part of him hovered overhead looking down, as if he were already dead, seeing himself lurch across the rock and hearing the shameful noise he made. He tripped on a boulder and went down hard, skinning his palms and knees. He got up and it was like running in his dreams, in slo-mo, weak as a crawdad, moving, moving but hardly making progress. On and on. At last he came to the chimney, sliding to his burning knees. He grabbed one of the two canisters and unscrewed the cap. Gas smell gouged him. His stomach clenched and wound up. He would not throw up. He would not. Eyes shut and tearing he turned away from the gas and breathed in and out. In and out. He fought it down. He turned back. His stomach sucker-punched him in the gut.

Beadles bent to the side and vomited a thin gruel of trail mix and yellow bile. He felt better. He leaned over the gas tank and went blotto.

What was he doing here?

An eerie clicking noise issued from the bowl. White noise with the pop of gristle coming at him like something crawling out of the depths of the sewers, rising in the pipe like vomit. Beadles tipped the canister forward and emptied the contents into the pipe sloshing it all around. He leaped for the second canister and did the same. The squeaking and chittering grew louder.

Beadles found his matches, lit several and tossed them into the chamber. FWOOSH. The top of the chimney lit up like the Olympic torch. Beadles staggered to his feet and back, his face flushed from the blast.

Black insect parts rose crackling from the tube like soot from a coal plant. They twisted in the wind and landed on Beadles' face and arms with an itching oily sensation. He frantically brushed them off backing away from the tube.

Flame belched up with a roaring sound sending whole snakes curling into the air performing arabesques. Beadles felt like dancing. He pumped his fist in the air.

"BURN YOU MOTHERFUCKERS!"

He danced and cackled like Walter Huston in *Treasure of the Sierra Madre*. He pumped his fist and did the Harlem Shake. He whooped like a cowboy at a rodeo.

He raced back to the vantage point and picked up the binocs. He looked down. The thing was gone. He felt light-headed. He cackled gleefully with an undertone of madness. He'd burned its army and now it was gone. GONE.

Was that all there was to it?

A sharp pain pierced his shoulder. He turned and beheld the devil's face.

CHAPTER SEVENTY-FIVE

THE DEVIL HIMSELF

It towered over him, its lipless mouth fixed in a zipper grin exposing vulpine fangs. Massive high cheekbones, forehead like a cliff, backhoe chin. It stank of despair and the passing of time. Its skin was sun-cured leather stretched taut over massive bones. Its eyes were yellow slits. Its hair was like corn silk. The hands were the worst.

Each digit was a scorpion's tail. Thumbs the size of cigars tapering into lethal stingers. The hand flickered and seized Beadles by the throat, five needles puncturing his skin injecting him with the poison of hatred and history. Effortlessly it lifted Beadles six inches in the air and studied him as one might study an insect. It exhaled the stench of hecatomb.

Beadles seized its massive wrist in both hands to relieve the pressure, his feet dangling. This was it. He'd had a nice run. Shame to go out a loser. He wished he could have held Lars in his arms again. Even Betty. Even Summer.

He closed his eyes and prayed. Prayed to God. Hadn't been to church or thought about religion in decades. He made his peace.

Stingers pierced his neck. An instant of shock. He felt light-headed. The light swam diagonally in flexible hexagons.

He stood on the ground beneath a merciless sun.

Accompanied by five of his fiercest warriors Skorpio approached the meeting of the blue-eyed devils with extreme trepidation. His mother Nagua had warned of this for years. They would come from the south, a strange invader that actually consisted of two beings fused together. The rider and his beast. So it was prophesied; so the Azuma alone of all the tribes understood that these were but men. Their creatures inspired awe. But the Azuma had seen deer and buffalo and knew that the creatures were children of the sun.

When the invaders first appeared word spread as fast as the runners and filled the land between the four sacred mountains.

The invaders arrived by sea—something neither Skorpio nor any member of his tribe had seen, although there were stories of such a place. Wherever the creatures rode they demanded gold and laid waste to the People with their bang sticks and with disease.

The Azuma were at war with the Navajo, the Apache and the Ute. But in the face of this existential threat all tribes were one.

Still grieving from the unexpected loss of his wife Xahnea, Skorpio sought the wisdom of the elders, especially his mother the medicine woman Nagua but also other wise men from other tribes. He sought council with Braza of the Ute, Wyanute of the Navajo and Creote of the Chiracahua. He prayed and fasted five days on the butte. He sang the songs to Monster Slayer promising a cruel end to the blue-eyed devils. He sent runners to follow the four-legged fiends. His warriors captured one of the intruders and were surprised to find him on foot, an ordinary man, not even equal to their youngest fighter. Skorpio told them what to do so they brought their captive with them until it was time to make a statement.

The invaders reacted with fury, destroying a Navajo village that had dared to defy Skorpio. In this way he knew that his prayers had been answered.

Naguna warned him what would happen. It turned his liver white. The invaders would flood the land like a plague of grasshoppers. They would bring unimaginable vice and strife. They were liars and killers. There could be no peace with them. The People would fall on harsh times and know servility and degradation.

The alien leader sent his pet Navajo to ask Skorpio to the pow-wow.

And so it was a on a blistering day in the Month of the Least Heat Moon Skorpio set out on foot with five of his fiercest warriors to meet the invader at a secret watering hole until recently known only to the Navajo. Now the invaders had come with their beasts and foul habits.

Skorpio and his dog soldiers walked across an endless plain of blistering heat, their feet inured by years running barefoot over rock and sand. Ahead they saw the clump of trees huddled around the secret spring where the invader leader waited with only his Navajo interpreter.

Both leaders agreed to bring five warriors. Skorpio and his men entered the ring of stones with their hands empty to show their peaceful intentions, although each warrior was armed with bow, arrows, and an obsidian knife.

The alien leader came forward to greet them, astonished by Skorpio's size. Skorpio towered over the little man who had black kinky hair and a full beard, sweat pouring down his face in the intense heat. He wore a metal breastplate over a leather cuirass and Skorpio knew he was crazy. His soldiers had stripped in the heat and wore only shirts, leggings and boots. They all stared at Skorpio in astonishment. They had never seen an Indian so large.

Skorpio's men stared back. They'd never seen men so white and hairy, or the monstrous deer-like creatures they rode. Each warrior had the same thought. What if we rode those beasts as well? To see the horse was to covet the horse. The unspoken flashed among them like the sun's word: we must steal these creatures.

The white devil bade Skorpio and his men sit in a circle while he passed around water in hollowed gourds but the Azuma refused the water and fetched their own from the spring after carefully tasting it. The invaders stank. With the Navajo interpreting the invader identified himself as da Gama and asked why the Azuma had killed his man.

Skorpio brushed the question aside. "Why have you come?"

Da Gama claimed that he brought a new religion that would uplift and transform the Azuma and that he was also interested in gold. He gave Skorpio a knife. It was the first steel the chief had ever seen and he was in awe. Imagine what the Azuma could accomplish with weapons like this—or even the thundersticks. Some of his runners had seen the thundersticks in action while following the white devils. Two of them were with Skorpio that day.

Da Gama stood, took off his sword, and bade Skorpio accompany him and the Navajo interpreter and leave all others behind. Skorpio, da Gama and the Navajo walked around the spring to the far side and hunkered behind a juniper bush. Da Gama extended sympathies on the death of Skorpio's beloved wife Xahnea. Skorpio masked his amazement but quickly realized da Gama could have gained this information from any number of rival tribes. It was not exactly a secret.

Da Gama stunned Skorpio with what he said next, "I will bring her back to you, but you must come alone and you must bring gold."

Naguna said the invaders were liars. It was a trap. But such was Skorpio's love for Xahnea that he convinced himself the invaders spoke the truth. Had they not done as they had said? Had they not slain dozens if not hundreds of the People? Did not their thunder sticks bring down a man with a single bark? And if they were the future as Naguna had warned what was the point of resistance? If they killed him his spirit would join Xahnea's in the place of pinons.

Skorpio agreed to the meeting. For four days he fasted, praying to the four sacred colors, four sacred plants and four sacred mountains. On the appointed day he went to the oasis. From the distance a woman beckoned to him. She might have been Xahnea. There was only one way to find out. As he approached she ran away and the Spaniards emerged from hiding. They had learned concealment from the Navajo. The invaders seized him but not before he killed two with his bare hands. They tied him to a wagon wheel, carried him into the desert, gouged out his eyes, castrated him and left him to die in the sun.

CHAPTER SEVENTY-SIX

A DAY SPLIT IN TWO

The agony of that long-ago day merged with the agony encircling Beadles' neck. He fought through the pain and opened his eyes. Skorpio stared at him through merciless yellow slits. Its grip tightened. Its corpse's mouth spread in a ghastly grin. Beadles felt death gather like the surf and prepare to rush him. Skorpio spun him as helplessly as a rabbit so that the sun seared directly into his eyes. Sunlight weighed on him like a coat of iron, crushing the breath from him. It transformed his skin to a tenuous red membrane as if it might split at any second and his insides would gush forth like garbage from a split plastic bag.

He tried to close his eyes. The giant chuckled, a sound like a gargling drain, and shook him violently, enjoying his agony. Beadles disassociated and looked down. Only this time he saw not himself but Skorpio, bound to the wheel, eye sockets seeping, hands writhing in agony. The fingers were human. His crotch a bloody swamp.

The monsters segmented talons slowly crushed Beadles' neck. He hovered over the mesa death creeping in like morning fog. His vision dimmed. He saw the creature's grin. A shadow fell across them, an unexpected coolness. The giant's eyes grew wide and looked up like baby birds opening their beaks to catch food. The temperature dropped.

The thing staggered. It released Beadles who fell to the hard earth. A line of darkness marched across the butte. Beadles rolled over on his back and looked up.

The moon had eclipsed the sun. For an exquisite nanosecond all was peace.

The moon moved on. Blazing sunlight took the stage. With a rasp of defiance Skorpio drew himself to his full height and turned with fury toward Beadles.

A silver point emerged from the giant's sternum. He looked down stupidly. The point withdrew, whirled through the air and severed the giant's head from its body. The head smacked the rock and rolled inexorably toward Beadles who lay gasping, unable to move, watching in dread.

It bumped to a stop against his feet. Gasping, Summer stood where the giant lay holding the Spanish sword. She walked toward Beadles. She dropped the sword and ran toward Beadles. She knelt and took his head.

"Are you all right?"

Beadles gasped and bathed in her glow. He tried to say something but could barely breath. She placed a finger against his lips, unlooped the canteen, unscrewed the lid, held his head up and tilted. Beadles drank thirstily although it hurt to swallow. He tentatively touched his neck and felt raw welts.

After awhile he said, "I thought you…"

Again she touched his lips. "I did. But then I came back."

Beadles reached for water. He sat up and took the canteen himself.

"All my life I've made the worst choices in men," Summer said. "One loser after another. But you. I could tell from the way you presented yourself you were for real."

Beadles tried to laugh and began coughing. Summer pounded him on the back.

"Don't do that!" she said when he stopped. "I meant what I said. You hardly talk about yourself, y'know? You're not boastful of your achievements or insecure. I believe you were framed. And I know you're not perfect."

Beadles smiled through the intense pain encircling his throat which felt hoarse and raw. But not from the stingers, from trying to breath. Skorpio's flashback was imprinted on his brain. He had difficulty separating what happened and what he'd seen from reality. He couldn't believe it had happened.

"Did you…" he croaked.

Summer's forehead crumpled in concern. "Don't."

"Did you…get any pictures?"

She shook her head sadly realizing the immensity of the lost opportunity.

He craned his neck, straining to see.

Summer helped him to his feet. The sword lay on the rock. There was no sign of the ghost. They staggered under the cottonwoods as the sun continued its journey to the west. She found the first aid kit, applied ointment and bandages to the five punctures in his neck. He ached all over. Even his hair ached.

Faint insect buzzing. It grew louder. It was a plane. Beadles and Summer got to their feet and came out from under the trees looking up. It was a one-engine plane headed their way from the southwest. Beadles and Summer waved their arms, screaming and jumping up and down. The plane came closer. Beadles wished he'd saved some of the gas although it was hot and bright out.

The plane came closer. It descended to within a couple hundred feet of the summit and dipped its wings.

SAVED

The helo arrived three hours later. It was a Llama from Page Municipal Airport. It flew them to Kayenta where police debriefed them about Vince. The State Police dispatched a ground team to investigate. The police took Beadles and Summer to Agranda Hospital in Kayenta to be treated for exposure and observation.

They tried to hook Beadles up to an IV but he would have none of it. A freelancer monitoring police frequencies connected Beadles with the Creighton scandal and tried to get into his room. A deputy sheriff kept him out.

At seven p.m. a huge squarish man with a beard in a plain gray suit and a Stetson entered Beadles' room and handed Beadles his card. "Sir, I'm State Criminal Investigator Wallace Ford. Can you tell us what happened? The last information we received from Sheriff Conway was that you were one of the patrons at the Last Chance when he took Mr. Sealy into custody?"

Beadles sucked on the straw in a big plastic glass. "I guess," he said in a hoarse voice.

"You told one of the flight crew that Vince had followed you out there?"

Beadles nodded.

"Tuesday some ranchers spotted a concentration of turkey buzzards off County Road XX. They found Sheriff Conway's body."

Ford pulled a small recorder from inside his jacket and laid it on the bed table. "I'm going to record this if you don't mind."

Beadles nodded. "Go ahead."

"It appeared Conway's larynx had been crushed although we're still waiting for the autopsy. Somehow Sealy got out of the handcuffs and overpowered the sheriff. We found the car in Gap this morning. He'd hidden it behind some dumpsters. Nobody could believe anyone would flee into the desert."

Ford looked expectantly at Beadles. Speaking slowly because of the pain Beadles told the investigator everything that had happened since the Sheriff drove off. Ford leaned back in the steel and fabric chair and listened impassively.

"And then your plane found us," Beadles said.

Ford was still as an icebox. He stared limpidly without blinking.

At last he said, "You say Sealy was stung to death by scorpions?"

"That's what I think. I'm no expert, but there should be something of him left to autopsy. I'm sure it would show up. Am I under suspicion or something? I didn't kill him."

"We can't rule anything out until we know more. You left your last position under a cloud, didn't you?"

Beadles shrugged. He'd been expecting the question and now that it came he felt nothing. No anxiety, no anger. He was in the zone. He was on the zen. He was in a state of grace. Nothing mattered and what if it did. He knew it wouldn't last but he enjoyed it now that it was here, as much as one could enjoy in his condition.

Summer was the only thing he cared about.

"I believe I was framed. I know—everybody tells you that. I'm not here to plead my case. But I do intend to fight these false accusations and sue."

Ford consulted some notes in a spiral pad. "We have been unable to locate Mr. Preston who is wanted on federal cyber terrorism charges. Did you know he is wanted by the FBI?"

"No, sir. I knew he was a crook! But he was a smart crook."

"His accomplice, Gregorio Peterson, was wanted for robbing the First National Bank of Decatur."

"Do I need a lawyer?" Beadles said.

"Not if your story checks out. The DA has no plans to charge you. But I got some problems with your story. All this shit about a ghost and a river of scorpions. Sure you weren't hallucinating?"

"No, sir I am not. Let me know when you find the gold."

"Oh yes, the gold," the investigator said. "That's gonna put a burr under someone's saddle. Personally, I hope you're just raving. This is enough of a mess as it is."

"Inspector, I can't emphasize enough how important it is that your men leave the site alone. It has overwhelming historical significance."

"Well we're trying to conduct an investigation but we'll do our best."

"No crimes were committed on top of that butte. It would be best if you left it to experts in anthropology and archaeology."

Ford doodled in his pad. "I hear you. That may not be possible. We're going to have to put some inspectors on top of the butte but I'll advise them to tread lightly."

Ford left. Beadles changed from his hospital gown into his own clothes, still covered with desert silt, and went across the hall where another statie was interviewing Summer. There was a state cop standing outside the stairwell. Beadles waited until the investigator finished and went into the room. Summer opened her arms and he fell into them.

"Now what?" Summer said.

Beadles shrugged. "We'll see. No one can take this away from us. I think word got out. They got a cop stationed at the stairwell. It's not to keep us in. It's to keep reporters out."

"Oh fuck," Summer said. "Are we going to be in tabloids? I promised my mom I wouldn't end up in the tabloids."

"Yeah well, get set. You got your cop killing, grisly murder, ghosts, buried treasure and sex."

Summer held him tight. "Where do we go?"

"Don't worry. We've done nothing wrong. Good things are about to happen, you'll see."

He'd abandoned his laptop in the Jeep but if he could get online he could check his email. He needed to contact Panny. Beadles had suddenly become a hot property. There would be offers. It was the way things worked. He needed money to hire Panny to pursue Stephanie Byrd. He needed to contact Mel Berenson. He was going to sue the university for false termination.

There was a knock and a young nurse slipped in through the partially opened door. She carried a clipboard and wore blue slacks, a white blouse with the tails out and a name badge. Beadles stood.

"Professor Beadles?" she said. He nodded.

"I'm Melanie Hecht with *The National Enquirer*. Could I ask you a few questions?"

CHAPTER SEVENTY-EIGHT
THE NARRATIVE

*ISGRACED PROF FINDS LOST TRIBE, TREASURE*

By Melanie Hecht exclusive to National Enquirer

Vaughan Beadles, former Distinguished Professor of Anthropology at Creighton University, Creighton, IL, claims to have discovered a heretofore undocumented Amerindian tribe, remains of a long-lost Spanish expedition, and a fortune in gold. Beadles has long maintained that the Azuma differed from other Navajo and Hopi-related Amerindian Tribes occupying the Colorado Plateau from the fifteenth to the nineteenth century. The Azuma are said to have been among the most bellicose of all tribes, making up for their lack of numbers with their ferocity and tactics. Even the Apache feared them.

Beadles was let go from Creighton four weeks ago, charged with stealing from the priceless Azuma Collection of which he was the curator. Beadles had also been charged with manslaughter in the bizarre death of a student, Rob Whitfield. Whitfield died of a scorpion sting when he was allowed to handle, against university policy, priceless Azuma artifacts. Those charges were later dropped.

Beadles has maintained his innocence regarding charges of grand larceny and vows to fight them. The University has declined to comment.

Beadles claims to have discovered the epicenter of the Azuma civilization atop a butte in the Four Corners region. He also claims to have discovered the bodies of two Creighton University students who went missing in the eighties.

Curt Mayweather and Ronnie Potts may also have been in search of the Azuma legend when they disappeared in May, 1985, outside Gap, AZ, population 217. Ronnie's father Daniel Potts, Class of '64, recently gave two million to the Creighton Dept. of Anthropology in his son's name. Mr. Potts could not be reached for comment.

The story of how Prof. Beadles tracked down the Azuma involves suicide, ghosts, strippers and the even more bizarre death of ex-con and cagefighter Vincent Sealy of Los Vegas. Sealy's remains were found next to the burnt-out husk of his Hummer at the base of the Azuma stronghold. Although autopsy reports are still pending Beadles claims Sealy died of literally hundreds of scorpion stings.

Shortly after the police jailed Beadles on manslaughter charges his wife of six years, Betty Halverson-Beadles, initiated divorce proceedings. The Beadles have a two-year-old son. Betty Halverson-Beadles could not be reached for comment.

There was an aerial photograph of the butte, an old file photo of Beadles from his Discovery special, and the centerpiece, a publicity still of Summer from her model portfolio. The Babe. The Mystery Woman. The Hooker With a Heart of Gold was out shopping in a rental car to fill the larder of the apartment Beadles had rented with his advance from a publisher. The apartment was in Creighton, where the University had asked him to assume the directorship of the Anthropology Department following the abrupt resignation of Joel Liggett. Stephanie Byrd had returned from Belize on advice of her attorney and confessed that Liggett had paid her to hide the stolen pottery in Beadles' home.

Beadles tossed the tabloid on the coffee table in the sparsely furnished living room. He'd picked it up at the Stop 'N' Go that morning. The clerk didn't give him a second look. That was about to change. He was booked on The Morning Show and 60 Minutes had contacted him about doing a segment. His FB page, on which he'd posted some pictures from the canyon and the butte, had reached the limit and his message folder was filled with inquiries from agents and publishers.

Only a week had passed since their rescue from the butte and already his life had shifted into high gear. Daniel Potts agreed to pay Beadles the fifty thousand dollar reward for news of Ronnie. Beadles had a new phone. Only Summer, Berenson and Panny had his number. He referred all media requests to Berenson. The State Police had retrieved his laptop from the Jeep and forwarded it to him. He intended to transfer his files to his new laptop which he'd picked up yesterday. He'd already begun writing.

But there was a problem. A big problem. How could he write what happened without coming off as a crackpot? The police had documented the wounds to his neck but what did it prove? Like most anthropologists he regarded Erich Van Daniken as a sensationalist kook. Any student who cited Van Daniken earned an automatic D or worse. How could Beadles claim he was assaulted by a six-hundred year old seven foot ghost? He could not. It would destroy his academic credibility.

Sealy's autopsy report stated, "Subject appears to have died from massive quantities of scorpion venom. Subject's face and body bore innumerable scorpion stings, well in excess of a hundred." If there was talk of revenge-seeking ghosts let The Enquirer carry that banner. He took out Melanie Hecht's business card and stared at it.

No. Better let that dog lie. If Beadles had learned nothing else during his years in academia, he had absorbed the most fundamental rule: control the narrative. In America that's all there was, really. The narrative. He who controlled the narrative controlled the media and he who controlled the media controlled everything. He was meeting Berenson that afternoon to choose an agent. Berenson had gone to college with Johnny Depp and had put in a call to Depp's office. If it was good enough for the

Deppster it was good enough for Beadles.

No one had found the skull. Beadles was saving it for TV.

There was a knock on the door. Beadles was sure he'd given Summer a key. He opened the door. Ninja swept by wearing a beige Calvin Klein suit over a black T, trailing the scent of Acqua di Gio and a European man purse. He stood in the middle of the sparsely furnished living room and did a slow 360.

"What a dump," he said in perfect imitation of Bette Davis.

"Ninja!" Beadles said. "What are you doing here?"

"We had a deal, professor. I want my gold."

"Are you shitting me? The State of Arizona seized the gold!"

Ninja showed his perfect grill. "Surprised to see me? You shouldn't be. You know what I can do. I'm surprised you didn't try to contact me! I'm gonna be in the next issue of the Enquirer!"

"Melanie Hecht?" Beadles said going into the kitchenette. "You want a Mr. Pibb or something?"

Ninja flopped down on the leather sofa. "That be fine. I got something to show you. Something you might like."

Beadles retrieved two Pibbs from the refrigerator and returned to the living room. Ninja removed his laptop from the man purse and spooled up. He poked and stroked.

"Take a look at this, Professor. What do you make of that?" Ninja rotated the screen toward Beadles.

It showed an intense satellite magnification of an arid desert. A tag said Bolivia followed by a series of numbers. The photograph was black and white overlaid with green and yellow lines. In the center was a red circle from which radiated a series of squiggly lines.

About the Author

Born in Wisconsin, Mike Baron is best known for his comics work on *Nexus, Badger, Punisher, Flash, Deadman, Star Wars, and Robotech*. A perennial fan favorite, he is the winner of the prestigious Inkpot Award and the Eisner Award. He has written for every major comics publisher.

He broke into comics with *Nexus*, co-created with artist Steve Rude. *Nexus* currently appears monthly in Dark Horse Presents. Baron also created *Badger*, one of the longest-lived and most intriguing of independent superheroes. The Badger is a multiple personality, only one of whom dons a costume to fight crime. *Badger* returns this winter from a resurgent First Comics.

Skorpio is his fourth novel following *Helmet Head, Whack Job,* and *Biker*. Baron lives in Colorado with his wife Ann and a bunch of mutts. bloodyredbaron.net.

www.ingramcontent.com/pod-product-compliance
Lightning Source LLC
Chambersburg PA
CBHW030524120726
47904CB00005B/1607